THE NEW WINDMILL BOOK OF

STORIES THEN AND NOW

EDITED BY BRIAN HAWTHORN AND
KATHERINE HAWTHORN

with contributions by Marian Slee

Consultant: *ANDREW BENNETT,*
Principal Examiner for GCSE English

Heinemann
New Windmills

Heinemann Educational Publishers
Halley Court, Jordan Hill, Oxford OX2 8EJ
a division of Reed Educational & Professional Publishing Ltd
OXFORD MELBOURNE AUCKLAND
JOHANNESBURG BLANTYRE GABORONE
IBADAN PORTSMOUTH (NH) USA CHICAGO

First published in the New Windmill Series 1997

08 07 06 05 04 03 02 01 00
20 19 18 17 16 15 14 13
ISBN 0 435 12482 X

Acknowledgements

The author and publisher should like to thank the following for permission to use copyright material:

A P Watt Ltd. on behalf of The Literary Executors of the Estate of H G Wells for 'The Red Room' by H G Wells, page 3; Richard Scott Simon Ltd. for 'Farthing House' by Susan Hill © Susan Hill 1992, first published in *Good Housekeeping*, December 1992/January 1993, page 16; Permission granted by Don Congdon Associates, Inc. Copyright 1950, renewed 1977 by Ray Bradbury, for 'The Whole Town's Sleeping', page 37; David Higham Associates for 'The Landlady' from *Kiss, Kiss* by Roald Dahl, published by Penguin, page 80; Macmillan General Books, Papermac for 'Tony Kytes, the Arch-Deceiver' by Thomas Hardy, page 95; Mrs Ernestine Naughton for 'Seeing a Beauty Queen Home' by Bill Naughton, page 106; Laurence Pollinger Limited and the Estate of Frieda Lawrence Ravagli for 'Tickets, Please' from *The Complete Short Stories of D H Lawrence* published by William Heinemann Ltd., page 118; David Higham Associates for 'Lamb to the Slaughter' from *Someone Like You* by Roald Dahl, published by Penguin, page 137; 'The Speckled Band' from *The Adventures of Sherlock Holmes* by Sir Arthur Conan Doyle, Copyright © Sheldon Reynolds 1996. Reproduced by kind permission of Jonathan Clowes Ltd., London on behalf of Sheldon Reynolds, page 150; Macmillan General Books, Papermac for 'The Son's Veto' by Thomas Hardy, page 185; David Higham Associates for 'Survival' from *The Seeds of Time* by John Wyndham, published by Michael Joseph 1956, page 206.

Every effort has been made to contact copyright holders. We should be glad to rectify any omissions at the next reprint if notice is given to the publisher.

Cover painting 'The Beach' by Moreau-Nelaton reproduced by kind permission of the Bridgeman Art Library; cover photograph reproduced by kind permission of Zefa UK Ltd
Cover design by The Point
Typeset by Books Unlimited (Nottm) NG19 7QZ
Printed and bound in the United Kingdom by Clays Ltd, St Ives plc

Contents

Introduction iv

Ghost Stories

The Red Room – H G Wells 3

Farthing House – Susan Hill 16

Fear

The Whole Town's Sleeping – Ray Bradbury 37

A Terribly Strange Bed – Wilkie Collins 57

The Landlady – Roald Dahl 80

Men and Women

Tony Kytes, the Arch-Deceiver – Thomas Hardy 95

Seeing a Beauty Queen Home – Bill Naughton 106

Tickets, Please – D H Lawrence 118

Murder Mysteries

Lamb to the Slaughter – Roald Dahl 137

The Speckled Band – Sir Arthur Conan Doyle 150

Sacrifice

The Son's Veto – Thomas Hardy 185

Survival – John Wyndham 206

Activities and Assignments 241

Introduction

This anthology aims to help you explore some of the similarities and differences between stories written before 1900 and stories written during the twentieth century. It contains a rich mix of stories arranged in thematic pairs or groups which offer wide opportunities for lively discussion and response.

The short story became a popular form of fiction during the nineteenth century and has remained so ever since. The comparison of twentieth-century and pre-twentieth-century stories helps us to think about changes in the ways people live, behave, speak and write over time. Yet these comparisons also show us how similar people remain in their hopes and fears and, above all, in their relationships with other people.

All of the pre-twentieth-century authors included here appear on the National Curriculum reading list. The twentieth-century authors are major writers with established reputations.

At the end of the book you will find activities and assignments for each pair or group of stories. These activities and assignments offer lots of suggestions for comparing the stories – you will of course find your own ways of comparing stories, too.

If you particularly enjoy one of the short stories in this selection you may wish to read more short stories by the same author. There is a list of single-author short story selections from Heinemann on page 268. This anthology offers something for everyone: we hope you enjoy reading it.

Brian and Katherine Hawthorn

Ghost Stories

The Red Room by H G Wells (1896)

Farthing House by Susan Hill (1992/1993)

The Red Room

H G Wells

'I can assure you,' said I, 'that it will take a very tangible ghost to frighten me.' And I stood up before the fire with my glass in my hand.

'It is your own choosing,' said the man with the withered arm, and glanced at me askance.

'Eight-and-twenty years,' said I, 'I have lived, and never a ghost have I seen as yet.'

The old woman sat staring hard into the fire, her pale eyes wide open. 'Ah,' she broke in: 'and eight-and-twenty years you have lived and never seen the likes of this house, I reckon. There's a many things to see, when one's still but eight-and-twenty.' She swayed her head slowly from side to side. 'A many thing to see and sorrow for.'

I half suspected the old people were trying to enhance the spiritual terrors of their house by their droning insistence. I put down my empty glass on the table and looked about the room, and caught a glimpse of myself, abbreviated and broadened to an impossible sturdiness, in the queer old mirror at the end of the room. 'Well,' I said, 'if I see anything tonight, I shall be so much the wiser. For I come to the business with an open mind.'

'It's your own choosing,' said the man with the withered arm once more.

I heard the sound of a stick and a shambling step on the flags in the passage outside, and the door creaked on its hinges as a second old man entered, more bent, more wrinkled, more aged even than the first. He supported himself by a single crutch, his eyes were covered by a shade, and his lower lip, half averted, hung pale and pink from his decaying yellow teeth. He made straight for an armchair on the opposite side of the table, sat down clumsily, and began to cough. The man with the withered arm gave this newcomer a short glance of positive dislike; the old woman took no notice of his arrival, but remained with her eyes fixed steadily on the fire.

'I said – it's your own choosing,' said the man with the withered arm, when the coughing had ceased for a while.

'It's my own choosing,' I answered.

The man with the shade became aware of my presence for the first time, and threw his head back for a moment and sideways, to see me. I caught a momentary glimpse of his eyes, small and bright and inflamed. Then he began to cough and splutter again.

'Why don't you drink?' said the man with the withered arm, pushing the beer towards him. The man with the shade poured out a glassful with a shaky arm that splashed half as much again on the deal table. A monstrous shadow of him crouched upon the wall and mocked his action as he poured and drank. I must confess I had scarce expected these grotesque custodians*. There is to my mind something inhuman in senility, something crouching and atavistic*; the human qualities seem to drop from old people insensibly day by day. The three of them made me feel uncomfortable, and with their gaunt silences, their bent carriage*, their evident unfriendliness to me and to one another.

* custodians: caretakers
atavistic: resembling a remote ancestral type
carriage: posture

'If,' said I, 'you will show me to this haunted room of yours, I will make myself comfortable there.'

The old man with the cough jerked his head back so suddenly that it startled me, and shot another glance of his red eyes at me from under the shade; but no one answered me. I waited a minute, glancing from one to the other.

'If,' I said a little louder, 'if you will show me to this haunted room of yours, I will relieve you from the task of entertaining me.'

'There's a candle on the slab outside the door,' said the man with the withered arm, looking at my feet as he addressed me. 'But if you go to the red room tonight – '

('This night of all nights!' said the old woman.)

'You go alone.'

'Very well,' I answered. 'And which way do I go?'

'You go along the passage for a bit,' said he, 'until you come to a door, and through that is a spiral staircase, and halfway up that is a landing and another door covered with baize. Go through that and down the long corridor to the end, and the red room is on your left up the steps.'

'Have I got that right?' I said, and repeated his directions. He corrected me in one particular.

'And are you really going?' said the man with the shade, looking at me again for the third time, with that queer unnatural tilting of the face.

('This night of all nights?' said the old woman.)

'It is what I came for,' I said, and moved towards the door. As I did so the old man with the shade rose and staggered round the table, so as to be closer to the others and to the fire. At the door I turned and looked at them, and saw they were all close together, dark against the firelight, staring at me over their shoulders, with an intent expression on their ancient faces.

'Good night,' I said, setting the door open.

'It's your own choosing,' said the man with the withered arm.

I left the door wide open until the candle was well alight, and then I shut them in and walked down the chilly, echoing passage.

I must confess that the oddness of these three old pensioners in whose charge her ladyship had left the castle, and the deep-toned, old-fashioned furniture of the housekeeper's room in which they forgathered, affected me in spite of my efforts to keep myself at a matter of fact phase. They seemed to belong to another age, an older age, an age when things spiritual were different from this of ours, less certain; an age when omens and witches were credible, and ghosts beyond denying. Their very existence was spectral; the cut of their clothing, fashions born in dead brains. The ornaments and conveniences* of the room about them were ghostly – the thoughts of vanished men, which still haunted rather than participated in the world of today. But with an effort I sent such thoughts to the right-about. The long, draughty, subterranean* passage was chilly and dusty, and my candle flared and made the shadows cower and quiver. The echoes rang up and down the spiral staircase, and a shadow came sweeping up after me, and one fled before me into the darkness overhead. I came to the landing and stopped there for a moment, listening to a rustling that I fancied I heard; then, satisfied of the absolute silence, I pushed open the baize-covered door and stood in the corridor.

* conveniences: furnishings subterranean: underground

The effect was scarcely what I expected, for the moonlight coming in by the great window on the grand staircase picked out everything in vivid black shadow or silvery illumination. Everything was in its place; the house might have been deserted on the yesterday instead of eighteen months ago. There were candles in the sockets of the sconces* and whatever dust had gathered on the carpets or upon the polished flooring was distributed so evenly as to be invisible in the moonlight. I was about to advance, and stopped abruptly. A bronze group stood upon the landing, hidden from me by the corner of the wall, but its shadow fell with marvellous distinctness upon the white panelling and gave me the impression of some one crouching to waylay me. I stood rigid for half a minute perhaps. Then, with my hand in the pocket that held my revolver, I advanced, only to discover a Ganymede and Eagle* glistening in the moonlight. That incident for a time restored my nerve, and a porcelain Chinaman on a buhl* table, whose head rocked silently as I passed him, scarcely startled me.

The door to the red room and the steps up to it were in a shadowy corner. I moved my candle from side to side, in order to see clearly the nature of the recess in which I stood before opening the door. Here it was, thought I, that my predecessor was found, and the memory of that story gave me a sudden twinge of apprehension. I glanced over my shoulder at the Ganymede in the moonlight, and opened the door of the red room rather hastily, with my face half-turned to the pallid silence of the landing.

* sconce: wall-mounted candlestick
Ganymede and Eagle: a classical statue
buhl: decorative inlay

I entered, closed the door behind me at once, turned the key I found in the lock within, and stood with the candle held aloft, surveying the scene of my vigil, the great red room of Lorraine Castle, in which the young duke had died. Or, rather, in which he had begun his dying, for he had opened the door and fallen headlong down the steps I had just ascended. That had been the end of his vigil, of his gallant attempt to conquer the ghostly tradition of the place, and never, I thought, had apoplexy* better served the ends of superstition. And there were other and older stories that clung to the room, back to the half-credible beginning of it all, the tale of a timid wife and the tragic end that came to her husband's jest of frightening her. And looking around that large sombre room, with its shadowy window bays, its recesses and alcoves, one could well understand the legends that had sprouted in its black corners, its germinating darkness. My candle was a little tongue of light in its vastness, that failed to pierce the opposite end of the room, and left an ocean of mystery and suggestion beyond its island of light.

I resolved to make a systematic examination of the place at once, and dispel the fanciful suggestions of its obscurity before they obtained a hold upon me. After satisfying myself of the fastening of the door, I began to walk about the room, peering round each article of furniture, tucking up the valances of the bed, and opening its curtains wide. I pulled up the blinds and examined the fastenings of the several windows before closing the shutters, leant forward and looked up the blackness of the wide chimney, and tapped the dark oak panelling for any secret opening. There were two big mirrors in the room, each with a pair of sconces

* apoplexy: sudden seizure

bearing candles, and on the mantelshelf, too, were more candles in china candlesticks. All these I lit one after the other. The fire was laid, an unexpected consideration from the old housekeeper – and I lit it, to keep down any disposition to shiver, and when it was burning well, I stood round with my back to it and regarded the room again. I had pulled up a chintz-covered armchair and a table, to form a kind of barricade before me, and on this lay my revolver ready to hand. My precise examination had done me good, but I still found the remoter darkness of the place, and its perfect stillness, too stimulating for the imagination. The echoing of the stir and crackling of the fire was no sort of comfort to me. The shadow in the alcove at the end in particular had that undefinable quality of a presence, that odd suggestion of a lurking, living thing, that comes so easily in silence and solitude. At last, to reassure myself, I walked with a candle into it, and satisfied myself that there was nothing tangible there. I stood that candle upon the floor of the alcove, and left it in that position.

By this time I was in a state of considerable nervous tension, although to my reason there was no adequate cause for the condition. My mind, however, was perfectly clear. I postulated quite unreservedly that nothing supernatural could happen, and to pass the time I began to string some rhymes together, Ingoldsby fashion*, of the original legend of the place. A few I spoke aloud, but the echoes were not pleasant. For the same reason I also abandoned, after a time, a conversation with myself upon the impossibility of ghosts and haunting. My mind reverted to the three old and distorted people downstairs, and I tried to keep

* Ingoldsby fashion: style of verse in *The Ingoldsby Legends*

it upon that topic. The sombre reds and blacks of the room troubled me; even with seven candles the place was merely dim. The one in the alcove flared in a draught, and the fire's flickering kept the shadows and penumbra* perpetually shifting and stirring. Casting about for a remedy, I recalled the candles I had seen in the passage, and, with a slight effort, walked out into the moonlight, carrying a candle and leaving the door open, and presently returned with as many as ten. These I put in various knick-knacks of china with which the room was sparsely adorned, lit and placed where the shadows had lain deepest, some on the floor, some in the window recesses, until at last my seventeen candles were so arranged that not an inch of the room but had the direct light of at least one of them. It occurred to me that when the ghost came, I could warn him not to trip over them. The room was now quite brightly illuminated. There was something very cheery and reassuring in these little streaming flames, and snuffing them gave me an occupation, and afforded a helpful sense of the passage of time.

Even with that, however, the brooding expectation of the vigil weighed heavily upon me. It was after midnight that the candle in the alcove suddenly went out, and the black shadow sprang back to its place there. I did not see the candle go out; I simply turned and saw that the darkness was there, as one might start and see the unexpected presence of a stranger. 'By Jove!' said I aloud; 'that draught's a strong one!' and taking the matches from the table, I walked across the room in a leisurely manner to relight the corner again. My first match would not strike, and as I succeeded with the second, something seemed to blink

* penumbra: half-shadow

on the wall before me. I turned my head involuntarily, and saw that the two candles on the little table by the fireplace were extinguished. I rose at once to my feet.

'Odd!' I said. 'Did I do that myself in a flash of absent-mindedness?'

I walked back, relit one, and as I did so, I saw the candle in the right sconce of one of the mirrors wink and go right out, and almost immediately its companion followed it. There was no mistake about it. The flame vanished, as if the wicks had been suddenly nipped between a finger and thumb, leaving the wick neither glowing nor smoking, but black. While I stood gaping, the candle at the foot of the bed went out, and the shadows seemed to take another step towards me.

'This won't do!' said I, and first one and then another candle on the mantelshelf followed.

'What's up?' I cried, with a queer high note getting into my voice somehow. At that the candle on the wardrobe went out, and the one I had relit in the alcove followed.

'Steady on!' I said. 'These candles are wanted,' speaking with a half-hysterical facetiousness*, and scratching away at a match the while for the mantel candlesticks. My hands trembled so much that twice I missed the rough paper of the matchbox. As the mantel emerged from darkness again, two candles in the remoter end of the window were eclipsed. But with the same match I also relit the larger mirror candles, and those on the floor near the doorway, so that for the moment I seemed to gain on the extinctions. But then in a volley there vanished four lights at once in different corners of the room, and I struck another

* facetiousness: attempt at humour

match in quivering haste, and stood hesitating whither to take it.

As I stood undecided, an invisible hand seemed to sweep out the two candles on the table. With a cry of terror, I dashed at the alcove, then into the corner, and then into the window, relighting three, as two more vanished by the fireplace; then, perceiving a better way, I dropped the matches on the iron-bound deedbox in the corner, and caught up the bedroom candlestick. With this I avoided the delay of striking matches; but for all that the steady process of extinction went on, and the shadows I feared and fought against returned, and crept in upon me, first a step gained on this side of me and then on that. It was like a ragged stormcloud sweeping out the stars. Now and then one returned for a minute, and was lost again. I was now almost frantic with the horror of the coming darkness, and my self-possession deserted me. I leapt panting and dishevelled from candle to candle in a vain struggle against that remorseless advance.

I bruised myself on the thigh against the table, I sent a chair headlong, I stumbled and fell and whisked the cloth from the table in my fall. My candle rolled away from me, and I snatched another as I rose. Abruptly this was blown out, as I swung it off the table, by the wind of my sudden movement, and immediately the two remaining candles followed. But there was light still in the room, a red light that staved off the shadows from me. The fire! Of course I could still thrust my candle between the bars and relight it!

I turned to where the flames were still dancing between the glowing coals, and splashing red reflections upon the furniture, made two steps towards the grate, and incontinently* the flames

* incontinently: all at once

dwindled and vanished, the glow vanished, the reflections rushed together and vanished, and as I thrust the candle between the bars darkness closed upon me like the shutting of an eye, wrapped about me in a stifling embrace, sealed my vision, and crushed the last vestiges of reason from my brain. The candle fell from my hand. I flung out my arms in a vain effort to thrust that ponderous blackness away from me, and, lifting up my voice, screamed with all my might – once, twice, thrice. Then I think I must have staggered to my feet. I know I thought suddenly of the moonlit corridor, and, with my head bowed and my arms over my face, made a run for the door.

But I had forgotten the exact position of the door, and struck myself heavily against the corner of the bed. I staggered back, turned, and was either struck or struck myself against some other bulky furniture. I have a vague memory of battering myself thus, to and fro in the darkness, of a cramped struggle, and of my own wild crying as I darted to and fro, of a heavy blow at last upon my forehead, a horrible sensation of falling that lasted an age, of my last frantic effort to keep my footing, and then I remember no more.

I opened my eyes in daylight. My head was roughly bandaged, and the man with the withered arm was watching my face. I looked about me, trying to remember what had happened, and for a space I could not recollect. I rolled my eyes into the corner, and saw the old woman, no longer abstracted, pouring out some drops of medicine from a little blue phial into a glass. 'Where am I?' I asked; 'I seem to remember you, and yet I cannot remember who you are.'

They told me then, and I heard of the haunted red room as one who hears a tale. 'We found you at dawn,' said he, 'and there was blood on your forehead and lips.'

It was very slowly I recovered my memory of my experience. 'You believe now,' said the old man, 'that the room is haunted?' He spoke no longer as one who greets an intruder, but as one who grieves for a broken friend.

'Yes,' said I; 'the room is haunted.'

'And you have seen it. And we, who have lived here all our lives, have never set eyes upon it. Because we have never dared . . . Tell us, is it truly the old earl who – '

'No,' said I; 'it is not.'

'I told you so,' said the old lady, with the glass in her hand. 'It is his poor young countess who was frightened – '

'It is not,' I said. 'There is neither ghost of earl nor ghost of countess in that room, there is no ghost there at all; but worse, far worse – '

'Well?' they said.

'The worst of all the things that haunt poor mortal man,' said I; 'and that is, in all its nakedness – *Fear!* Fear that will not have light nor sound, that will not bear with reason, that deafens and darkens and overwhelms. It followed me through the corridor, it fought against me in the room – '

I stopped abruptly. There was an interval of silence. My hand went up to my bandages.

Then the man with the shade sighed and spoke. 'That is it,' said he. 'I knew that was it. A power of darkness. To put such a curse upon a woman! It lurks there always. You can feel it even in the daytime, even of a bright summer's day, in the hangings, in the curtains, keeping behind you however you face about. In the dusk it creeps along the corridor and follows you, so that you dare not turn. There is Fear in that room of hers – black Fear, and there will be – so long as this house of sin endures.'

Farthing House

Susan Hill

I have never told you any of this before – I have never told anyone, and indeed, writing it down and sealing it up in an envelope to be read at some future date may still not count as 'telling'. But I shall feel better for it, I am sure of that. Now it has all come back to me, I do not want to let it go again, I must set it down.

It is true, and for that very reason you must not hear it just now. You will be prey to enough anxieties and fancies without my adding ghosts to them; the time before the birth of a child one is so very vulnerable.

I daresay that it has made me vulnerable too, that this has brought the events to mind.

I began to be restless several weeks ago. I was burning the last of the leaves. It was a most beautiful day, clear and cold and blue and a few of them were swirling down as I raked and piled. And then a light wind blew suddenly across the grass, scuttling the leaves and making the woodsmoke drift towards me, and as I caught the smell of it, that most poignant, melancholy, nostalgic of all smells, something that had been drifting on the edges of my consciousness blurred and insubstantial, came into focus, and in a rush I remembered . . .

It was as though a door had been opened on to the past, and I had stepped through and gazed at what I saw there again. I saw the house, the drive sweeping up to it, the countryside around it, on that late November afternoon, saw the red sun setting behind the beech copse, beyond the rising, brown fields, saw the bonfire the gardener had left to smoulder on gently by itself, and the thin pale smoke coiling up from its heart. I was there, all over again.

I went in a daze into the house, made some tea, and sat, still in my old, outdoor clothes at the kitchen table, as it went quite dark outside the window, and I let myself go back to that day, and the nights that followed, watched it all unfold again, remembered. So that it was all absolutely clear in my mind when the newspaper report appeared, a week later.

I was going to see Aunt Addy. It was November, and she had been at the place called Farthing House since the New Year, but it was only now that I had managed to get away and make the two hundred-mile journey to visit her.

We had written, of course, and spoken on the telephone, and so far as I could tell she sounded happy. Yes, they were very nice people, she said, and yes, it was such a lovely house, and she did so like her room, everyone was most kind, oh yes dear, it was the right thing, I should have done it long ago, I really am very settled.

And Rosamund said that she was, too, said that it was fine, really, just as Addy told me, a lovely place, such kind people, and Alec had been and he agreed.

All the same, I was worried, I wasn't sure. She had been so independent always, so energetic, so very much her own person all her life, I couldn't see her in a Home, however nice and however sensible a move it was – and she was eighty-six and had had two nasty falls the previous winter – I liked to think of her as she was when we were children, and went to stay at the house in Wales, striding over the hills with the dogs, rowing on the lake, getting up those colossal picnics for us all. I always loved her, she was such fun. I wish you had known her.

And of course, I wish that one of us could have had her, but there really wasn't room to make her comfortable and, oh, other feeble-sounding reasons, which are real reasons, nonetheless.

She had never asked me to visit her, that wasn't her way. Only the more she didn't ask, the more I knew that I should, the guiltier I felt. It was just such a terrible year, what with one thing and another.

But now I was going. It had been a beautiful day for the drive too. I had stopped twice, once in a village, once in a small market town and explored churches and little shops, and eaten lunch and had a pot of tea and taken a walk along the banks of a river in the late sunshine, and the berries, I remember had been thick and heavy, clustered on the boughs. I'd seen a jay and two deer and once, like magic, a kingfisher, flashing blue as blue across a hump-backed bridge. I'd had a sort of holiday really. But now I was tired, I would be glad to get there. It was very nice that they had a guest-room, and I didn't have to stay alone in some hotel. It meant I could really spend all my time with Aunt Addy. Besides, you know how I've always hated hotels, I lie awake thinking of the hundreds of people who've slept in the bed before me.

Little Dornford 1½m.

But as I turned right and the road narrowed to a single track, between trees, I began to feel nervous, anxious, I prayed that it really would be all right, that Aunt Addy had been telling the truth.

'You'll come to the church', they had said, and a row of three cottages, and then there is the sign to Farthing House, at the bottom of the drive.

I had seen no other car since leaving the cathedral town seven miles back on the main road. It was very quiet, very out of the way. I wondered if Addy minded. She had always been alone up there in her own house but somehow now that she was so old and infirm, I thought she might have liked to be nearer some bustle, perhaps actually in a town. And what about the others, a lot of old women isolated out here together? I shivered suddenly and peered forwards along the darkening lane. The church was just ahead, the car lights swept along a yew hedge, a lych gate*, caught the shoulder of a gravestone. I slowed down.

FARTHING HOUSE. It was a neat, elegantly lettered sign, not too prominent and at least it did not proclaim itself Residential Home.

The last light was fading in the sky behind a copse of bare beech trees, the sun dropping down, a great red, frost-rimmed ball. I saw the drive, a wide lawn, the remains of a bonfire of leaves, smouldering by itself in a corner. Farthing House.

I don't know exactly what my emotions had been up to that moment. I was very tired, with that slightly dazed, confused sensation that comes after a long drive and the attendant concentration. And I was apprehensive. I so wanted to be happy about Aunt Addy, to be sure that she was in the right place to spend the rest of her life – or maybe I just wanted to have my conscience cleared so I could bowl off home again in a couple of days with a blithe heart, untroubled by guilt and be able to enjoy the coming Christmas.

But as I stood on the black and white marbled floor of the entrance porch I felt something else and it made

* lych gate: gate at the entrance to a churchyard

me hesitate before ringing the bell. What was it? Not fear or anxiety, no shudders. I am being very careful now, it would be too easy to claim that I had sensed something sinister, that I was shrouded at once in the atmosphere of a haunted house.

But I did not, nothing of that sort crossed my mind. I was only overshadowed by a curious sadness – I don't know exactly how to describe it – a sense of loss, a melancholy. It descended like a damp veil about my head and shoulders. But it lifted, or almost, the cloud passed after a few moments. Well, I was tired, I was cold, it was the back end of the year, and perhaps I had caught a chill, which often manifests itself first as a sudden change of mood into a lower key.

The only other thing I noticed was the faintest smell of hospital antiseptic. That depressed me a bit more. Farthing House wasn't a hospital or even a nursing home proper and I didn't want it to seem so to Aunt Addy, not even in this slight respect.

But in fact, once I was inside, I no longer noticed it at all, there was only the pleasant smell of furniture polish, and fresh chrysanthemums and, somewhere in the background, a light, spicy smell of baking.

The smells that greeted me were all of a piece with the rest of the welcome. Farthing House seemed like an individual, private home. The antiques in the hall were good, substantial pieces and they had been well cared for over the years, there were framed photographs on a sideboard, flowers in jugs and bowls, there was an old, fraying, tapestry-covered armchair on which a fat cat slept beside a fire. It was quiet, too, there was no rattling of trolleys or buzzing of bells. And the matron did not call herself one.

'You are Mrs Flower – how nice to meet you.' She put out her hand. 'Janet Pearson.'

She was younger than I had expected, probably in her late forties. A small King Charles spaniel hovered about her waving a frond-like tail. I relaxed.

I spent a good evening in Aunt Addy's company; she was so settled and serene, and yet still so full of life. Farthing House was well run, warm and comfortable, and there was good, home-cooked dinner, with fresh vegetables and an excellent lemon meringue pie. The rooms were spacious, the other residents pleasant but not over-obtrusive.

Something else was not as I had expected. It had been necessary to reserve the guest-room and bathroom well in advance, but when Mrs Pearson herself took my bag and led me up the handsome staircase, she told me that after a serious leak in the roof had caused damage, it was being redecorated. 'So I've put you in Cedar – it happens to be free just now.' She barely hesitated as she spoke. 'And it's such a lovely room, I'm sure you'll like it.'

How could I have failed? Cedar Room was one of the two largest in the house, on the first floor, with big bay windows overlooking the garden at the back – though now the deep red curtains had been drawn against the early evening darkness.

'Your aunt is just across the landing.'

'So they've put you in Cedar,' Addy said later when we were having a drink in her own room. It wasn't so large but I preferred it simply, I think, because there was so much familiar furniture, her chair, her own oak dresser, the painted screen, even the club fender we used to sit on to toast our toes as children.

'Yes. It seems a bit big for one person, but it's very handsome. I'm surprised it's vacant.'

Addy winked at me. 'Well, of course it *wasn't* . . .'

'Oh.' For an instant, that feeling of unease and melancholy passed over me like a shadow again.

'Now buck up, don't look wan, there isn't time.' And she plunged me back into family chat and cheerful recollections, interspersed with sharp observations about her fellow residents, so that I was almost entirely comfortable again.

I remained so until we parted at getting on for half past eleven. We had spent much of the evening alone together, and then joined some of the others in one of the lounges, where an almost party-like atmosphere had developed, with laughter and banter and happy talk, which had all helped to revive my first impressions of Farthing House and Addy's place there.

It was not until I closed the door of my room and was alone that I was forced to acknowledge again what had been at the back of my mind all the time, almost like having a person at my shoulder, though just out of sight. I was in this large, high-ceilinged room because it was free, its previous occupant having recently died. I knew no more, and did not want to know, had firmly refrained from asking any questions. Why should it matter? It did not. As a matter of fact it still does not, it had no bearing at all on what happened, but I must set it down because I feel I have to tell the whole truth and part of that truth is that I was in an unsettled, slightly nervous frame of mind as I got ready for bed, because of what I knew, and because I could not help wondering whether whoever had occupied Cedar Room had died in it, perhaps even in this bed. I was, as you might say, almost expecting to have bad dreams or to see a ghost.

There is just one other thing.

When we were all in the lounge, the talk had inevitably been of former homes and families, the past in general, and Addy had wanted some photographs from upstairs. I had slipped out to fetch them for her.

It was very quiet in the hall. The doors were heavy and soundproof, though from behind one I could just hear some faint notes of recorded music, but the staff quarters down the passage were closed off and silent.

So I was quite certain that I heard it, the sound was unmistakable. It was a baby crying. Not a cat, not a dog. They are quite different, you know. What I heard from some distant room on the ground floor was the cry of a newborn baby.

I hesitated. Stopped. But it was over at once, and it did not come again. I waited, feeling uncertain. But then, from the room with the music, I heard the muffled signature tune of the ten o'clock news. I went on up the staircase. The noise had come from the television then.

Except, you see, that deep down and quite surely, I knew that it had not.

I may have had odd frissons[*] about my room but once I was actually in bed and settling down to read a few pages of *Sense and Sensibility* before going to sleep, I felt quite composed and cheerful. The only thing wrong was that the room still seemed far too big for one person. There was ample furniture and yet it was as though someone else ought to be there. I find it difficult to explain precisely.

I was very tired. And Addy was happy, Farthing House was everything I had hoped it would be, I had had a most enjoyable evening, and the next day we were to go out and see something of the countryside and later, hear sung evensong at the cathedral.

I switched out the lamp.

* frissons: shivers

At first I thought it was as quiet outside the house as in, but after a few minutes, I heard the wind sifting through the bare branches and sighing towards the windows and away. I felt like a child again, snug in my little room under the eaves.

I slept.

I dreamed almost at once and with extraordinary vividness, and it was, at least to begin with, a most happy dream. I was in St Mary's, the night after you were born, lying in my bed in that blissful, glowing, untouchable state when the whole of the rest of life seems suspended and everything irrelevant but this. You were there in your crib beside me, though I did not look at you. I don't think anything happened in the dream and it did not last very long. I was simply there in the past and utterly content.

I woke with a start, and as I came to, it was with that sound in my ears, the crying of the baby that I had heard as I crossed the hall earlier that evening. The room was quite dark. I knew at once where I was and yet I was still half within my dream – I remember that I felt a spurt of disappointment that it had *been* a dream and I was actually there, a new young mother again with you beside me in the crib.

How strange, I thought, I wonder why. And then something else happened – or no, not 'happened'. There just *was* something else, that is the only way I can describe it.

I had the absolutely clear sense that someone else had been in my room – not the hospital room of my dream, but this room in Farthing House. No one was here now, but minutes before I woke, I knew that they had been. I remember thinking, someone is in the next bed. But of course, there was no next bed, just mine.

After a while I switched on the lamp. All was as it had been when I had gone to sleep. Only that sensation, that atmosphere was still there. If nothing else had happened at Farthing House, I suppose in time I would have decided I had half-dreamed, half-imagined it, and forgotten. It was only because of what happened afterwards that I remembered so clearly and knew with such certainty that my feeling had been correct.

I got up, went over to the tall windows and opened the curtains a little. There was a clear, star-pricked sky and a thin paring of moon. The gardens and the dark countryside all around were peaceful and still.

But I felt oppressed again by the most profound melancholy of spirit, the same terrible sadness and sense of loss that had overcome me on my arrival. I stood there for a long time, unable to release myself from it, before going back to bed to read another chapter of Jane Austen, but I could not concentrate properly and in the end grew drowsy. I heard nothing, saw nothing, and I did not dream again.

The next morning my mood had lightened. There had been a slight frost during the night, and the sun rose on a countryside dusted over with rime*. The sky was blue, trees set in dark pencil strokes against it.

We had a good day, Aunt Addy and I, enjoying one another's company, exploring churches and antique shops, having a pub lunch, and an old-fashioned muffin and fruitcake tea after the cathedral service.

It was as we were eating it that I asked suddenly, 'What do you know about Farthing House?'

Seeing Addy's puzzled look, I went on, 'I just mean, how long has Mrs Pearson been there, who had it

* rime: white frost

before, all that sort of thing. Presumably it was once a family house.'

'I have an idea someone told me it had been a military convalescent home during the war. Why do you ask?'

I thought of Cedar Room the previous night, and that strange sensation. *What* had it been? Or who? But I found that I couldn't talk about it for some reason, it made me too uneasy. 'Oh, nothing. Just curious.' I avoided Addy's eye.

That evening, the matron invited me to her own room for sherry, and to ask if I was happy about my aunt. I reassured her, saying all the right, polite things. Then she said, 'And have you been quite comfortable?'

'Oh yes.' I looked straight at her. I thought she might have been giving me an opening – I wasn't sure. And I almost did tell her. But again, I couldn't speak of it. Besides, what was there to tell? I had heard a baby crying – from the television. I'd had an unusual dream, and an odd, confused sensation when I woke from it that someone had just left my room.

Nothing.

'I've been extremely comfortable,' I said firmly. 'I feel quite happy about everything.'

Did she relax just visibly, smile a little too eagerly, was there a touch of relief in her voice when she next spoke?

I don't know whether or not I dreamed that night. It seemed that one minute I was in a deep sleep, and the next that something had woken me. As I came to, I know I heard the echo of crying in my ears, or in my inner ear, but a different sort of crying this time, not that of a baby, but a desperate, woman's sobbing. The antiseptic smell was faintly there again too, my awareness of it was mingled with that of the sounds.

I sat bolt upright. The previous night, I had had the sensation of someone having just been in my room.

Now, I saw her.

There was another bed in the opposite corner of the room, close to the window, and she was getting out of it. The room felt horribly cold. I remember being conscious of the iciness on my hands and face.

I was wide awake, I am quite sure of that, I could hear my own heart pounding, see the bedside table, and the lamp and the blue binding of *Sense and Sensibility* in the moonlight. I know I was not dreaming, so much so that I almost spoke to the woman, wondering as I saw her what on earth they were thinking of to put her and her bed in my room while I was asleep.

She was young, with a flowing, embroidered nightgown, high necked and long sleeved. Her hair was long too, and as pale as her face. Her feet were bare. But I could not speak to her, my throat felt paralysed. I tried to swallow, but even that was difficult, the inside of my mouth was so dry.

She seemed to be crying. I suppose that was what I had heard. She moved across the room towards the door and she held out her arms as if she were begging someone to give her something. And that terrible melancholy came over me again, I felt inconsolably hopeless and sad.

The door opened. I know that because a rush of air came in to the room, and it went even colder, but somehow, I did not see her put her hand to the knob and turn it. All I know is that she had gone, and that I was desperate to follow her, because I felt that she needed me in some way.

I did not switch on the lamp or put on my dressing gown, I half-ran to catch her up.

The landing outside was lit as if by a low, flickering candle flame. I saw the door of Aunt Addy's room but the wood looked darker, and there were some pictures on the walls that I had not noticed before. It was still so cold my breath made little haws of white in front of my face.

The young woman had gone. I went to the head of the staircase. Below, it was pitch dark. I heard nothing, no footstep, no creak of the floorboards. I was too frightened to go any further.

As I turned, I saw that the flickering light had faded and the landing was in darkness too. I felt my way, trembling, back to my own room and put my hand on the doorknob. As I did so I heard from far below, in the recesses of the house, the woman's sobbing and a calling – it might have been of a name, but it was too faint and far away for me to make it out.

I managed to stumble across the room and switch on the lamp. All was normal. There was just one bed, my own. Nothing had changed.

I looked at the clock. It was a little after three. I was soaked in sweat, shaking, terrified. I did not sleep again that night but sat up in the chair wrapped in the eiderdown with the lamp on, until the late grey dawn came around the curtains. That I had seen a young woman, that she had been getting out of another bed in my room, I had no doubt at all. I had not been dreaming, as I certainly had on the previous night. The difference between the two experiences was quite clear to me. She had been there.

I had never either believed or disbelieved in ghosts, scarcely ever thought about the subject at all. Now, I knew that I had seen one. And I could not throw off not only my fear but the depression her presence inflicted on me. Her distress and agitation, whatever their cause, had affected me profoundly, and from the first moment of my arrival at the door of Farthing House. It was a dark, dreadful, helpless feeling and with it there also went a sense of foreboding.

I was due to leave for home the following morning but when I joined Aunt Addy for breakfast I felt wretched, tense and strained, quite unfit for a long drive. When I went to Mrs Pearson's office and explained simply that I had not slept well, she expressed concern at once and insisted that I stay on another night. I wanted to, but I did not want to remain in Cedar Room. When I mentioned it, very diffidently, Mrs Pearson gave me a close look and I waited for her to question me but she did not, only told me, slipping her pen nervously round and round between her fingers that there simply was not another vacant room in the house. So I said that of course it did not matter, it was only that I had always felt uneasy sleeping in very large rooms, and laughed it off, trying to reassure her. She pretended that I had.

That morning, Aunt Addy had an appointment with the visiting hairdresser. I didn't feel like sitting about reading papers and chatting in the lounge. They were nice women, the other residents, kind and friendly and welcoming but I was on edge and still enveloped in sadness and foreboding. I needed time to myself.

The weather didn't help. It had gone a degree or two warmer and the rise in temperature had brought a dripping fog and low cloud that masked the lines of the countryside. I trudged around Farthing House gardens but the grass was soaking wet and the sight of the dreary bushes and black trees lowered my spirits further. I set off down the lane, past the three cottages. A dog barked from one, but the others were silent and apparently empty. I suppose that by then I had begun to wallow slightly in my mood and I decided that I might as well go the whole hog and visit the church and its overgrown little graveyard. It was bitterly cold inside. There were some good brasses and a wonderful ornate eighteenth-century monument to a pious local squire, with florid rhymes and madly grieving angels. But the stained glass was in ugly 'uncut moquette'* colours, as Stephen would have said, and besides it was actually colder inside the church than out.

I had a prowl around the graveyard, looking here and there at epitaphs. There were a couple of minor gems but otherwise, all was plain, names and dates and dullness and I was about to leave when my eye was caught by some gravestones at the far side near to the field wall. They were set a little apart and neatly arranged in two rows. I bent down and deciphered the faded inscriptions. They were all the graves of babies, newborn or a few days old, and dating from the early years of the century. I wondered why so many, and why all young babies. They had different surnames, though one or two recurred. Had there been some dreadful epidemic in the village? Had the village been much larger then, if there had been so many young families?

At the far end of the row were three adult sized stones. The inscriptions on two had been mossed over but one was clear.

Eliza Maria Dolly.
Died January 20 1902. Aged 19 years.
And also her infant daughter.

* 'uncut moquette': type of furnishing fabric

As I walked thoughtfully back I saw an elderly man dismount from a bicycle beside the gate and pause, looking towards me.

'Good morning! Gerald Manberry, vicar of the parish. Though really I am semi-retired, there isn't a great deal for a full-time man to take care of nowadays. I see you have been looking at the poor little Farthing House graves.'

'Farthing House?'

'Yes, just down the lane. It was a home for young women and their illegitimate babies from the turn of the century until the last war. Then a military convalescent home, I believe. It's a home for the elderly now, of course.'

How bleak that sounded. I told him that I had been staying there. 'But the graves . . .' I said.

'I suppose a greater number of babies died around the time of birth then, especially in those circumstances. And mothers too, I fear. Poor girls. It's all much safer now. A better world. A better world.'

I watched him wheel his ancient bicycle round to the vestry door, before beginning to walk back down the empty lane towards Farthing House. But I was not seeing my surroundings or hearing the caw-cawing of the rooks in the trees above my head. I was seeing the young woman in the nightgown, her arms outstretched, and hearing her cry and feeling again that terrible sadness and distress. I thought of the grave of Eliza Maria Dolly, 'and also her infant daughter'.

I was not afraid any more, not now that I knew who she was and why she had been there, getting out of her bed in Cedar Room, to go in search of her baby. Poor, pale, distraught young thing, she could do no one harm.

*

I slept well that night, I saw nothing, heard nothing, although in the morning I knew, somehow, that she had been there again, there was the same emptiness in the room and the imprint of her sad spirit upon it.

The fog had cleared and it was a pleasant winter day, intermittently sunny. I left for home after breakfast, having arranged that Aunt Addy was to come to us for Christmas.

She did so and we had a fine time, as happy as we all used to be together, with Stephen and I, Rosamund, Alec and the others. I shall always be glad of that, for it was Addy's last Christmas. She fell down the stairs at Farthing House the following March, broke her hip and died of a stroke a few days later. They took her to hospital and I saw her there, but afterwards, when her things were to be cleared up, I couldn't face it. Stephen and Alec did everything. I never went back to Farthing House.

I often thought about it though, even dreamed of it. An experience like that affects you profoundly and for ever. But I could not have spoken about it, not to anyone at all. If ever a conversation touched upon the subject of ghosts I kept silent. I had seen one. I knew. That was all.

Some years afterwards, I learned that Farthing House had closed to residents, been sold and then demolished, to make room for a new development – the nearby town was spreading out now. Little Dornford had become a suburb.

I was sad. It had been, in most respects, such a good and happy place.

Then, only a week ago, I saw the name again, quite by chance, it leaped at me from the newspaper. You may remember the case, though you would not have known of any personal connection.

A young woman stole a baby, from its pram outside a shop. The child had only been left for a moment or two but apparently she had been following and keeping watch, waiting to take it. It was found eventually, safe and well. She had looked after it, so I suppose things could have been worse, but the distress caused to the parents was obviously appalling. You can imagine that now, can't you?

They didn't send her to prison, she was taken into medical care. Her defence was that she had stolen the child when she was out of her right mind after the death of her own baby not long before. The child was two days old. Her address was given as Farthing House Close, Little Dornford.

I think of it constantly, see the young, pale, distraught woman, her arms outstretched, searching, hear her sobbing, and the crying of her baby.

But I imagine that she has gone, now that she has what she was looking for.

Fear

The Whole Town's Sleeping by Ray Bradbury (1950)

A Terribly Strange Bed by Wilkie Collins (1856)

The Landlady by Roald Dahl (1960)

The Whole Town's Sleeping

Ray Bradbury

It was a warm summer night in the middle of Illinois country. The little town was deep far away from everything, kept to itself by a river and a forest and a ravine. In the town the sidewalks were still scorched. The stores were closing and the streets were turning dark. There were two moons: a clock moon with four faces in four night directions above the solemn black courthouse, and the real moon that was slowly rising in vanilla whiteness from the dark east.

In the downtown drugstore, fans whispered in the high ceiling air. In the rococo* shade of porches, invisible people sat. On the purple bricks of the summer twilight streets, children ran. Screen doors whined their springs and banged. The heat was breathing from the dry lawns and trees.

On her solitary porch, Lavinia Nebbs, aged thirty-seven, very straight and slim, sat with a twinkling lemonade in her white fingers, tapping to her lips, waiting.

'Here I am, Lavinia.'

Lavinia turned. There was Francine, at the bottom porch step, in the smell of zinnias and hibiscus. Francine was all in snow white and didn't look thirty-five.

Miss Lavinia Nebbs rose and locked her front door, leaving her lemonade glass standing empty on the porch rail.

'It's a fine night for the movie.'

* rococo: frivolous

'Where you going, ladies?' cried Grandma Hanlon from her shadowy porch across the street.

They called back through the soft ocean of darkness: 'To the Elite Theatre to see Harold Lloyd in *Welcome, Danger*!'

'Won't catch me out on no night like this,' wailed Grandma Hanlon. 'Not with the Lonely One strangling women. Lock myself in with my *gun*!'

Grandma's door slammed and locked.

The two maiden ladies drifted on. Lavinia felt the warm breath of the summer night shimmering off the oven-baked sidewalk. It was like walking on a hard crust of freshly warmed bread. The heat pulsed under your dress and along your legs with a stealthy sense of invasion.

'Lavinia, you don't believe all that gossip about the Lonely One, do you?'

'Those women like to see their tongues dance.'

'Just the same, Hattie McDollis was killed a month ago. And Roberta Ferry the month before. And now Eliza Ramsell has disappeared . . . '

'Hattie McDollis walked off with a travelling man, I bet.'

'But the others – strangled – four of them, their tongues sticking out their mouths, they say.'

They stood upon the edge of the ravine that cut the town in two. Behind them were the lighted houses and faint radio music; ahead was deepness, moistness, fireflies and dark.

'Maybe we shouldn't go to the movie,' said Francine. 'The Lonely One might follow us and kill. I don't like that ravine. Look how black, smell it, and *listen*.'

The ravine was a dynamo that never stopped running, night or day: there was a great moving hum among the secret mists and washed shales and the odours of a rank greenhouse. Always the black dynamo was humming, with electric sparkles where fireflies hovered.

'And it won't be me,' said Francine, 'coming back through this terrible dark ravine tonight, late. It'll be you, Lavinia, you down the steps and over that rickety bridge and maybe the Lonely One standing behind a tree. I'd never have gone over to church this afternoon if I had to walk through here all alone, even in daylight.'

'Bosh,' said Lavinia Nebbs.

'It'll be you alone on the path, listening to your shoes, not me. And shadows. You *all alone* on the way back home. Lavinia, don't you get lonely living by yourself in that house?'

'Old maids love to live alone,' said Lavinia. She pointed to a hot shadowy path. 'Let's walk the short cut.'

'I'm afraid.'

'It's early. The Lonely One won't be out till late.' Lavinia, as cool as mint ice-cream, took the other woman's arm and led her down the dark winding path into cricket warmth and frog-sound, and mosquito-delicate silence.

'Let's run,' gasped Francine.

'No.'

If Lavinia hadn't turned her head just then, she wouldn't have seen it. But she did turn her head, and it was there. And then Francine looked over and she saw it too, and they stood there on the path, not believing what they saw.

In the singing deep night, back among a clump of bushes – half hidden, but laid out as if she had put herself down there to enjoy the soft stars – lay Eliza Ramsell.

Francine screamed. The woman lay as if she were floating there, her face moon-freckled, her eyes like white marble, her tongue clamped in her lips.

Lavinia felt the ravine turning like a gigantic black merry-go-round underfoot. Francine was gasping and choking and a long while later Lavinia heard herself say, 'We'd better get the police'.

'Hold me, Lavinia, please hold me, I'm cold. Oh, I've never been so cold since winter.'

Lavinia held Francine and the policemen were all around in the ravine grass. Flashlights darted about, voices mingled, and the night grew towards eight-thirty.

'It's like December, I need a sweater,' said Francine, eyes shut against Lavinia's shoulder.

The policeman said, 'I guess you can go now, ladies. You might drop in by the station tomorrow for a little more questioning.'

Lavinia and Francine walked away from the police and the delicate sheet-covered thing upon the ravine grass.

Lavinia felt her heart going loudly within her and she was cold too, with a February cold. There were bits of sudden snow all over her flesh and the moon washed her brittle fingers whiter, and she remembered doing all the talking while Francine just sobbed.

A police voice called, 'You want an escort, ladies?'

'No, we'll make it,' said Lavinia, and they walked on. I can't remember anything now, she thought. I can't remember how she looked lying there, or anything. I don't believe it happened. Already I'm forgetting, I'm making myself forget.

'I've never *seen* a dead person before,' said Francine.

Lavinia looked at her wristwatch, which seemed impossibly far away. 'It's only eight-thirty. We'll pick up Helen and get onto the show.'

'The show!'

'It's what we *need.*'

'Lavinia, you don't *mean* it!'

'We've got to forget this. It's not good to remember.'

'But Eliza's back there now and – '

'We need to laugh. We'll go to the show as if nothing happened.'

'But Eliza was once your friend, *my* friend – '

'We can't help her; we can only help ourselves forget. I insist. I won't go home and brood over it. I won't think of it. I'll fill my mind with everything else *but.*'

They started up the side of the ravine on a stony path in the dark. They heard voices and stopped.

Below, near the creek waters, a voice was murmuring, 'I am the Lonely One. I am the Lonely One. I *kill* people.'

'And I'm Eliza Ramsell. Look. And I'm dead, see my tongue out my mouth, see!'

Francine shrieked. 'You there! Children, you nasty children! Get home, get out of the ravine, you hear me? Get home, get home, get home!'

The children fled from their game. The night swallowed their laughter away up the distant hills into the warm darkness.

Francine sobbed again and walked on.

'I thought you ladies'd never come!' Helen Greer tapped her foot atop her porch steps. 'You're only an hour late, that's all.'

'We – ' started Francine.

Lavinia clutched her arms. 'There was a commotion. Someone found Eliza Ramsell dead in the ravine.'

Helen gasped. 'Who found her?'

'We don't know.'

The three maiden ladies stood in the summer night looking at one another. 'I've a notion to lock myself in my house,' said Helen at last.

But finally she went to fetch a sweater, and while she was gone Francine whispered frantically, 'Why didn't you *tell* her?'

The three women moved along the street under the black trees through a town that was slamming and locking doors, pulling down windows and shades and turning on blazing lights. They saw eyes peering out at them from curtained windows.

How strange, thought Lavinia Nebbs, the Popsicle night, the ice-cream night with the children thrown like jackstones on the streets, now turned in behind wood and glass, the Popsicles dropped in puddles of lime and chocolate where they fell when the children were scooped indoors. Baseballs and bats lie on the unfootprinted lawns. A half-drawn white chalk hopscotch line is there on the seamed sidewalk.

'We're crazy out on a night like this,' said Helen.

'Lonely One can't kill three ladies,' said Lavinia. 'There's safety in numbers. Besides, it's too soon. The murders come a month separated.'

A shadow fell across their faces. A figure loomed. As if someone had struck an organ a terrible blow, the three women shrieked.

'*Got* you!' The man jumped from behind a tree. Rearing into the moonlight, he laughed. Leaning on the tree, he laughed again.

'Hey, I'm the Lonely One!'

'Tom Dillon!'

'Tom!'

'Tom,' said Lavinia. 'If you ever do a childish thing like that again, may you be riddled with bullets by mistake!'

Francine began to cry.

Tom Dillon stopped smiling. 'Hey, I'm sorry.'

'Haven't you heard about Eliza Ramsell?' snapped Lavinia. 'She's dead, and you scaring women. You should be ashamed. Don't speak to us again.'

'Aw – '

He moved to follow them.

'Stay right there, Mr Lonely One, and scare yourself,' said Lavinia. 'Go see Eliza Ramsell's face and see if it's funny!' She pushed the other two on along the street of trees and stars, Francine holding a handkerchief to her face.

'Francine,' pleaded Helen, 'it was only a joke. Why is she crying so hard?'

'I guess we better tell you, Helen. *We* found Eliza. And it wasn't pretty. And we're trying to forget. We're going to the show to help and let's not talk about it. Enough's enough. Get your ticket money ready, we're almost downtown.'

The drugstore was a small pool of sluggish air which the great wooden fans stirred in tides of arnica* and tonic and soda-smell out into the brick streets.

'A nickel's worth of green mint chews,' said Lavinia to the druggist. His face was set and pale, like all the faces they had seen on the half-empty street. 'For eating in the show,' she explained, as the druggist dropped the mints into a bag with a silver shovel.

'Sure look pretty tonight,' said the druggist. 'You looked cool this noon, Miss Lavinia, when you was in

* arnica: plant-extract used in medicine

here for chocolates. So cool and nice that someone asked after you.'

'Oh?'

'You're getting popular. Man sitting at the counter – ' he rustled a few more mints in the bag – 'watched you walk out and he said to me, "Say, who's *that*?" Man in dark suit, thin pale face. "Why, that's Lavinia Nebbs, prettiest maiden lady in town," *I* said. "Beautiful," *he* said. "Where's she live?"' Here the druggist paused and looked away.

'You *didn't*?' wailed Francine. 'You didn't give him her address, I hope! You *didn't*!'

'Sorry, guess I didn't think. I said, "Oh, over on Park Street, you know, near the ravine." Casual remark. But now, tonight, them finding the body. I heard a minute ago, I suddenly thought, what've I *done*!' He handed over the package, much too full.

'You fool!' cried Francine, and tears were in her eyes.

'I'm sorry. 'Course maybe it was nothing.'

'Nothing, nothing!' said Francine.

Lavinia stood with the three people looking at her, staring at her. She didn't know what or how to feel. She felt nothing – except perhaps the slightest prickle of excitement in her throat. She held out her money automatically.

'No charge for those peppermints.' The druggist turned down his eyes and shuffled some papers.

'Well, I know what we're going to do right *now*!' Helen stalked out of the drug store. 'We're going right straight home. I'm not going to be part of any hunting party for you, Lavinia. That man asking for you. You're *next*! You want to be dead in that ravine?'

'It was just a man,' said Lavinia slowly, eyes on the streets.

'So's Tom Dillon a man but maybe he's the Lonely One!'

'We're all overwrought,' said Lavinia reasonably. 'I won't miss the movie now. If I'm the next victim, let me *be* the next victim. A lady has all too little excitement in her life, especially an old maid, a lady thirty-seven like me, so you don't mind if I enjoy it. And I'm being sensible. Stands to reason he won't be out tonight, so soon after a murder. A month from now yes, when the police've relaxed and when he *feels* like another murder. You've got to *feel* like murdering people you know. At least that kind of murderer does. And he's just resting up now. And anyway I'm not going home to stew in my juices.'

'But Eliza's face, there in the ravine!'

'After the first look I never looked again. I didn't *drink* it in, if that's what you mean. I can see a thing and tell myself I never saw it, that's how strong *I* am. And the whole argument's silly anyhow, because I'm not beautiful.'

'Oh, but you are, Lavinia. You're the loveliest maiden lady in town, now that Eliza's – ' Francine stopped. 'If you'd only relaxed, you'd been married years ago – '

'Stop snivelling, Francine. Here's the box office. You and Helen go on home. I'll sit alone and go home alone.'

'Lavinia, you're crazy. We can't leave you here – '

They argued for five minutes. Helen started to walk away but came back when she saw Lavinia thump down her money for a solitary movie ticket. Helen and Francine followed her silently into the theatre.

The first show was over. In the dim auditorium, as they sat in the odour of ancient brass polish, the manager appeared before worn red velvet curtains for an announcement:

'The police have asked for an early closing tonight. So everyone can be home at a decent hour. So we're cutting our short subjects and putting on our feature film again now. The show will be over at eleven. Everyone's advised to go straight home and not linger on the streets. Our police force is pretty small and will be spread around pretty thin.'

'That means us, Lavinia. *Us*!' Lavinia felt the hands tugging at her elbows on either side.

Harold Lloyd in Welcome, Danger! said the screen in the dark.

'Lavinia,' Helen whispered.

'What?'

'As we came in, a man in a dark suit, across the street, crossed over. He just came in. He just sat in the row behind us.'

'Oh, Helen.'

'He's right behind us *now*.'

Lavinia looked at the screen.

Helen turned slowly and glanced back. 'I'm calling the manager!' she cried and leaped up. 'Stop the film! Lights!'

'Helen, come back!' said Lavinia, eyes shut.

When they set down their empty soda glasses, each of the ladies had a chocolate moustache on her upper lip. They removed them with their tongues, laughing.

'You see how *silly* it was?' said Lavinia. 'All that riot for nothing. How embarrassing!'

The drugstore clock said eleven twenty-five. They had come out of the theatre and the laughter and the enjoyment feeling new. And, now they were laughing at Helen and Helen was laughing at herself.

Lavinia said, 'When you ran up that aisle crying "Lights!" I thought I'd die!'

'That poor man!'

'The theatre manager's brother from Racine!'

'I apologized,' said Helen.

'You *see* what a panic can do?'

The great fans still swirled and whirled in the warm night air, stirring and restirring the smells of vanilla, raspberry, peppermint and disinfectant in the drugstore.

'We shouldn't have stopped for those sodas. The police said – '

'Oh, bosh the police,' Lavinia laughed. 'I'm not afraid of anything. The Lonely One is a million miles away now. He won't be back for weeks, and the police'll get him then, just wait. Wasn't the film *funny*!'

The streets were clean and empty. Not a car or a truck or a person was in sight. The bright lights were still lit in the small store windows where the hot wax dummies stood. Their blank blue eyes watched as the ladies walked past them, down the night street.

'Do you suppose if we screamed they'd do anything?'

'Who?'

'The dummies, the window people.'

'Oh, *Francine*.'

'Well . . . '

There were a thousand people in the windows, stiff and silent, and three people on the street, the echoes following like gunshots when they tapped their heels on the baked pavement.

A red neon sign flickered dimly, buzzing like a dying insect. They walked past it.

Baked and white, the long avenue lay ahead. Blowing and tall in a wind that touched only their leafy summits, the trees stood on either side of the three small women.

'First we'll walk you home, Francine.'

'No, I'll walk *you* home.'

'Don't be silly. You live the nearest. If you walked me home, you'd have to come back across the ravine alone yourself. And if so much as a leaf fell on you, you'd drop dead.'

Francine said, 'I can stay the night at your house. You're the *pretty* one!'

'No.'

So they drifted like three prim clothes-forms over a moonlit sea of lawn and concrete and tree. To Lavinia, watching the black trees flit by, listening to the voices of her friends, the night seemed to quicken. They seemed to be running while walking slowly. Everything seemed fast, and the colour of hot snow.

'Let's sing,' said Lavinia.

They sang sweetly and quietly, arm in arm, not looking back. They felt the hot sidewalk cooling underfoot, moving, moving.

'Listen,' said Lavinia.

They listened to the summer night, to the crickets and the far-off tone of the courthouse clock making it fifteen minutes to twelve.

'Listen.'

A porch swing creaked in the dark. And there was Mr Terle, silent, alone on his porch as they passed, having a last cigar. They could see the pink cigar fire idling to and fro.

Now the lights were going, going, gone. The little house lights and big house lights, the yellow lights and green hurricane lights, the candles and oil lamps and porch lights, and everything felt locked up in brass and iron and steel. Everything, thought Lavinia, is boxed and wrapped and shaded. She imagined the people in their moonlit beds, and their breathing in the summer night's rooms, safe and together. And here we are, she thought, listening to our solitary footsteps on the baked summer evening sidewalk. And above us the lonely street lights shining down, making a million wild shadows.

'Here's your house, Francine. Good night.'

'Lavinia, Helen, stay here tonight. It's late, almost midnight now. Mrs Murdoch has an extra room. I'll make hot chocolate. It'd be ever such fun!' Francine was holding them both close to her.

'No thanks,' said Lavinia.

And Francine began to cry.

'Oh, not *again*, Francine,' said Lavinia.

'I don't want you dead,' sobbed Francine, the tears running straight down her cheeks. 'You're so fine and nice, I want you alive. Please, oh, please.'

'Francine, I didn't realize how much this has affected you. But I promise you I'll phone when I get home, right away.'

'Oh, *will* you?'

'And tell you I'm safe, yes. And tomorrow we'll have a picnic lunch at Electric Park, all right? With ham sandwiches I'll make myself. How's that? You'll see; I'm going to live for ever!'

'You'll phone?'

'I promised, didn't I?'

'Good night, good night!' Francine was gone behind her door, locked tight in an instant.

'Now,' said Lavinia to Helen. 'I'll walk you home.'

The courthouse clock struck the hour. The sounds went across a town that was empty, emptier than it had ever been before. Over empty streets, and empty lots and empty lawns the sound went.

'Ten, eleven, *twelve*,' counted Lavinia, with Helen on her arm.

'Don't you feel *funny*?' asked Helen.

'How do you mean?'

'When you think of us being out here on the sidewalk, under the trees, and all those people safe behind locked doors lying in their beds. We're practically the only walking people out in the open in a thousand miles, I bet.' The sound of the deep warm dark ravine came near.

In a minute they stood before Helen's house, looking at each other for a long time. The wind blew the odour of cut grass and wet lilacs between them. The moon in a sky that was beginning to cloud over. 'I don't suppose it's any use asking you to stay, Lavinia?'

'I'll be going on.'

'Sometimes . . . '

'Sometimes what?'

'Sometimes I think people *want* to die. You've certainly acted odd all evening.

'I'm just not afraid,' said Lavinia. 'And I'm curious, I suppose. And I'm using my head. Logically, the Lonely One can't be around. The police and all.'

'*Our* police? *Our* little old force? They're home in bed too, the covers up over their ears.'

'Let's just say I'm enjoying myself, precariously but safely. If there were any *real* chance of anything happening to me, I'd stay here with you, you can be sure of that.'

'Maybe your subconscious doesn't want you to live any more.'

'You and Francine, honestly.'

'I feel so guilty. I'll be drinking hot coffee just as you reach the ravine bottom and walk on the bridge in the dark.'

'Drink a cup for me. Good night.'

Lavinia Nebbs walked down the midnight street, down the late summer night silence. She saw the houses with their dark windows and far away she heard a dog barking. In five minutes, she thought, I'll be safe home. In five minutes I'll be phoning silly little Francine. I'll –

She heard a man's voice singing far away among the trees.

She walked a little faster.

Coming down the street towards her in the dimming moon lights was a man. He was walking casually.

I can run and knock on one of these doors, thought Lavinia. If necessary.

The man was singing 'Shine On, Harvest Moon', and he carried a long club in his hand. 'Well, look who's here! What a time of night for you to be out, Miss Nebbs!'

'Officer Kennedy!'

And that's who it was, of course – Officer Kennedy on his beat.

'I'd better see you home.'

'Never mind, I'll make it.'

'But you live across the ravine.'

Yes, she thought, but I won't walk the ravine with *any* man. How do I know *who* the Lonely One is? 'No thanks,' she said.

'I'll wait right here then,' he said. 'If you need help give a yell. I'll come running.'

She went on, leaving him under a light humming to himself, alone.

Here I am, she thought.

The ravine.

She stood on the top of the one hundred and thirteen steps down the steep, brambled bank that led across the creaking bridge one hundred yards and up through the black hills to Park Street. And only one lantern to see by. Three minutes from now, she thought, I'll be putting my key in my house door. Nothing can happen in just one hundred and eighty seconds.

She started down the dark green steps into the deep ravine night.

'One, two, three, four, five, six, seven, eight, nine steps,' she whispered.

She felt she was running, but she was not running.

'Fifteen, sixteen, seventeen, eighteen, nineteen steps,' she counted aloud.

'One-fifth of the way!' she announced to herself.

The ravine was deep, deep and black, black. And the world was gone, the world of safe people in bed. The locked doors, the town, the drugstore, the theatre, the lights, everything was gone. Only the ravine existed and lived, black and huge about her.

'Nothing's happened, has it? No one around, *is* there? Twenty-four, twenty-five steps. Remember that old ghost story you told each other when you were children?'

She listened to her feet on the steps.

'The story about the man coming in your house and you upstairs in bed. And now he's at the *first* step, coming up to your room. Now he's at the second step. Now he's at the third and the fourth, and the *fifth* step! Oh, how you laughed and screamed at that story! And now the horrid man is at the twelfth step, opening your door, and now he's standing by your bed. I got *you*!'

She screamed. It was like nothing she had ever heard, that scream. She had never screamed that loud in her life. She stopped, she froze, she clung to the wooden banister. Her heart exploded in her. The sound of its terrified beating filled the universe.

'There, there!' she screamed to herself. 'At the bottom of the steps. A man, under the light! No, now he's gone! He was *waiting* there!'

She listened.

Silence. The bridge was empty.

Nothing, she thought, holding her heart. Nothing. Fool. That story I told myself. How silly. What shall I do?

Her heartbeats faded.

Shall I call the officer, did he hear my scream? Or was it only loud to *me*? Was it really just a small scream after all?

She listened. Nothing. Nothing.

I'll go back to Helen's and sleep the night. But even while she thought this, she moved down again. No, it's nearer home now. Thirty-eight, thirty-nine steps, careful, don't fall. Oh, I *am* a fool. Forty steps. Forty-one. Almost half-way now. She froze again.

'Wait,' she told herself. She took a step.

There was an echo.

She took another step. Another echo – just a fraction of a moment later.

'Someone's following me,' she whispered to the ravine, to the black crickets and dark green frogs and the black stream. 'Someone's on the steps behind me. I don't dare turn around.'

Another step, another echo.

Every time I take a step, *they* take one.

A step and an echo.

Weakly she asked of the ravine, 'Officer Kennedy? Is that *you*?'

The crickets were suddenly still. The crickets were listening. The night was listening to *her*. For a moment, all of the far summer night meadows and close summer night trees were suspending motion. Leaf, shrub, star and meadowgrass had ceased their particular tremors and were listening to Lavinia Nebb's heart. And perhaps a thousand miles away, across locomotive-lonely country, in an empty way station a lonely night traveller reading a dim newspaper under a naked light-bulb might raise his head, listen, and think, What's that? and decide, Only a Woodchuck, surely, beating a hollow log. But it was Lavinia Nebbs, it was most surely the heart of Lavinia Nebbs.

Faster. Faster. She went down the steps.

Run!

She heard music. In a mad way, a silly way, she heard the huge surge of music that pounded at her, and she realized as she ran – as she ran in panic and terror – that some part of her mind was dramatizing, borrowing from the turbulent score of some private film. The music was rushing and plunging her faster, faster, plummeting and scurrying, down and down into the pit of the ravine!

'Only a little way,' she prayed. 'One hundred ten, eleven, twelve, thirteen steps! The bottom! Now run! Across the bridge!'

She spoke to her legs, her arms, her body, her terror; she advised all parts of herself in this white and terrible instant. Over the roaring creek waters, on the hollow, swaying, almost-alive bridge planks she ran, followed by the wild footsteps behind, with the music following too, the music shrieking and babbling!

He's following. Don't turn, don't look – if you see him, you'll not be able to move! You'll be frightened, you'll freeze! Just run, run, *run*!

She ran across the bridge.

Oh, God! God, please, please let me get up the hill! Now up, up the path, now between the hills. Oh, God, it's dark, and everything so far away! If I screamed now it wouldn't help; I can't scream anyway! Here's the top of the path, here's the street. Thank God I wore my low-heeled shoes. I can run, I can run! Oh, God please let me be safe! If I get home safe I'll never go out alone, I was a fool, let me admit it, a fool! I didn't know what terror was, I wouldn't let myself think, but if you let me home from this I'll never go out without Helen or Francine again! Across the street now!

She crossed the street and rushed up the sidewalk.

Oh, God, the porch! My house!

In the middle of her running, she saw the empty lemonade glass where she had left it hours before, in the good, easy, lazy time, left it on the railing. She wished she were back in that time now, drinking from it, the night still young and not begun.

'Oh, please, please, give me time to get inside and lock the door and I'll be safe!'

She heard her clumsy feet on the porch, felt her hands scrabbling and ripping at the lock with the key. She heard her heart. She heard her inner voice shrieking.

The key fitted.

'Unlock the door, quick, quick!'

The door opened.

'Now inside. *Slam* it!'

She slammed the door

'Now lock it, bar it, lock it!' she cried wretchedly. 'Lock it *tight*!'

The door was locked and barred and bolted.

The music stopped.

She listened to her heart again and the sound of it diminishing into silence.

Home. Oh, safe at home. Safe, safe, and safe at home! She slumped against the door. Safe, safe. Listen. Not a sound. Safe, safe, oh, thank God, safe at home. I'll never go out at night again. Safe, oh safe, safe, home, so good, so good, safe. Safe inside, the door locked. *Wait*. Look out the window.

She looked. She gazed out the window for a full half-minute.

'Why there's nothing there at all! Nobody! There was no one following me at all. Nobody running after me.' She caught her breath and almost laughed at herself. 'It stands to reason. If a man *had* been following me, he'd have *caught* me. I'm not a fast runner. There's no one on the porch or in the yard. How silly of me. I wasn't running from anything except *me*. That ravine was safer than safe. Just the same, though, it's nice to be home. Home's the really good warm safe place, the *only* place to be.'

She put her hand out to the light switch and stopped.

'What?' she asked. 'What? *What*?'

Behind her, in the black living-room, someone cleared his throat . . .

A Terribly Strange Bed

Wilkie Collins

Shortly after my education at college was finished I happened to be staying at Paris with an English friend. We were both young men then, and lived, I am afraid, rather a wild life in the delightful city of our sojourn*. One night we were idling about the neighbourhood of the Palais Royal, doubtful to what amusement we should next betake ourselves. My friend proposed a visit to Frascati's; but his suggestion was not to my taste. I knew Frascati's, as the French saying is, by heart; had lost and won plenty of five-franc pieces there, merely for amusement's sake, until it was amusement no longer, and was thoroughly tired, in fact, of all the ghastly respectabilities of such a social anomaly* as a respectable gambling-house. 'For Heaven's sake,' said I to my friend, 'let us go somewhere where we can see a little genuine, blackguard, poverty-stricken gaming, with no false gingerbread glitter thrown over it at all. Let us get away from fashionable Frascati's, to a house where they don't mind letting in a man with a ragged coat, or a man with no coat, ragged or otherwise.' 'Very well,' said my friend, 'we needn't go out of the Palais Royal to find the sort of company you want. Here's the place just before us, as blackguard a place, by all report, as you could possibly wish to see.' In another minute we arrived at the door and entered the house.

When we got upstairs, and had left our hats and sticks with the doorkeeper, we were admitted into the

* sojourn: temporary residence anomaly: contradiction

chief gambling-room. We did not find many people assembled there. But, few as the men were who looked up at us on our entrance, they were all types – lamentably true types – of their respective classes.

We had come to see blackguards; but these men were something worse. There is a comic side, more or less appreciable, in all blackguardism – here there was nothing but tragedy – mute, weird tragedy. The quiet in the room was horrible. The thin, haggard, long-haired young man, whose sunken eyes fiercely watched the turning up of the cards, never spoke; the flabby, fat-faced, pimply player, who pricked his piece of pasteboard perseveringly to register how often black won and how often red – never spoke; the dirty, wrinkled old man, with the vulture eyes and the darned greatcoat, who had lost his last *sou*[*], and still looked on desperately after he could play no longer – never spoke. Even the voice of the croupier sounded as if it were strangely dulled and thickened in the atmosphere of the room. I had entered the place to laugh, but the spectacle before me was something to weep over. I soon found it necessary to take refuge in excitement from the depression of spirits which was fast stealing on me. Unfortunately I sought the nearest excitement by going to the table and beginning to play. Still more unfortunately, as the event will show, I won – won prodigiously, won incredibly; won at such a rate that the regular players at the table crowded round me; and, staring at my stakes with hungry, superstitious eyes, whispered to one another that the English stranger was going to break the bank.

The game was *Rouge et Noir*. I had played at it in every city in Europe, without, however, the care or the

* *sou*: small coin of low value

wish to study the Theory of Chances – that philosopher's stone* of all gamblers! And a gambler, in the strict sense of the word, I had never been. I was heart-whole from the corroding passion for play. My gaming was a mere idle amusement. I never resorted to it by necessity, because I never knew what it was to want money. I never practised it so incessantly as to lose more than I could afford, or to gain more than I could coolly pocket without being thrown off my balance by my good luck. In short, I had hitherto frequented gaming-tables – just as I frequented ball-rooms and opera-houses – because they amused me, and because I had nothing better to do with my leisure hours.

But on this occasion it was very different – now, for the first time in my life, I felt what the passion for play really was. My success first bewildered, and then, in the most literal meaning of the word, intoxicated me. Incredible as it may appear, it is nevertheless true, that I only lost when I attempted to estimate chances, and played according to previous calculation. If I left everything to luck, and staked without any care or consideration, I was sure to win – to win in the face of every recognized probability in favour of the bank. At first, some of the men present ventured their money safely enough on my colour; but I speedily increased my stakes to sums which they dared not risk. One after another they left off playing, and breathlessly looked on at my game.

Still, time after time, I staked higher and higher, and still won. The excitement in the room rose to fever pitch. The silence was interrupted by a deep-muttered

* philosopher's stone: imaginary stone which was thought to turn base metals into gold

chorus of oaths and exclamations in different languages every time the gold was shovelled across to my side of the table – even the imperturbable* croupier dashed his rake on the floor in a (French) fury of astonishment at my success. But one man present preserved his self-possession, and that man was my friend. He came to my side, and, whispering in English, begged me to leave the place, satisfied with what I had already gained. I must do him the justice to say that he repeated his warnings and entreaties several times, and only left me and went away after I had rejected his advice (I was to all intents and purposes gambling-drunk) in terms which rendered it impossible for him to address me again that night.

Shortly after he had gone a hoarse voice behind me cried, 'Permit me, my dear sir! – permit me to restore to their proper place two Napoleons which you have dropped. Wonderful luck, sir! I pledge you my word of honour, as an old soldier, in the course of my long experience in this sort of thing, I never saw such luck as yours! – never! Go on, sir – *Sacré mille bombes!* Go on boldly, and break the bank!'

I turned round and saw, nodding and smiling at me with inveterate* civility, a tall man, dressed in a frogged and braided surtout*.

If I had been in my senses I should have considered him, personally, as being rather a suspicious specimen of an old soldier. He had goggling blood-shot eyes, mangy mustachios, and a broken nose. His voice betrayed a barrack-room intonation of the worst order, and he had the dirtiest pair of hands I ever saw

* imperturbable: calm inveterate: ingrained
frogged and braided surtout: overcoat with ornamental surface decoration

– even in France. These little personal peculiarities exercised, however, no repelling influence on me. In the mad excitement, the reckless triumph of that moment, I was ready to 'fraternize' with anybody who encouraged me in my game. I accepted the old soldier's offered pinch of snuff, clapped him on the back, and swore he was the honestest fellow in the world, the most glorious relic of the Grand Army that I had ever met with. 'Go on!' cried my military friend, snapping his fingers in ecstasy. 'Go on, and win! Break the bank – *Mille tonnerres!* my gallant English comrade, break the bank!'

And I *did* go on – went on at such a rate, that in another quarter of an hour the croupier called out, 'Gentlemen! the bank has discontinued for tonight.' All the notes and all the gold in that 'bank' now lay in a heap under my hands; the whole floating capital of the gambling-house was waiting to pour into my pockets!

'Tie up the money in your pocket-handkerchief, my worthy sir,' said the old soldier, as I wildly plunged my hands into my heap of gold. 'Tie it up, as we used to tie up a bit of dinner in the Grand Army; your winnings are too heavy for any breeches pockets that ever were sewed. There? that's it! Shovel them in, notes and all! *Credié!* what luck! – Stop! another Napoleon on the floor! *Ah! sacré petit polisson de Napoleon!* have I found thee at last? Now then, sir – two tight double knots each way with your honourable permission, and the money's safe. Feel it! feel it, fortunate sir! hard and round as a cannon ball – *Ah, bah!* if they had only fired such cannon balls at us at Austerlitz – *nom d'une pipe!* if they only had! And now, as an ancient grenadier, as an ex-brave of the French army, what remains for me to do? I ask what? Simply this: to entreat my valued English friend to drink a bottle of champagne with me, and toast the goddess Fortune in foaming goblets before we part!'

Excellent ex-brave! Convivial ancient grenadier! Champagne by all means! An English cheer for an old soldier! Hurrah! hurrah! Another English cheer for the goddess Fortune! Hurrah! hurrah! hurrah!

'Bravo! the Englishman; the amiable, gracious Englishman, in whose veins circulates the vivacious blood of France! Another glass? *Ah, bah!* – the bottle is empty! Never mind! *Vive le vin!* I, the old soldier, order another bottle – and half a pound of *bon-bons* with it!'

'No, no, ex-brave; never – ancient grenadier! *Your* bottle last time, *my* bottle this. Behold it! Toast away! The French Army! – the great Napoleon! – the present company! the croupier! the honest croupier's wife and daughters – if he has any! the ladies generally! Everybody in the world!'

By this time the second bottle of champagne was emptied. I felt as if I had been drinking liquid fire – my brain seemed all aflame. No excess in wine had ever had this effect on me before in my life. Was it the result of a stimulant acting upon my system when I was in a highly excited state? Was my stomach in a particularly disordered condition? Or was the champagne amazingly strong?

'Ex-brave of the French Army!' cried I, in a mad state of exhilaration, '*I* am on fire! how are *you?* You have set me on fire! Do you hear, my hero of Austerlitz? Let us have a third bottle of champagne to put the flame out!'

The old soldier wagged his head, rolled his goggle eyes, until I expected to see them slip out of their sockets; placed his dirty forefinger by the side of his broken nose, solemnly ejaculated, 'Coffee!' and immediately ran off into an inner room.

The word pronounced by the eccentric veteran seemed to have a magical effect on the rest of the company present. With one accord they all rose to depart. Probably they had expected to profit by my intoxication; but finding that my new friend was benevolently bent on preventing me from getting dead drunk, had now abandoned all hope of thriving pleasantly on my winnings. Whatever their motive might be, at any rate they went away in a body. When the old soldier returned and sat down again opposite to me at the table, we had the room to ourselves. I could see the croupier, in a sort of vestibule which opened out of it, eating his supper in solitude. The silence was now deeper than ever.

A sudden change, too, had come over the 'ex-brave'. He assumed a portentously* solemn look, and when he spoke to me again his speech was ornamented by no oaths, enforced by no finger-snapping, enlivened by no apostrophes or exclamations.

'Listen, my dear sir,' said he, in mysteriously confidential tones, – 'listen to an old soldier's advice. I have been to the mistress of the house (a very charming woman, with a genius for cookery!) to impress on her the necessity of making us some particularly strong and good coffee. You must drink this coffee in order to get rid of your little amiable exaltation of spirits before you think of going home – you *must*, my good and gracious friend! With all that money to take home to-night, it is a sacred duty to yourself to have your wits about you. You are known to be a winner to an enormous extent by several gentlemen present to-night, who, in a certain point of view, are very worthy and excellent fellows; but they

* portentously: ominously

are mortal men, my dear sir, and they have their amiable weaknesses! Need I say more? Ah, no, no! you understand me! Now, this is what you must do. Send for a cabriolet* when you feel quite well again, draw up all the windows when you get into it, and tell the driver to take you home only through the large and well-lighted thoroughfares. Do this, and you and your money will be safe. Do this, and to-morrow you will thank an old soldier for giving you a word of honest advice.'

Just as the ex-brave ended his oration in very lachrymose* tones, the coffee came in, ready poured out in two cups. My attentive friend handed me one of the cups with a bow. I was parched with thirst, and drank it off at a draught. Almost instantly afterwards I was seized with a fit of giddiness, and felt more completely intoxicated than ever. The room whirled round and round furiously; the old soldier seemed to be regularly bobbing up and down before me like the piston of a steam-engine. I was half deafened by a violent singing in my ears; a feeling of utter bewilderment, helplessness, idiocy overcame me. I rose from my chair, holding on by the table to keep my balance, and stammered out that I felt dreadfully unwell, so unwell that I did not know how I was to get home.

'My dear friend,' answered the old soldier – and even his voice seemed to be bobbing up and down as he spoke – 'my dear friend, it would be madness to go home in *your* state; you would be sure to lose your money; you might be robbed and murdered with the greatest ease. *I* am going to sleep here: do *you* sleep

* cabriolet: two-wheeled horse-drawn carriage
lachrymose: sorrowful

here, too – they make up capital beds in this house – take one; sleep off the effects of the wine, and go home safely with your winnings tomorrow – tomorrow, in broad daylight.'

I had but two ideas left: one, that I must never let go hold of my handkerchief full of money; the other, that I must lie down somewhere immediately and fall off into a comfortable sleep. So I agreed to the proposal about the bed, and took the offered arm of the old soldier, carrying my money with my disengaged hand. Preceded by the croupier, we passed along some passages and up a flight of stairs into the bedroom which I was to occupy. The ex-brave shook me warmly by the hand, proposed that we should breakfast together, and then, followed by the croupier, left me for the night.

I ran to the wash-hand stand, drank some of the water in my jug, poured the rest out, and plunged my face into it, then sat down in a chair and tried to compose myself. I soon felt better. The change for my lungs from the fetid* atmosphere of the gambling-room to the cool air of the apartment I now occupied; the almost equally refreshing change for my eyes from the glaring gas-lights of the 'Salon' to the dim, quiet flicker of one bedroom candle, aided wonderfully the restorative effects of cold water. The giddiness left me, and I began to feel a little like a reasonable being again. My first thought was of the risk of sleeping all night in a gambling-house; my second, of the still greater risk of trying to get out after the house was closed, and of going home alone at night, through the streets of Paris, with a large sum of money about me. I had slept in worse places than this on my

* fetid: foul-smelling

travels; so I determined to lock, bolt, and barricade my door and take my chance till the next morning.

Accordingly, I secured myself against all intrusion, looked under the bed and into the cupboard, tried the fastening of the window, and then, satisfied that I had taken every proper precaution, pulled off my upper clothing, put my light, which was a dim one, on the hearth among a feathery litter of wood ashes, and got into bed, with the handkerchief full of money under my pillow.

I soon felt not only that I could not go to sleep, but that I could not even close my eyes. I was wide awake, and in a high fever. Every nerve in my body trembled – every one of my senses seemed to be preternaturally* sharpened. I tossed and rolled, and tried every kind of position, and perseveringly sought out the old corners of the bed, and all to no purpose. Now, I thrust my arms over the clothes; now, I poked them under the clothes; now, I violently shot my legs straight out down to the bottom of the bed; now, I convulsively coiled them up as near my chin as they would go; now, I shook out my crumpled pillow, changed it to the cool side, patted it flat, and lay down quietly on my back; now, I fiercely doubled it in two, set it up on end, thrust it against the board of the bed, and tried a sitting posture. Every effort was in vain; I groaned with vexation, as I felt that I was in for a sleepless night.

What could I do? I had no book to read. And yet, unless I found out some method of diverting my mind, I felt certain that I was in the condition to imagine all sorts of horrors; to rack my brain with forebodings of every possible and impossible danger; in short, to pass

* preternaturally: abnormally

the night in suffering all conceivable varieties of nervous terror.

I raised myself on my elbow, and looked about the room, which was brightened by a lovely moonlight pouring straight through the window – to see if it contained any pictures or ornaments that I could at all clearly distinguish. While my eyes wandered from wall to wall, a remembrance of Le Maistre's delightful little book, *Voyage autour de ma Chambre*, occurred to me. I resolved to imitate the French author, and find occupation and amusement enough to relieve the tedium of my wakefulness by making a mental inventory of every article of furniture I could see, and by following up to their sources the multitude of associations which even a chair, a table, or a wash-hand stand may be made to call forth.

In the nervous unsettled state of my mind at that moment I found it much easier to make my inventory than to make my reflections, and thereupon soon gave up all hope of thinking in Le Maistre's fanciful track – or, indeed, of thinking at all. I looked about the room at the different articles of furniture, and did nothing more.

There was, first, the bed I was lying in; a four-post bed, of all things in the world to met with in Paris! – yes, a thorough clumsy British four-poster, with the regular top lined with chintz – the regular fringed valance all round – the regular stifling unwholesome curtains, which I remembered having mechanically drawn back against the posts without particularly noticing the bed when I first got into the room. Then there was the marble-topped wash-hand stand, from which the water I had spilt, in my hurry to pour it out, was still dripping, slowly and more slowly, on to the brick floor. Then two small chairs, with my coat, waistcoat, and trousers flung on them. Then a large elbow-chair covered with dirty-white dimity*, with my cravat and shirt-collar thrown over the back. Then a chest of drawers with two of the brass handles off, and a tawdry, broken china inkstand placed on it by way of ornament for the top. Then the dressing-table, adorned by a very small looking-glass, and a very large pincushion. Then the window – an unusually large window. Then a dark old picture, which the feeble candle dimly showed me. It was the picture of a fellow in a high Spanish hat, crowned with a plume of towering feathers. A swarthy, sinister ruffian, looking upward, shading his eyes with his hand, and looking intently upward – it might be at some tall gallows at which he was going to be hanged. At any rate, he had the appearance of thoroughly deserving it.

This picture put a kind of constraint upon me to look upward too – at the top of the bed. It was a gloomy and not an interesting object, and I looked back at the picture. I counted the feathers in the man's hat – they stood out in relief – three white, two green. I observed the crown of his hat, which was of a conical shape, according to the fashion supposed to have been favoured by Guido Fawkes. I wondered what he was looking up at. It couldn't be at the stars; such a desperado was neither astrologer nor astronomer. It must be at the high gallows, and he was going to be hanged presently. Would the executioner come into possession of his conical-crowned hat and plume of feathers? I counted the feathers again – three white, two green.

While I still lingered over this very improving and intellectual employment, my thoughts insensibly*

* dimity: cotton fabric insensibly: unconsciously

began to wander. The moonlight shining into the room reminded me of a certain moonlight night in England – the night after a picnic party in a Welsh valley. Every incident of the drive homeward, through lovely scenery, which the moonlight made lovelier than ever, came back to my remembrance, though I had never given the picnic a thought for years; though, if I had *tried* to recollect it, I could certainly have recalled little or nothing of that scene long past. Of all the wonderful faculties that help to tell us we are immortal, which speaks the sublime truth more eloquently than memory? Here was I, in a strange house of the most suspicious character, in a situation of uncertainty and even of peril, which might seem to make the cool exercise of my recollection almost out of the question; nevertheless, remembering, quite involuntarily, places, people, conversations, minute circumstances of every kind, which I had thought forgotten for ever, which I could not possibly have recalled at will, even under the most favourable auspices*. And what cause had produced in a moment the whole of this strange, complicated, mysterious effect? Nothing but some rays of moonlight shining in at my bedroom window. I was still thinking of the picnic – of our merriment on the drive home – of the sentimental young lady who *would* quote *Childe Harold* because it was moonlight. I was absorbed by these past scenes and past amusements, when, in an instant, the thread on which my memories hung snapped asunder: my attention immediately came back to present things more vividly than ever, and I found myself, I neither knew why nor wherefore, looking hard at the picture again.

Looking for what?

* auspices: omens

Good God! the man had pulled his hat down on his brows – No! – the hat itself was gone! Where was the conical crown? Where the feathers – three white, two green? Not there! In place of the hat and feathers, what dusky object was it that now hid his forehead, his eyes, his shading hand?

Was the bed moving?

I turned on my back and looked up. Was I mad? drunk? dreaming? giddy again? or was the top of the bed really moving down – sinking slowly, regularly, silently, horribly right down throughout the whole of its length and breadth – right down upon me as I lay underneath?

My blood seemed to stand still. A deadly paralysing coldness stole all over me as I turned my head round on the pillow and determined to test whether the bed-top was really moving or not by keeping my eye on the man in the picture.

The next look in that direction was enough. The dull, black, frowsy outline of the valance above me was within an inch of being parallel with his waist. I still looked breathlessly. And steadily, and slowly – very slowly – I saw the figure, and the line of frame below the figure, vanish as the valance moved down before it.

I am, constitutionally, anything but timid. I have been on more than one occasion in peril of my life, and have not lost my self-possession for an instant; but when the conviction first settled on my mind that the bed-top was really moving, was steadily and continuously sinking down upon me, I looked up shuddering, helpless, panic-stricken, beneath the hideous machinery for murder, which was advancing closer and closer to suffocate me where I lay.

I looked up, motionless, speechless, breathless. The candle, fully spent, went out; but the moonlight still brightened the room. Down and down, without pausing and without sounding, came the bed-top, and still my panic-terror seemed to bind me faster and faster to the mattress on which I lay – down and down it sank, till the dusty odour from the lining of the canopy came stealing into my nostrils.

At that final moment the instinct of self-preservation startled me out of my trance and I moved at last. There was just room for me to roll myself sideways off the bed. As I dropped noiselessly to the floor the edge of the murderous canopy touched me on the shoulder.

Without stopping to draw my breath, without wiping the cold sweat from my face, I rose instantly on my knees to watch the bed-top. I was literally spell-bound by it. If I had heard footsteps behind me, I could not have turned round; if a means of escape had been miraculously provided for me, I could not have moved to take advantage of it. The whole life in me was, at that moment, concentrated in my eyes.

It descended – the whole canopy, with the fringe round it, came down – down – close down, so close that there was not room now to squeeze my finger between the bed-top and the bed. I felt at the sides, and discovered that what had appeared to me from beneath to be the ordinary light canopy of a four-post bed was in reality a thick, broad mattress, the substance of which was concealed by the valance and its fringe. I looked up and saw the four posts rising hideously bare. In the middle of the bed-top was a huge wooden screw that had evidently worked it down through a hole in the ceiling, just as ordinary presses are worked down on the substance selected for compression. The frightful apparatus moved without making the faintest noise. There had been no creaking as it came down; there was now not the faintest sound from the room above. Amid a dead and awful silence I beheld before me – in the nineteenth century, and in the civilized capital of France – such a machine for secret murder by suffocation as might have existed in the worst days of the Inquisition, in the lonely inns among the Hartz Mountains, in the mysterious tribunals of Westphalia! Still, as I looked on it I could not move, I could hardly breathe, but I began to recover the power of thinking, and in a moment I discovered the murderous conspiracy framed against me in all its horror. My cup of coffee had been drugged, and drugged too strongly. I had been saved from being smothered by having taken an overdose of some narcotic. How I had chafed and fretted at the fever-fit which had preserved my life by keeping me awake! How recklessly I had confided myself to the two wretches who had led me into this room, determined, for the sake of my winnings, to kill me in my sleep by the surest and most horrible contrivance for secretly accomplishing my destruction! How many men, winners like me, had slept, as I had proposed to sleep, in that bed and had never been seen or heard of more! I shuddered at the bare idea of it.

But ere long all thought was again suspended by the sight of the murderous canopy moving once more. After it had remained on the bed – as nearly as I could guess – about ten minutes, it began to move up again. The villains who worked it from above evidently believed that their purpose was now accomplished. Slowly and silently, as it had descended, that horrible bed-top rose towards its former place. When it reached the upper extremities of the four posts, it reached the ceiling too. Neither hole nor screw could be seen; the bed became in appearance an ordinary bed again – the canopy an ordinary canopy – even to the most suspicious eyes.

Now, for the first time, I was able to move – to rise from my knees – to dress myself in my upper clothing – and to consider of how I should escape. If I betrayed, by the smallest noise, that the attempt to suffocate me had failed, I was certain to be murdered. Had I made any noise already? I listened intently, looking towards the door.

No! no footsteps in the passage outside – no sound of a tread, light or heavy, in the room above – absolute silence everywhere. Besides locking and bolting my door I had moved an old wooden chest against it, which I had found under the bed. To remove this chest (my blood ran cold as I thought of what its contents *might* be!) without making some disturbance was impossible; and, moreover, to think of escaping through the house, now barred up for the night, was sheer insanity. Only one chance was left me – the window. I stole to it on tiptoe.

My bedroom was on the first floor, above an *entresol*[*], and looked into the back street. I raised my hand to open the window, knowing that on that action hung, by the merest hair's-breadth, my chance of safety. They keep vigilant watch in a House of Murder. If any part of the frame cracked, if the hinge creaked, I was a lost man! It must have occupied me at least five minutes, reckoning by time – five *hours*, reckoning by suspense – to open that window. I succeeded in doing it silently – in doing it with all the dexterity of a housebreaker – and then looked down into the street. To leap the distance beneath me would be almost certain destruction! Next, I looked round at the sides

* *entresol*: mezzanine floor

of the house. Down the left side ran the thick water-pipe – it passed close by the outer edge of the window. The moment I saw the pipe I knew I was saved. My breath came and went freely for the first time since I had seen the canopy of the bed moving down upon me!

To some men the means of escape which I had discovered might have seemed difficult and dangerous enough – to *me* the prospect of slipping down the pipe into the street did not suggest even a thought of peril. I had always been accustomed, by the practice of gymnastics, to keep up my schoolboy powers as a daring and expert climber, and knew that my head, hands, and feet would serve me faithfully in any hazards of ascent or descent. I had already got one leg over the window-sill when I remembered the handkerchief filled with money under my pillow. I could well have afforded to leave it behind me, but I was revengefully determined that the miscreants* of the gambling-house should miss their plunder as well as their victim. So I went back to the bed and tied the heavy handkerchief at my back by my cravat. Just as I had made it tight and fixed it in a comfortable place, I thought I heard a sound of breathing outside the door. The chill feeling of horror ran through me again as I listened. No! dead silence still in the passage – I had only heard the night-air blowing softly into the room. The next moment I was on the window-sill – and the next I had a firm grip on the water-pipe with my hands and knees.

I slid down into the street easily and quietly, as I thought I should, and immediately set off at the top of my speed to a branch 'Prefecture' of Police, which I

* miscreants: wrongdoers

knew was situated in the immediate neighbourhood. A 'Sub-prefect' and several picked men among his subordinates happened to be up, maturing, I believe, some scheme for discovering the perpetrator of a mysterious murder which all Paris was talking of just then. When I began my story, in a breathless hurry and in very bad French, I could see that the Sub-prefect suspected me of being a drunken Englishman who had robbed somebody; but he soon altered his opinion as I went on, and before I had anything like concluded, he shoved all the papers before him into a drawer, put on his hat, supplied me with another (for I was bare-headed), ordered a file of soldiers, desired his expert followers to get ready all sorts of tools for breaking open doors and ripping up brick-flooring, and took my arm in the most friendly and familiar manner possible to lead me with him out of the house. I will venture to say that when the Sub-prefect was a little boy, and was taken for the first time to the play, he was not half as much pleased as he was now at the job in prospect for him at the gambling-house!

Away we went through the streets, the Sub-prefect cross-examining and congratulating me in the same breath as we marched at the head of our formidable *posse comitatus**. Sentinels were placed at the back and front of the house the moment we got to it; a tremendous battery of knocks was directed against the door; a light appeared at the window; I was told to conceal myself behind the police – then came more knocks, and a cry of 'Open in the name of the law!' At that terrible summons bolts and locks gave way before an invisible hand, and the moment after the

* *posse comitatus*: band of law-enforcers (Latin)

Sub-prefect was in the passage, confronting a waiter half-dressed and ghastly pale. This was the short dialogue which immediately took place:

'We want to see the Englishman who is sleeping in this house.'

'He went away hours ago.'

'He did no such thing. His friend went away; *he* remained. Show us to his bedroom!'

'I swear to you, Monsieur le Sous-prefect, he is not here! he – '

'I swear to you, Monsieur le Garçon, he is. He slept here – he didn't find your bed comfortable – he came to us to complain of it – here he is among my men – and here am I ready to look for a flea or two in his bedstead. Renaudin! (calling to one of the subordinates and pointing to the waiter) collar that man and tie his hands behind him. Now, then, gentlemen, let us walk upstairs!'

Every man and woman in the house was secured – the 'Old Soldier' the first. Then I identified the bed in which I had slept, and then we went into the room above.

No object that was at all extraordinary appeared in any part of it. The Sub-prefect looked round the place, commanded everybody to be silent, stamped twice on the floor, called for a candle, looked attentively at the spot he had stamped on, and ordered the flooring there to be carefully taken up. This was done in no time. Lights were produced, and we saw a deep raftered cavity between the floor of this room and the ceiling of the room beneath. Through this cavity there ran perpendicularly a sort of case of iron thickly greased, and inside the case appeared the screw which communicated with the bed-top below. Extra lengths of screw, freshly oiled; levers covered with felt; all the complete upper works of a heavy press – constructed with infernal ingenuity so as to join the fixtures below, and when taken to pieces again to go into the smallest possible compass – were next discovered and pulled out on the floor. After some little difficulty the Sub-prefect succeeded in putting the machinery together, and, leaving his men to work it, descended with me to the bedroom. The smothering canopy was then lowered, but not so noiselessly as I had seen it lowered. When I mentioned this to the Sub-prefect, his answer, simple as it was, had a terrible significance. 'My men,' said he, 'are working down the bed-top for the first time – the men whose money you won were in better practice.'

We left the house in the sole possession of two police agents – every one of the inmates being removed to prison on the spot. The Sub-prefect, after taking down my '*procès-verbal*'* in his office, returned with me to my hotel to get my passport. 'Do you think,' I asked as I gave it to him, 'that any men have really been smothered in that bed as they tried to smother *me*?'

'I have seen dozens of drowned men laid out at the Morgue,' answered the Sub-prefect, 'in whose pocket-books were found letters stating that they had committed suicide in the Seine, because they had lost everything at the gaming-table. Do I know how many of those men entered the same gambling-house that *you* entered? won as *you* won? took that bed as *you* took it? slept in it? were smothered in it? and were privately thrown into the river with a letter of explanation written by the murderers and placed in their pocket-books? No man can say how many or how few have suffered the fate from which you have

* '*procès-verbal*': statement

escaped. The people of the gambling-house kept their bedstead machinery a secret from *us* – even from the police! The dead kept the rest of the secret for them. Goodnight, or rather good morning, Monsieur Faulkner! Be at my office again at nine o'clock – in the meantime, *au revoir*!'

The rest of my story is soon told. I was examined and re-examined; the gambling-house was strictly searched all through from top to bottom; the prisoners were separately interrogated, and two of the less guilty among them made a confession. *I* discovered that the Old Soldier was the master of the gambling-house – *justice* discovered that he had been drummed out of the army as a vagabond years ago; that he had been guilty of all sorts of villainies since; that he was in possession of stolen property, which the owners identified; and that he, the croupier, another accomplice, and the woman who had made my cup of coffee were all in the secret of the bedstead. There appeared some reason to doubt whether the inferior persons attached to the house knew anything of the suffocating machinery, and they received the benefit of that doubt by being treated simply as thieves and vagabonds. As for the Old Soldier and his two head-myrmidons*, they went to the galleys; the woman who had drugged my coffee was imprisoned for I forget how many years; the regular attendants at the gambling-house were considered 'suspicious' and placed under 'surveillance'; and I became, for one whole week (which is a long time), the head 'lion' in Parisian society. My adventure was dramatized by three illustrious playmakers, but never saw theatrical daylight, for the censorship forbade the introduction

* myrmidons: followers

on the stage of a correct copy of the gambling-house bedstead.

One good result was produced by my adventure which any censorship must have approved: it cured me of ever again trying *Rouge et Noir* as an amusement. The sight of a green cloth, with packs of cards and heaps of money on it, will henceforth be for ever associated in my mind with the sight of a bed-canopy descending to suffocate me in the silence and darkness of the night.

The Landlady

Roald Dahl

Billy Weaver had travelled down from London on the slow afternoon train, with a change at Swindon on the way, and by the time he got to Bath it was about 9 o'clock in the evening and the moon was coming up out of a clear starry sky over the houses opposite the station entrance. But the air was deadly cold and the wind was like a flat blade of ice on his cheeks.

'Excuse me,' he said, 'but is there a fairly cheap hotel not too far away from here?'

'Try The Bell and Dragon,' the porter answered, pointing down the road. 'They might take you in. It's about a quarter of a mile along on the other side.'

Billy thanked him and picked up his suitcase and set out to walk the quarter-mile to The Bell and Dragon. He had never been to Bath before. He didn't know anyone who lived there. But Mr Greenslade at the Head Office in London had told him it was a splendid city. 'Find your own lodgings,' he had said, 'and then go along and report to the Branch Manager as soon as you've got yourself settled.'

Billy was seventeen years old. He was wearing a new navy-blue overcoat, a new brown trilby hat, and a new brown suit, and he was feeling fine. He walked briskly down the street. He was trying to do everything briskly these days. Briskness, he had decided, was *the* one common characteristic of all successful businessmen. The big shots up at Head Office were absolutely fantastically brisk all the time. They were amazing.

There were no shops on this wide street that he was walking along, only a line of tall houses on each side, all of them identical. They had porches and pillars and four or five steps going up to their front doors, and it was obvious that once upon a time they had been very swanky residences. But now, even in the darkness, he could see that the paint was peeling from the woodwork on their doors and windows, and that the handsome white façades were cracked and blotchy from neglect.

Suddenly, in a downstairs window that was brilliantly illuminated by a street-lamp not six yards away, Billy caught sight of a printed notice propped up against the glass in one of the upper panes. It said BED AND BREAKFAST. There was a vase of pussy willows, tall and beautiful, standing just underneath the notice.

He stopped walking. He moved a bit closer. Green curtains (some sort of velvety material) were hanging down on either side of the window. The pussy willows looked wonderful beside them. He went right up and peered through the glass into the room, and the first thing he saw was a bright fire burning in the hearth. On the carpet in front of the fire, a pretty little dachshund was curled up asleep with its nose tucked into its belly. The room itself, so far as he could see in the half-darkness, was filled with pleasant furniture. There was a baby-grand piano and a big sofa and several plump armchairs; and in one corner he spotted a large parrot in a cage. Animals were usually a good sign in a place like this, Billy told himself; and all in all, it looked to him as though it would be a pretty decent house to stay in. Certainly it would be more comfortable than The Bell and Dragon.

On the other hand, a pub would be more congenial than a boarding-house. There would be beer and darts in the evenings, and lots of people to talk to, and it would probably be a good bit cheaper, too. He had stayed a couple of nights in a pub once before and he had liked it. He had never stayed in any boarding-houses, and, to be perfectly honest, he was a tiny bit frightened of them. The name itself conjured up images of watery cabbage, rapacious landladies, and a powerful smell of kippers in the living-room.

After dithering about like this in the cold for two or three minutes, Billy decided that he would walk on and take a look at The Bell and Dragon before making up his mind. He turned to go.

And now a queer thing happened to him. He was in the act of stepping back and turning away from the window when all at once his eye was caught and held in the most peculiar manner by the small notice that was there. BED AND BREAKFAST, it said. BED AND BREAKFAST, BED AND BREAKFAST, BED AND BREAKFAST. Each word was like a large black eye staring at him through the glass, holding him, compelling him, forcing him to stay where he was and not to walk away from that house, and the next thing he knew, he was actually moving across from the window to the front door of the house, climbing the steps that led up to it, and reaching for the bell.

He pressed the bell. Far away in a back room he heard it ringing, and then *at once* – it must have been at once because he hadn't even had time to take his finger from the bell-button – the door swung open and a woman was standing there.

Normally you ring the bell and you have at least a half-minute's wait before the door opens. But this dame was like a jack-in-the-box. He pressed the bell – and out she popped! It made him jump.

She was about forty-five or fifty years old, and the moment she saw him, she gave him a warm welcoming smile.

'*Please* come in,' she said pleasantly. She stepped aside, holding the door wide open, and Billy found himself automatically starting forward into the house. The compulsion or, more accurately, the desire to follow after her into that house was extraordinarily strong.

'I saw the notice in the window,' he said, holding himself back.

'Yes, I know.'

'I was wondering about a room.'

'It's *all* ready for you, my dear,' she said. She had a round pink face and very gentle blue eyes.

'I was on my way to The Bell and Dragon,' Billy told her. 'But the notice in your window just happened to catch my eye.'

'My dear boy,' she said, 'why don't you come in out of the cold?'

'How much do you charge?'

'Five and sixpence a night, including breakfast.'

It was fantastically cheap. It was less than half of what he had been willing to pay.

'If that is too much,' she added, 'then perhaps I can reduce it just a tiny bit. Do you desire an egg for breakfast? Eggs are expensive at the moment. It would be sixpence less without the egg.'

'Five and sixpence is fine,' he answered. 'I should like very much to stay here.'

'I knew you would. Do come in.'

She seemed terribly nice. She looked exactly like the mother of one's best school-friend welcoming one into the house to stay for the Christmas holidays. Billy took off his hat, and stepped over the threshold.

'Just hang it there,' she said, 'and let me help you with your coat.'

There were no other hats or coats in the hall. There were no umbrellas, no walking-sticks – nothing.

'We have it *all* to ourselves,' she said, smiling at him over her shoulder as she led the way upstairs. 'You see, it isn't very often I have the pleasure of taking a visitor into my little nest.'

The old girl is slightly dotty, Billy told himself. But at five and sixpence a night, who gives a damn about that? 'I should've thought you'd be simply swamped with applicants,' he said politely.

'Oh, I am, my dear, I am, of course I am. But the trouble is that I'm inclined to be just a teeny weeny bit choosy and particular – if you see what I mean.'

'Ah, yes.'

'But I'm always ready. Everything is always ready day and night in the house just on the off-chance that an acceptable young gentleman will come along. And it is such a pleasure, my dear, such a very great pleasure when now and again I open the door and I see someone standing there who is just *exactly* right.' She was half-way up the stairs, and she paused with one hand on the stair-rail, turning her head and smiling down at him with pale lips. 'Like you,' she added, and her blue eyes travelled slowly all the way down the length of Billy's body, to his feet, and then up again.

On the first-floor landing she said to him, 'This floor is mine.'

They climbed up a second flight. 'And this one is *all* yours,' she said. 'Here's your room. I do hope you'll like it.' She took him into a small but charming front bedroom, switching on the light as she went in.

'The morning sun comes right in the window, Mr Perkins. It *is* Mr Perkins, isn't it?'

'No,' he said. 'It's Weaver.'

'Mr Weaver. How nice. I've put a water-bottle between the sheets to air them out, Mr Weaver. It's such a comfort to have a hot water-bottle in a strange bed with clean sheets, don't you agree? And you may light the gas fire at any time if you feel chilly.'

'Thank you,' Billy said. 'Thank you ever so much.' He noticed that the bedspread had been taken off the bed, and that the bedclothes had been neatly turned back on one side, all ready for someone to get in.

'I'm so glad you appeared,' she said, looking earnestly into his face. 'I was beginning to get worried.'

'That's all right,' Billy answered brightly. 'You mustn't worry about me.' He put his suitcase on the chair and started to open it.

'And what about supper, my dear? Did you manage to get anything to eat before you came here?'

'I'm not a bit hungry, thank you,' he said. 'I think I'll just go to bed as soon as possible because tomorrow I've got to get up rather early and report to the office.'

'Very well, then. I'll leave you now so that you can unpack. But before you go to bed, would you be kind enough to pop into the sitting-room on the ground floor and sign the book? Everyone has to do that because it's the law of the land, and we don't want to go breaking any laws at *this* stage in the proceedings, do we?' She gave him a little wave of the hand and went quickly out of the room and closed the door.

Now, the fact that his landlady appeared to be slightly off her rocker didn't worry Billy in the least. After all, she was not only harmless – there was no question about that – but she was also quite obviously a kind and generous soul. He guessed that she had probably lost a son in the war, or something like that, and had never got over it.

So a few minutes later, after unpacking his suitcase and washing his hands, he trotted downstairs to the ground floor and entered the living-room. His landlady wasn't there, but the fire was glowing in the hearth, and the little dachshund was still sleeping in front of it. The room was wonderfully warm and cosy. I'm a lucky fellow, he thought, rubbing his hands. This is a bit of all right.

He found the guest-book lying open on the piano, so he took out his pen and wrote down his name and address. There were only two other entries above his on the page, and, as one always does with guest-books, he started to read them. One was a Christopher Mulholland from Cardiff. The other was Gregory W. Temple from Bristol.

That's funny, he thought suddenly. Christopher Mulholland. It rings a bell.

Now where on earth had he heard that rather unusual name before?

Was he a boy at school? No. Was it one of his sister's numerous young men, perhaps, or a friend of his father's? No, no, it wasn't any of those. He glanced down again at the book.

Christopher Mulholland *231 Cathedral Road, Cardiff.*
Gregory W. Temple *27 Sycamore Drive, Bristol*

As a matter of fact, now he came to think of it, he wasn't at all sure that the second name didn't have almost as much of a familiar ring about it as the first.

'Gregory Temple?' he said aloud, searching his memory. 'Christopher Mulholland? . . . '

'Such charming boys,' a voice behind him answered, and he turned and saw his landlady sailing into the room with a large silver tea-tray in her hands. She was holding it well out in front of her, and rather high up, as though the tray were a pair of reins on a frisky horse.

'They sound somehow familiar,' he said.

'They do? How interesting.'

'I'm almost positive I've heard those names before somewhere. Isn't that queer? Maybe it was in the newspapers. They weren't famous in any way, were they? I mean famous cricketers or footballers or something like that?'

'Famous,' she said, setting the tea-tray down on the low table in front of the sofa. 'Oh no, I don't think they were famous. But they were extraordinarily handsome, both of them, I can promise you that. They were tall and young and handsome, my dear, just exactly like you.'

Once more, Billy glanced down at the book. 'Look here,' he said, noticing the dates. 'This last entry is over two years old.'

'It is?'

'Yes, indeed. And Christopher Mulholland's is nearly a year before that – more than *three years ago*.'

'Dear me,' she said, shaking her head and heaving a dainty little sigh. 'I would never have thought it. How time does fly away from us all, doesn't it, Mr Wilkins?'

'It's Weaver,' Billy said. 'W-e-a-v-e-r.'

'Oh, of course it is!' she cried, sitting down on the sofa. 'How silly of me. I do apologize. In one ear and out the other, that's me, Mr Weaver.'

'You know something?' Billy said. 'Something that's really quite extraordinary about all this?'

'No, dear, I don't.'

'Well, you see – both of these names, Mulholland and Temple, I not only seem to remember each one of them separately, so to speak, but somehow or other, in some peculiar way, they both appear to be sort of connected together as well. As though they were both famous for the same sort of thing, if you see what I mean – like . . . well . . . like Dempsey and Tunney, for example, or Churchill and Roosevelt.'

'How amusing,' she said. 'But come over here now, dear, and sit down beside me on the sofa and I'll give you a nice cup of tea and a ginger biscuit before you go to bed.'

'You really shouldn't bother,' Billy said. 'I didn't mean you to do anything like that.' He stood by the piano, watching her as she fussed about with the cups and saucers. He noticed that she had small, white, quickly moving hands, and red fingernails.

'I'm almost positive it was in the newspapers I saw them,' Billy said. 'I'll think of it in a second. I'm sure I will.'

There is nothing more tantalizing than a thing like this which lingers just outside the borders of one's memory. He hated to give up.

'Now wait a minute,' he said. 'Wait just a minute. Mulholland . . . Christopher Mulholland . . . wasn't *that* the name of the Eton schoolboy who was on a walking-tour through the West Country, and then all of a sudden . . . '

'Milk?' she said. 'And sugar?'

'Yes, please. And then all of a sudden . . . '

'Eton schoolboy?' she said, 'Oh no, my dear, that can't possibly be right because *my* Mr Mulholland was certainly not an Eton schoolboy when he came to me. He was a Cambridge undergraduate. Come over here now and sit next to me and warm yourself in front of this lovely fire. Come on. Your tea's all ready for you.' She patted the empty place beside her on the sofa, and she sat there smiling at Billy and waiting for him to come over.

He crossed the room slowly, and sat down on the edge of the sofa. She placed his teacup on the table in front of him.

'*There* we are,' she said. 'How nice and cosy this is, isn't it?'

Billy started sipping his tea. She did the same. For half a minute or so, neither of them spoke. But Billy knew that she was looking at him. Her body was half-turned towards him and he could feel her eyes resting on his face, watching him over the rim of her teacup. Now and again he caught a whiff of a peculiar smell that seemed to emanate* directly from her person. It was not in the least unpleasant, and it reminded him – well, he wasn't quite sure what it reminded him of. Pickled walnuts? New leather? Or was it the corridors of a hospital?

'Mr Mulholland was a great one for his tea,' she said at length. 'Never in my life have I seen anyone drink as much tea as dear, sweet Mr Mulholland.'

'I suppose he left fairly recently,' Billy said. He was positive now that he had seen them in the newspapers – in the headlines.

'Left?' she said, arching her brows. 'But my dear boy, he never left. He's still here. Mr Temple is also here. They're on the third floor, both of them together.'

Billy set down his cup slowly on the table, and stared at his landlady. She smiled back at him, and then she put out one of her white hands and patted him comfortingly on the knee.

'How old are you, my dear?' she asked.

* emanate: proceed

'Seventeen.'

'Seventeen!' she cried. 'Oh, it's the perfect age! Mr Mulholland was also seventeen. But I think he was a trifle shorter than you are, in fact I'm sure he was, and his teeth weren't *quite* so white. You have the most beautiful teeth, Mr Weaver, did you know that?'

'They're not as good as they look,' Billy said. 'They've got simply masses of fillings in them at the back.'

'Mr Temple, of course, was a little older,' she said, ignoring his remark. 'He was actually twenty-eight. And yet I never would have guessed it if he hadn't told me, never in my whole life. There wasn't a *blemish* on his body.'

'A what?' Billy said.

'His skin was *just* like a baby's.'

There was a pause. Billy picked up his teacup and took another sip of his tea, then he set it down again gently in its saucer. He waited for her to say something else, but she seemed to have lapsed into another of her silences. He sat there staring ahead of him into the far corner of the room, biting his lower lip.

'That parrot,' he said at last. 'You know something? It had me completely fooled when I first saw it through the window from the street. I could have sworn it was alive.'

'Alas, no longer.'

'It's most terribly clever the way it's been done,' he said. 'It doesn't look in the least bit dead. Who did it?'

'I did.'

'*You* did?'

'Of course,' she said. 'And have you met my little Basil as well?' She nodded towards the dachshund curled up so comfortably in front of the fire. Billy looked at it. And suddenly, he realized that this animal had all the time been just as silent and motionless as the parrot. He put out a hand and touched it gently on the top of its back. The back was hard and cold, and when he pushed the hair to one side with his fingers, he could see the skin underneath, greyish-black and dry, and perfectly preserved.

'Good gracious me,' he said. 'How absolutely fascinating.' He turned away from the dog and stared with deep admiration at the little woman beside him on the sofa. 'It must be most awfully difficult to do a thing like that.'

'Not in the least,' she said. 'I stuff *all* my little pets myself when they pass away. Will you have another cup of tea?'

'No, thank you,' Billy said. The tea tasted faintly of bitter almonds, and he didn't much care for it.

'You did sign the book, didn't you?'

'Oh, yes.'

'That's good. Because later on, if I happen to forget what you were called, then I can always come down here and look it up. I still do that almost every day with Mr Mulholland and Mr . . . Mr . . . '

'Temple,' Billy said. 'Gregory Temple. Excuse me asking, but haven't there been *any* other guests here except them in the last two or three years?'

Holding her teacup high in one hand, inclining her head slightly to the left, she looked up at him out of the corners of her eyes and gave him another gentle little smile.

'No, my dear,' she said. 'Only you.'

Men and Women

Tony Kytes, the Arch-Deceiver by Thomas Hardy
(1894)

Seeing a Beauty Queen Home by Bill Naughton
(1959)

Tickets, Please by D H Lawrence
(1922/24)

Tony Kytes, the Arch-Deceiver

Thomas Hardy

'I shall never forget Tony's face,' said the carrier. ''Twas a little, round, firm, tight face, with a seam here and there left by the smallpox, but not enough to hurt his looks in a woman's eye, though he'd had it badish when he was a boy. So very serious looking and unsmiling 'a was, that young man, that it really seemed as if he couldn't laugh at all without great pain to his conscience. He looked very hard at a small speck in your eye when talking to 'ee. And there was no more sign of a whisker or beard on Tony Kytes's face than on the palm of my hand. He used to sing "The Tailor's Breeches" with a religious manner, as if it were a hymn: –

> "O the petticoats went off,
> and the breeches they went on!"

and all the rest of the scandalous stuff. He was quite the women's favourite, and in return for their likings he loved 'em in shoals.

'But in course of time Tony got fixed down to one in particular, Milly Richards, a nice, light, small, tender little thing; and it was soon said that they were engaged to be married. One Saturday he had been to market to do business for his father, and was driving home the waggon in the afternoon. When he reached the foot of the very hill we shall be going over in ten minutes, who should he see waiting for him at the top but Unity Sallet, a handsome girl, one of the young women he'd been very tender toward before he'd got engaged to Milly.

'As soon as Tony came up to her she said, "My dear Tony, will you give me a lift home?"

'"That I will, darling," said Tony. "You don't suppose I could refuse 'ee?"

'She smiled a smile, and up she hopped, and on drove Tony.

'"Tony," she says, in a sort of tender chide, "why did ye desert me for that other one? In what is she better than I? I should have made 'ee a finer wife, and a more loving one too. 'Tisn't girls that are so easily won at first that are the best. Think how long we've known each other – ever since we were children almost – now haven't we, Tony?"

'"Yes, that we have," says Tony, a-struck with the truth o't.

'"And you've never seen anything in me to complain of, have ye, Tony? Now tell the truth to me?"

'"I never have, upon my life," says Tony.

'"And – can you say I'm not pretty, Tony? Now look at me!"

'He let his eyes light upon her for a long while. "I really can't," says he. "In fact, I never knowed you was so pretty before!"

'"Prettier than she?"

'What Tony would have said to that nobody knows, for before he could speak, what should he see ahead, over the hedge past the turning, but a feather he knew well – the feather in Milly's hat – she to whom he had been thinking of putting the question as to giving out the banns that very week.

'"Unity," says he, as mild as he could, "here's Milly coming. Now I shall catch it mightily if she sees 'ee riding here with me; and if you get down she'll be turning the corner in a moment, and, seeing 'ee in the road, she'll know we've been coming on together. Now, dearest Unity, will ye, to avoid all unpleasantness, which I know ye can't bear any more than I, will ye lie down in the back part of the waggon, and let me cover you over with the tarpaulin till Milly has passed? It will all be done in a minute. Do! – and I'll think over what we've said; and perhaps I shall put a loving question to you after all, instead of Milly. 'Tisn't true that it is all settled between her and me."

'Well, Unity Sallet agreed, and lay down at the back end of the waggon, and Tony covered her over, so that the waggon seemed to be empty but for the loose tarpaulin; and then he drove on to meet Milly.

'"My dear Tony!" cries Milly, looking up with a little pout at him as he came near. "How long you've been coming home! Just as if I didn't live at Upper Longpuddle at all! And I've come to meet you as you asked me to do, and to ride back with you, and talk over our future home – since you asked me, and I promised. But I shouldn't have come else, Mr Tony!"

'"Ay, my dear, I did ask ye – to be sure I did, now I think of it – but I had quite forgot it. To ride back with me, did you say, dear Milly?"

'"Well, of course! What can I do else? Surely you don't want me to walk, now I've come all this way?"

'"O no, no! I was thinking you might be going on to town to meet your mother. I saw her there – and she looked as if she might be expecting 'ee."

'"O no; she's just home. She came across the fields, and so got back before you."

'"Ah! I didn't know that," says Tony. And here was no help for it but to take her up beside him.

'They talked on very pleasantly, and looked at the trees, and beasts, and birds, and insects, and at the ploughmen at work in the fields, till presently who should they see looking out of the upper window of a house that stood beside the road they were following, but Hannah Jolliver, another young beauty of the place at that time, and the very first woman that Tony had fallen in love with – before Milly and before Unity, in fact – the one that he had almost arranged to marry instead of Milly. She was a much more dashing girl than Milly Richards, though he'd not thought much of her of late. The house Hannah was looking from was her aunt's.

'"My dear Milly – my coming wife, as I may call 'ee," says Tony in his modest way, and not so loud that Unity could overhear, "I see a young woman alooking out of the window, who I think may accost me. The fact is, Milly, she had a notion that I was wishing to marry her, and since she's discovered I've promised another, and a prettier than she, I'm rather afeard of her temper if she sees us together. Now, Milly, would you do me a favour – my coming wife, as I may say?"

'"Certainly, dearest Tony," says she.

'"Then would ye creep under the empty sacks just here in the front of the waggon, and hide there out of sight till we've passed the house? She hasn't seen us yet. You see, we ought to live in peace and good-will since 'tis almost Christmas, and 'twill prevent angry passions rising, which we always should do."

'"I don't mind, to oblige you, Tony," Milly said; and though she didn't care much about doing it, she crept under, and crouched down just behind the seat, Unity being snug at the other end. So they drove on till they got near the road-side cottage. Hannah had soon seen him coming, and waited at the window, looking down upon him. She tosses her head a little disdainful and smiled off-hand.

'"Well, aren't you going to be civil enough to ask me to ride home with you!" she says, seeing that he was for driving past with a nod and a smile.

'"Ah, to be sure! What was I thinking of?" said Tony, in a flutter. "But you seem as if you was staying at your aunt's?"

'"No, I am not," she said. "Don't you see I have my bonnet and jacket on? I have only called to see her on my way home. How can you be so stupid, Tony?"

'"In that case – ah – of course you must come along wi' me," says Tony, feeling a dim sort of sweat rising up inside his clothes. And he reined in the horse and waited till she'd come downstairs, and then helped her up beside him. He drove on again, his face as long as a face that was a round one by nature well could be.

'Hannah looked round sideways into his eyes. "This is nice, isn't it, Tony?" she says. "I like riding with you."

'Tony looked back into her eyes. "And I with you," he said after a while. In short, having considered her, he warmed up, and the more he looked at her the more he liked her, till he couldn't for the life of him think why he had ever said a word about marriage to Milly or Unity while Hannah Jolliver was in question. So they sat a little closer and closer, their feet upon the foot-board and their shoulders touching, and Tony thought over and over again how handsome Hannah was. He spoke tenderer and tenderer, and called her "dear Hannah" in a whisper at last.

'"You've settled it with Milly by this time, I suppose," said she.

'"N-no, not exactly."

'"What? How low you talk, Tony."

'"Yes – I've a kind of hoarseness. I said, not exactly."

'"I suppose you mean to?"

'"Well, as to that –" His eyes rested on her face, and hers on his. He wondered how he could have been such a fool as not to follow up Hannah. "My sweet Hannah!"

he bursts out, taking her hand, not being really able to help it, and forgetting Milly and Unity, and all the world besides. "Settled it? I don't think I have!"

'"Hark!" says Hannah.

'"What?" says Tony, letting go her hand.

'"Surely I heard a sort of little screaming squeak under those sacks? Why, you've been carrying corn, and there's mice in this wagon, I declare!" She began to haul up the tails of her gown.

'"Oh no; 'tis the axle," said Tony in an assuring way. "It do go like that sometimes in dry weather."

'"Perhaps it was . . . Well, now, to be quite honest, dear Tony, do you like her better than me? Because – because, although I've held off so independent, I'll own at last that I do like 'ee Tony, to tell the truth; and I wouldn't say no if you asked me – you know what."

'Tony was so won over by this pretty offering mood of a girl who had been quite the reverse (Hannah had a backward way with her at times, if you can mind) that he just glanced behind, and then whispered very soft, "I haven't quite promised her, and I think I can get out of it, and ask you that question you speak of."

'"Throw over Milly? – all to marry me! How delightful!" broke out Hannah, quite loud, clapping her hands.

'At this there was a real squeak – an angry, spiteful squeak, and afterward a long moan, as if something had broke its heart, and a movement of the empty sacks.

'"Something's there!" said Hannah, starting up.

'"It's nothing, really," says Tony in a soothing voice, and praying inwardly for a way out of this. "I wouldn't tell 'ee at first, because I wouldn't frighten 'ee. But, Hannah, I've really a couple of ferrets in a bag under there, for rabbiting, and they quarrel sometimes. I don't wish it knowed, as 'twould be called poaching. Oh, they can't get out, bless ye – you are quite safe! And – and – what a fine day it is, isn't it, Hannah, for this time of year? Be you going to market next Saturday? How is your aunt now?" And so on, says Tony, to keep her from talking any more about love in Milly's hearing.

'But he found his work cut out for him, and wondering again how he should get out of this ticklish business, he looked about for a chance. Nearing home he saw his father in a field not far off, holding up his hand as if he wished to speak to Tony.

'"Would you mind taking the reins a moment, Hannah," he said, much relieved, "while I go and find out what father wants?"

'She consented, and away he hastened into the field, only too glad to get breathing time. He found that his father was looking at him with rather a stern eye.

'"Come, come, Tony," says old Mr Kytes, as soon as his son was alongside him, "this won't do, you know."

'"What?" says Tony.

'"Why, if you mean to marry Milly Richards, do it, and there's an end o't. But don't go driving about the country with Jolliver's daughter and making a scandal. I won't have such things done."

'"I only asked her – that is, she asked me, to ride home."

'"She? Why, now, if it had been Milly, 'twould have been quite proper; but you and Hannah Jolliver going about by yourselves –"

'"Milly's there too, father."

'"Milly? Where?"

'"Under the corn-sacks! Yes, the truth is, father, I've got rather into a nunny-watch*, I'm afraid! Unity

* nunny-watch: tangled mess (dialect)

Sallet is there too – yes, at the other end, under the tarpaulin. All three are in that waggon, and what to do with 'em I know no more than the dead! The best plan is, as I'm thinking, to speak out loud and plain to one of 'em before the rest, and that will settle it; not but what 'twill cause 'em to kick up a bit of a miff*, for certain. Now which would you marry, father, if you was in my place?"

'"Whichever of 'em did *not* ask to ride with thee."

'"That was Milly, I'm bound to say, as she only mounted by my invitation. But Milly –"

'"Then stick to Milly, she's the best . . . But look at that!"

'His father pointed toward the waggon. "She can't hold that horse in. You shouldn't have left the reins in her hands. Run on and take the horse's head, or there'll be some accident to them maids!"

'Tony's horse, in fact, in spite of Hannah's tugging at the reins, had started on his way at a brisk walking pace, being very anxious to get back to the stable, for he had had a long day out. Without another word Tony rushed away from his father to overtake the horse.

'Now of all things that could have happened to wean him from Milly there was nothing so powerful as his father's recommending her. No; it could not be Milly, after all. Hannah must be the one, since he could not marry all three. This he thought while running after the waggon. But queer things were happening inside it.

'It was, of course, Milly who had screamed under the sack-bags, being obliged to let off her bitter rage and shame in that way at what Tony was saying and never daring to show, for very pride and dread o' being

* miff: short outburst of temper

laughed at, that she was in hiding. She became more and more restless, and in twisting herself about, what did she see but another woman's foot and white stocking close to her head. It quite frightened her, not knowing that Unity Sallet was in the waggon likewise. But after the fright was over she determined to get to the bottom of all this, and she crept and crept along the bed of the waggon, under the tarpaulin, like a snake, when lo and behold she came face to face with Unity.

'"Well, if this isn't disgraceful!" says Milly in a raging whisper to Unity.

'"'Tis," says Unity, "to see you hiding in a young man's waggon like this, and no great character belonging to either of ye!"

'"Mind what you are saying!" replied Milly, getting louder. "I am engaged to be married to him, and haven't I a right to be here? What right have you, I should like to know? What has he been promising you? A pretty lot of nonsense, I expect! But what Tony says to other women is all mere wind, and no concern to me!"

'"Don't you be too sure!" says Unity. "He's going to have Hannah, and not you, nor me either; I could hear that."

'Now at these strange voices sounding from under the cloth Hannah was thunderstruck a'most into a swound*; and it was just at this time that the horse moved on. Hannah tugged away wildly, not knowing what she was doing; and as the quarrel rose louder and louder Hannah got so horrified that she let go the reins altogether. The horse went on at his own pace, and coming to the corner where we turn round to drop down the hill to Lower Longpuddle he turned too

* swound: fainting-fit

quick, the off wheels went up the bank, the waggon rose sideways till it was quite on edge upon the near axles, and out rolled the three maidens into the road in a heap.

'When Tony came up, frightened and breathless, he was relieved enough to see that neither of his darlings was hurt, beyond a few scratches from the brambles of the hedge. But he was rather alarmed when he heard how they were going on at one another.

'"Don't ye quarrel, my dears – don't ye!" says he, taking off his hat out of respect to 'em. And then he would have kissed them all around, as fair and square as a man could, but they were in too much of a taking to let him, and screeched and sobbed till they was quite spent.

'"Now I'll speak out honest, because I ought to," says Tony, as soon as he could get heard. "And this is the truth," says he. "I've asked Hannah to be mine, and she is willing, and we are going to put up the banns next –"

'Tony had not noticed that Hannah's father was coming up behind, nor had he noticed that Hannah's face was beginning to bleed from the scratch of a bramble. Hannah had seen her father, and had run to him, crying worse than ever.

'"My daughter is *not* willing, sir!" says Mr Jolliver hot and strong. "Be you willing, Hannah? I ask ye to have spirit enough to refuse him, if yer virtue is left to 'ee and you run no risk?"

'"She's as sound as a bell for me, that I'll swear!" says Tony flaring up. "And so's the others, come to that, though you may think it an onusual thing in me!"

'"I have spirit, and I do refuse him!" says Hannah, partly because her father was there, and partly, too, in a tantrum because of the discovery, and the scratch on her face. "Little did I think when I was so soft with him just now that I was talking to such a false deceiver!"

'"What, you won't have me, Hannah?" says Tony, his jaw hanging down like a dead man's.

'"Never – I would sooner marry no – nobody at all!" she gasped out, though with her heart in her throat, for she would not have refused Tony if he had asked her quietly, and her father had not been there, and her face had not been scratched by the bramble. And having said that, away she walked upon her father's arm, thinking and hoping he would ask her again.

'Tony didn't know what to say next. Milly was sobbing her heart out; but as his father had strongly recommended her he couldn't feel inclined that way so he turned to Unity.

'"Well, will you, Unity dear, be mine?" he says.

'"Take her leavings? Not I!" says Unity. "I'd scorn it!" And away walks Unity Sallet likewise, though she looked back when she'd gone some way, to see if he was following her.

'So there at last were left Milly and Tony by themselves, she crying in watery streams, and Tony looking like a tree struck by lightning.

'"Well, Milly," he says at last, going up to her, "it do seem as if fate had ordained that it should be you and I, or nobody. And what must be must be, I suppose. Hey, Milly?"

'"If you like, Tony. You didn't really mean what you said to them?"

'"Not a word of it!" declares Tony, bringing down his fist upon his palm.

'And then he kissed her, and put the waggon to rights, and they mounted together; and their banns were put up the very next Sunday. I was not able to go to their wedding, but it was a rare party they had, by all account. Everybody in Longpuddle was there almost.'

Seeing a Beauty Queen Home

Bill Naughton

One Saturday night I was dancing at the Floral Hall when the Ladies' 'Excuse me' dance came up before I'd time to get off the floor and have the usual ten-minute game of banker in the gents' cloakroom. Naturally the dames were all after me. It was the time when I *could* dance. I mean I never had to ask for a dance. I used to stroll up to the corner where the girls all stood in a circle, the cream of the town's dancers, and I'd run my eye over them, and the one my eye rested on would come running into the arm of my tight-sleeved pinstripe, barrelled jacket. Sometimes in their eagerness two would run out to me. If there happened to be a stranger, or one a bit posh, I might say, 'Lend us your body, baby,' but no more than that.

I had a rough passage in that 'Excuse me'. Every stumer* in the place wanted to have a dance with 'Rudy' – as they called me – especially the ones who were up in town for their Saturday night hop. I knew I was making their weekend for them, but charity can go too far. There was one wench at the finish who dragged me round the floor, and who wouldn't keep her damn big powdery chin off the lapel of my coat. Fortunately I was able to give the griffin* to Harry, the leader of the band, and he cut the dance short.

I got back to my mate, Eddie, and I said, 'Did you see that heavy-legged 'un who had me in tow, Eddie? My feet never touched the floor for five minutes.'

'Don't you know who that is?' said Eddie.

* stumer: failure, loser (slang)   griffin: warning signal

'Who?' I said.

'It's Maggie,' he said, 'the Cotton Town Beauty Queen.'

Beauty Queens were only just coming in at that time, and, in fact, so far as we were concerned, you could have all the beauties there were – we'd dance with the ugliest girl in town, as long as she could *move*, was *light*, and could follow a new blues or a quick-step Charleston. But it was getting towards the end of the evening, and since a chap had to take some girl home, it struck me that it might as well be a Beauty Queen. If Eddie hadn't told me what she was I don't suppose I'd have given her a second thought, let alone look, but you know how it is with those things – the world's opinion comes before your own.

I had to have a dance with my star partner, Ramona, just to recover, but when they struck up the last waltz I went across to Maggie. She got the shock of her life. I lugged her round, and though it was the waste of a good dance – a thing I detested – yet I knew she could hardly refuse to let me see her home after my sacrifice. And she didn't.

She lived in Raikes Row, a twopenny tram ride out of town, which in those days was nearly four miles. Now this was well beyond the limit of seeing girls home. Anything over two miles and you only saw them to the tram, having your smooch or whatever you got beside the railway footbridge that led to the tram centre. But being a Beauty Queen, I thought she was worth spending twopence on.

It was next to the last tram out. This isn't going to allow me much time at t'other end, I thought.

'What time does the last tram leave the terminus, Maggie?' I said.

'Three minutes to twelve,' she said.

The first kiss we had in the backstreet I knew at once I couldn't manage it. I could already hear the last tram on its way out. By the time the driver and his mate had changed wires and had a smoke it wouldn't allow me much more than ten minutes. Maggie wasn't a ten-minuter. Her smooching was like her dancing – on the slow side. She'd be good when she got warmed up, but I hadn't the time. I didn't reckon she was worth a four-mile walk with a bit more at the far end. But then she was a Beauty Queen. Many a chap would give anything to be in my shoes at this minute, I thought. And Eddie would want to know how I'd gone on. In the distance I could hear them switching the trolley pole over at the terminus.

'If you don't go now you'll miss it,' she said.

What I've had so far, I thought, hasn't been worth the tanner I'll have spent in tram fares. If I stayed she might not make it worth my while. *You're a fool if you stay*, something told me, *but you might as well chance it.*

'You'd better hurry,' she said.

'Suppose I miss it?' I said.

'You'll have to walk,' she said.

'Oh, let it go,' I said.

I was able to relax a bit when the tram clattered past, for now I knew there was no hurry. But after a time I felt myself getting chilly. Not only was the night getting cooler, but the effort of standing on my tiptoes all the time I was kissing her was a strain.

'My, you're shivering,' she said, 'are you cold?'

'Not much,' I said. 'Any chance of a cup of tea round here?'

I expected her to laugh it off, but she didn't; instead she hesitated and said.

'I'm not sure.'

At once I was on the scent. Not only for the tea – but the very thought of going in a girl's home intrigued me.

'Never mind, darling,' I put in quickly, 'I can't give you all that trouble.' Refuse anything nice a woman offers you, has always been my way of going about things, because they're sure to offer it again, and then it's like giving things twice over.

'I'm staying with my gran,' she said. 'I always do at weekends. Now if she's in bed we could creep in, and I'd make you a nice cup of tea or cocoa and happen a bit of toast.'

'Now I don't want to get you into any bother,' I said.

'You won't,' she said.

'But supposin' she hears us?' I said.

'If she's had her usual Sat'day night supper of fish an' chips and a gill* of stout,' she said, 'she'll be sleeping heavy. And anyway, she's hard of hearing.'

'How will we know whether she's in bed or not?' I said.

'If she is the light will be out,' she said. 'Come on.'

We held hands and walked quietly down the street. It was a nice little row of houses. Halfway down the street Maggie nodded. 'It's all right,' she whispered, 'she's in bed.'

We tiptoed to the door. There was a letter-box slot, and Maggie slipped her fingers through it and started pulling away at something.

'What's that?' I whispered.

'The key,' said Maggie.

After Maggie had carefully drawn out about three yards of string there was a *twang* inside the slot, and she fished out a big iron key. She put the key end in her

* gill: half-pint

mouth and sucked it. 'So's it won't make a din,' she said. Then she put it in the lock and quietly turned it. The door opened softly. She beckoned me in behind her, and closed the door after us.

The room was small and warm, with a bit of a glow coming from the fire in the kitchen range. It had a nice smell of home. Gran's had her fish and chips, I thought. There was a faint smell of liniment too – somebody's got the rheumatics. It was all so nice and homely that I put my arms round Maggie at once, pulling her to me, and gave her a right good long kiss.

'Let's wait till we've had something to eat,' she said.

This kid's got some savvy, I thought. Looks like it's going to be worth that walk home.

'Can you see all right?' she whispered.

'I can see you,' I said, 'and you're lovely.'

'I like the firelight glow,' she said. 'I'll not light the gas.' She took some nuts of coal from a scuttle beside the fender and placed them on the low red fire.

'They'll burn up in a couple of ticks,' she said. 'I'll go and make the tea.' And she went into the kitchen.

I heard her putting the kettle to the back kitchen tap. The next thing I heard a woman's voice yell from upstairs.

'Maggie!'

'Yes?' answered Maggie.

'Is that you?' came the voice again.

'Course it is!' snapped Maggie.

There was a pause.

'What time is it?'

'Summat to twelve,' said Maggie.

There was a sharp edge to her voice, and it was as different as chalk from cheese to the voice she'd been talking in all evening. She must think a lot about me, I thought, to go to so much trouble over the way she talks to me. When her gran spoke again her tone was mild.

'I've put your cocoa an' sugar in t'pint pot, Maggie.'

'You don't have to tell all t'neighbourhood,' said Maggie.

'Han' you locked the front door?'

'Course I have,' said Maggie.

'An' put bolt on?'

'Aye.'

'You didn't let cat out, did you?'

'Course I didn't.'

There was another pause, and then her gran called down in a very making-up sort of voice.

'Han' you had a good time, love?'

'Yes, Gran,' said Maggie.

'I'm glad. Goodnight, Maggie.'

This time Maggie's voice softened a little: 'Goodnight, Gran.'

The little nuts of coal had begun to burn, and in the jumping bits of light I was able to look round the place. It was clean, old-fashioned, and a bit bare. There was a horsehair sofa with a black prickly cover, a chest of drawers in reddish wood, and two pictures that each had an angel following a child. There was a framed certificate on the wall, and I was able to read it.

'*Presented to Thomas Henry Bibby, after forty-four years' faithful service at Workshaft's Model Bleaching Works: signed Ebenezer Workshaft.*'

All right for you, Ebenezer, I thought. Maggie came in with a pint pot of cocoa and a plate of bread and cheese. She had her finger to her lips.

'Did you hear her?' she whispered. I nodded. 'I had to shout,' went on Maggie, 'she's practically stone deaf.' She smiled at me. 'We'll have to sup out of same pot,' she said; 'do you mind?'

I felt I could have made a funny joke out of that, but I thought that perhaps I hadn't known her long enough.

'If you don't,' I said, 'I won't. Putting my lips where yours have been.'

She gave me a joking thump in the chest. 'Don't be daft, *Rudy*,' she said. I didn't answer. Matter of fact, I hadn't any wind for a minute or two.

'Nearly every house in the Row has one of them,' she said, looking up at the certificate. 'They got a blue 'un after forty years, an' a red 'un after fifty. Grandpa was going in for his red 'un, when one morning he slipped into a vat of acid. There was practically nothing left of him but his trouser-buttons when they pulled him out. 'Ere, come on, help yourself to the cheese. An' let's sit on the rug in front of the fire – it's more homely.'

We sat down on the rug, when suddenly a sharp knocking sounded on the ceiling.

Maggie put a finger to her lips for me to be quiet, and then she yelled: 'What's up?'

'Who's that?' called her gran.

'Who's what?'

'You've got somebody down there with you, lass – now who is it?'

'Don't be daft – it's only me.'

'I heard you talking to somebody,' called her gran. 'I had my suspicions when I heard you put all that water in the kettle. I'm coming down.'

'Sit down,' said Maggie to me. Then she went in the kitchen.

'If you must know,' she hissed up the stairs, 'it's Ernie Adams.'

'Ernie! What's he doing here?'

'He was over for the weekend, and I met him at the dance. And so I asked him in for a cup of cocoa, just for old time's sake, but you with your nattering an' squawking haven't given us a minute's peace.'

'Give her my love,' I sent a whisper into the kitchen.

'What's that?' called her gran.

'Ernie sends you his love,' said Maggie.

'Oh, it's all right if it's Ernie. Tell him to give my love to his mother. Tell him to be careful with his cigarette-ends. Goodnight.'

'For the last time,' bawled Maggie. 'Goodnight! an' good chuttons!'

Maggie tripped back and forced me down on the rug. 'She won't get up now,' she said. 'I've set her mind at rest.'

'Who's this Ernie Adams?' I said.

'A boy I used to know when I was sixteen,' she said. 'They lived in the next street and they used to have a black puddin' stall outside the Wanderers' football ground. Then they bought a boarding-house at Blackpool. Gran liked Ernie, he always made such a fuss of her.'

'Suppose she comes down an' sees me?' I said.

'Matter of fact,' said Maggie, 'you look that much like him, that she'd be hard put to tell the difference. She's very short-sighted, you know.'

'You said she was hard of hearing!'

'Don't you worry,' said Maggie, 'I know my gran. There's times when I could murder her.'

She had no sooner got the words out of her mouth than a couple of feet came clomping down the stairs.

'Stay where you are,' said Maggie to me, 'I'll handle her.' She went striding into the kitchen to meet her gran. I had a last sup of the cocoa and I was just ready for off, when a few thoughts stopped me. For one thing I didn't fancy hoofing it – that four miles home – not just for cocoa, anyway.

'Why've you no light on?' I heard her gran say as she trod off the stairs into the back kitchen, carrying a candle.

'I thought I'd save the gas,' said Maggie. 'Now you go back to bed, Gran, an' leave us in peace. I don't want you in there, and I'm sure Ernie doesn't.'

Now or never, I thought.

'Oh, yes I do!' I called out, at the same time running across to the door between the front kitchen and the back. 'How are you?' I said, shaking her hand and passing the candle to Maggie, who looked a bit flummoxed, but had the sense to blow it out. Living four miles away I'd a very different way of speaking from Raikes Row folk, but I knew the way they talked and I put it on for gran. 'I'm right fain to see you, Missis Bibby, I am that an' all. Here let me get you a chair. Isn't it grand in here – so cheery, yu' know, with the coal fire burnin'. Just like old times, eh, Maggie?'

Maggie didn't answer, and the old woman said, 'Well, I don't know – '

'You're lookin' champion, Missis Bibby,' I said.

She sat down. A little hardworked body she was, with a good hard stare coming out of her little wizened eyes. She was wearing a shawl over a flannel nightdress, and I thought that was perhaps why she didn't insist on Maggie lighting the gas. At last she spoke:

'If tha art Ernie Adams,' she said, 'tha's either changed a great deal, or my eyes are worse till I thought.'

'Course I've changed,' I said. 'What do you expect?'

'I'd expect thee to grow taller, not shorter,' she said.

'I am taller,' I said, and I stood up on my toes and stuck my chest out.

She looked at me, and I knew she had me as good as rumbled, and that I was out in the street unless I could strike something good. The liniment smell came a bit stronger to my nostrils and I took a chance. Suddenly I leant forward and said:

'How's your leg, Missis Bibby?'

'My leg?' she said. 'You mean *my* leg?'

'Yes, your bad leg,' I said. 'You know,' as though I didn't have to explain that.

'If anything,' she said, 'it's better till what it used to be.'

'You're all right if you keep on the move, Missis Bibby, eh?' I said.

'Aye, but if I have to sit down for any length of time it sets about me,' she said, and gave a bit of a groan.

'I'll bet you don't do much sitting down, Missis Bibby,' I said, 'unless you've changed a heck of a lot!'

'You're right there, Ernie,' she said warmly.

I'm in, I thought. 'I thought so,' I said.

'I forgot to ask you,' she said, 'how's your mother?'

'She'd be all right if it weren't for her arthritis,' I said. 'There's times when her hands get all curled up like that – it's the sea air, yu' know, doesn't do for her.'

'I'm right sorry to hear that,' she said. A flame from a nut of coal brightened up the room. She stared at my pinstripe suit and my painted-toe patent leather shoes, then looked up at my long-pointed collar and at me.

The look she had at first came back to her face. 'I can't get over the change in thee. Tha looks like a Woolworth's shop walker.' She changed the subject: 'How's your Fred?' she asked.

'He's gone into insurance,' I said. 'Started for the Prudential.'

'He never did like work,' she said.

The coal was catching on and the room was going brighter. Maggie was looking on, not saying a word.

'What about your Irene?' she said.

'She's got engaged,' I said.

'I thought she didn't like men,' she said.

'She's changed,' I said.

'Must be the sea air,' she said.

She wasn't satisfied. I sensed that. I must get back to her leg, I thought.

'How is – ' she said, turning to look at Maggie, and then looking quickly back at me, 'is your Harold?'

I nearly answered, but something in her manner warned me. '*Our Harold?*' I said.

'Aye, your Harold?' she said.

'Missis Bibby,' I said, 'I'm surprised at you. Wait till I tell my mam you were asking for *our Harold*!' And I burst out laughing.

'Blackpool's done thee no good,' she said, getting up from her chair. 'Maggie, don't be long. Don't forget to damp the fire down. I'm off.'

Maggie lit the candle for her, and gran gave a last look at me and went off. I waited until I heard the bedroom door close.

'Whew, Maggie,' I said, 'she nearly caught me then. I was going to lead off about brother Harold, but something came over me, and I knew I hadn't got one.'

The rug looked very nice and cosy. I was getting down to it when I saw Maggie.

'What's up?' I said.

'Get out that door,' she said.

I couldn't believe my own ears. I'd been waiting for the applause.

'Steady up, Maggie,' I said. As I stood up she stood in front of me. She seemed to be in some kind of temper that put inches on her height, and her bust. For the first time I was able to see the signs of a Queen in her.

'Out that door,' she said.

'But Maggie – '

'Out – ' she said. 'You might have taken *her* in, but you're not taking *me* in.'

'I'm going,' I said.

'Then get gone,' she said.

She opened the door.

'Maggie,' I said, 'it's pourin' down!'

'Yes,' she said, 'an' you can get out in it.'

'But I've no mac,' I said.

'A smart fella like you doesn't need one,' she said, seeing me off the doorstep.

'But Maggie,' I said, 'I'd have sworn you liked a smart boy.'

'I do,' said Maggie, holding the door open long enough to tell me, 'but there's one thing lets you down, mister – *you're too bloody smart*!' And with that she slammed the door in my face.

On that four-mile hoof back to town, along the cold wet streets, with the water seeping right into my patent leather shoes, and the rain taking the shape out of my barrelled jacket, I was able to weigh up her words over and over again, and realize for the first time in my life, how being right smart can not only get you in – but can also get you flung out.

Tickets, Please

D H Lawrence

There is in the Midlands a single-line tramway system which boldly leaves the country town and plunges off into the black, industrial countryside, up hill and down dale, through the long ugly villages of workmen's houses, over canals and railways, past churches perched high and noble over the smoke and shadows, through stark, grimy cold little market-places, tilting away in a rush past cinemas and shops down to the hollow where the collieries are, then up again, past a little rural church, under the ash trees, on in a rush to the terminus, the last little ugly place of industry, the cold little town that shivers on the edge of the wild, gloomy country beyond. There the green and creamy coloured tram-cars seem to pause and purr with curious satisfaction. But in a few minutes – the clock on the turret of the Co-operative Wholesale Society's shops gives the time – away it starts once more on the adventure. Again there are the reckless swoops downhill, bouncing the loops: again the chilly wait in the hill-top market-place: again the breathless slithering round the precipitous drop under the church: again the patient halts at the loops, waiting for the oncoming car: so on and on, for two long hours, till at last the city looms beyond the fat gas-works, the narrow factories draw near, we are in the sordid streets of the great town, once more we sidle to a standstill at our terminus, abashed by the great crimson and cream-coloured city cars, but still perky, jaunty, somewhat dare-devil, green as a jaunty sprig of parsley out of a black colliery garden.

To ride on these cars is always an adventure. Since we are in wartime, the drivers are men unfit for active service: cripples and hunchbacks. So they have the spirit of the devil in them. The ride becomes a steeplechase. Hurray! we have leapt in a clear jump over the canal bridge – now for the four-lane corner. With a shriek and a trail of sparks we are clear again. To be sure, a tram often leaps the rails – but what matter! It sits still in a ditch until other trams come to haul it out. It is quite common for a car, parked with one solid mass of living people, to come to a dead halt in the midst of unbroken blackness, the heart of nowhere on a dark night, and for the driver and the girl conductor to call: 'All get off – car's on fire!' Instead, however, of rushing out in a panic, the passengers stolidly reply: 'Get on – get on! We're not coming out. We're stopping where we are. Push on, George.' So till flames actually appear.

The reason for this reluctance to dismount is that the nights are howlingly cold, black, and windswept, and a car is a haven of refuge. From village to village the miners travel, for a change of cinema, of girl, of pub. The trams are desperately packed. Who is going to risk himself in the black gulf outside, to wait perhaps an hour for another tram, then to see the forlorn notice 'Depot Only', because there is something wrong! Or to greet a unit of three bright cars all so tight with people that they sail past with a howl of derision*. Trams that pass in the night.

This, the most dangerous tram-service in England, as the authorities themselves declare, with pride, is entirely conducted by girls, and driven by rash young men, a little crippled, or by delicate young men, who

* derision: triumphant mockery

creep forward in terror. The girls are fearless young hussies. In their ugly blue uniform, skirts up to their knees, shapeless old peaked caps on their heads, they have all the sang-froid* of an old non-commissioned officer. With a tram packed with howling colliers, roaring hymns downstairs and a sort of antiphony* of obscenities upstairs, the lasses are perfectly at their ease. They pounce on the youths who try to evade their ticket-machine. They push off the men at the end of their distance. They are not going to be done in the eye – not they. They fear nobody – and everybody fears them.

'Hello, Annie!'

'Hello, Ted!'

'Oh, mind my corn, Miss Stone. It's my belief you've got a heart of stone, for you've trod on it again.'

'You should keep it in your pocket,' replies Miss Stone, and she goes sturdily upstairs in her high boots.

'Tickets, please.'

She is peremptory*, suspicious, and ready to hit first. She can hold her own against ten thousand. The step of that tram-car is her Thermopylae*.

Therefore, there is a certain wild romance aboard these cars – and in the sturdy bosom of Annie herself. The time for soft romance is in the morning, between ten o'clock and one, when things are rather slack: that is, except market-day and Saturday. Thus Annie has time to look about her. Then she often hops off her car and into a shop where she has spied something, while the driver chats in the main road. There is very good feeling between the girls and the drivers. Are they not

* sang-froid: self-possession antiphony: organized response
peremptory: bossy
Thermopylae: narrow mountain pass in Greece where a small force of defenders held off the Persian army in 480 BC

companions in peril, shipments aboard this careering vessel of a tram-car, for ever rocking on the waves of a stormy land.

Then also, during the easy hours, the inspectors are most in evidence. For some reason, everybody employed in this tram-service is young: there are no grey heads. It would not do. Therefore the inspectors are of the right age, and one, the chief, is also good-looking. See him stand on a wet, gloomy morning, in his long oilskin, his peaked cap well down over his eyes, waiting to board a car. His face ruddy, his small brown moustache is weathered, he has a faint impudent smile. Fairly tall and agile, even in his waterproof, he springs aboard a car and greets Annie.

'Hello, Annie! Keeping the wet out?'

'Trying to.'

There are only two people in the car. Inspecting is soon over. Then for a long and impudent chat on the foot-board, a good, easy, twelve-mile chat.

The inspector's name is John Thomas Raynor – always called John Thomas, except sometimes, in malice, Coddy. His face sets in fury when he is addressed, from a distance, with this abbreviation. There is considerable scandal about John Thomas in half a dozen villages. He flirts with the girl conductors in the morning, and walks out with them in the dark night, when they leave their tram-car at the depot. Of course, the girls quit the service frequently. Then he flirts and walks out with the newcomer: always providing she is sufficiently attractive, and that she will consent to walk. It is remarkable, however, that most of the girls are quite comely*, they are all young, and this roving life aboard the car gives them a sailor's dash and recklessness. What

* comely: physically attractive

matter how they behave when the ship is in port? Tomorrow they will be aboard again.

Annie, however, was something of a Tartar*, and her sharp tongue had kept John Thomas at arm's length for many months. Perhaps, therefore, she liked him all the more; for he always came up smiling, with impudence. She watched him vanquish one girl, then another. She could tell by the movement of his mouth and eyes, when he flirted with her in the morning, that he had been walking out with this lass, or the other, the night before. A fine cock-of-the-walk he was. She could sum him up pretty well.

In this subtle antagonism they knew each other like old friends, they were as shrewd with one another almost as man and wife. But Annie had always kept him sufficiently at arm's length. Besides, she had a boy of her own.

The Statutes fair, however, came in November, at Bestwood. It happened that Annie had the Monday night off. It was a drizzling ugly night, yet she dressed herself up and went to the fair-ground. She was alone, but she expected soon to find a pal of some sort.

The roundabouts were veering round and grinding out their music, the side-shows were making as much commotion as possible. In the coconut shies there were no coconuts, but artificial wartime substitutes, which the lads declared were fastened into the irons. There was a sad decline in brilliance and luxury. None the less, the ground was muddy as ever, there was the same crush, the press of faces lighted up by the flares and the electric lights, the same smell of naphtha* and a few potatoes, and of electricity.

* Tartar: sharp-tongued woman
naphtha: by-product of coal-tar, used for lighting

Who should be the first to greet Miss Annie on the showground but John Thomas. He had a black overcoat buttoned up to his chin, and a tweed cap pulled down over his brows, his face between was ruddy and smiling and handy as ever. She knew so well the way his mouth moved.

She was very glad to have a 'boy'. To be at the Statutes without a fellow was no fun. Instantly, like the gallant he was, he took her on the Dragons, grim-toothed, roundabout switchbacks. It was not nearly so exciting as a tram-car actually. But, then, to be seated in a shaking, green dragon, uplifted above the sea of bubble faces, careering in a rickety fashion in the lower heavens, whilst John Thomas leaned over her, his cigarette in his mouth, was after all the right style. She was a plump, quick, alive little creature. So she was quite excited and happy.

John Thomas made her stay on for the next round. And therefore she could hardly for shame repulse him when he put his arm round her and drew her a little nearer to him, in a very warm and cuddly manner. Besides, he was fairly discreet, he kept his movement as hidden as possible. She looked down, and saw that his red, clean hand was out of sight of the crowd. And they knew each other so well. So they warmed up to the fair.

After the dragons they went on the horses. John Thomas paid each time, so she could but be complaisant*. He, of course, sat astride on the outer horse – named 'Black Bess' – and she sat sideways, towards him, on the inner horse – named 'Wildfire'. But of course John Thomas was not going to sit discreetly on 'Black Bess', holding the brass bar.

* but . . . complaisant: she could only agree

Round they spun and heaved, in the light. And round he swung on his wooden steed, flinging one leg across her mount, and perilously tipping up and down, across the space, half lying back, laughing at her. He was perfectly happy; she was afraid her hat was on one side, but she was excited.

He threw quoits on a table, and won for her two large, pale blue hat-pins. And then, hearing the noise of the cinemas, announcing another performance, they climbed the boards and went in.

Of course, during these performances pitch darkness falls from time to time, when the machine goes wrong. Then there is a wild whooping, and a loud smacking of simulated kisses. In these moments John Thomas drew Annie towards him. After all, he had a wonderfully warm, cosy way of holding a girl with his arm, he seemed to make such a nice fit. And, after all, it was pleasant to be so held: so very comforting and cosy and nice. He leaned over her and she felt his breath on her hair; she knew he wanted to kiss her on the lips. And, after all, he was so warm and she fitted in to him so softly. After all, she wanted him to touch her lips.

But the light sprang up; she also started electrically, and put her hat straight. He left his arm lying nonchalantly behind her. Well, it was fun, it was exciting to be at the Statutes with John Thomas.

When the cinema was over they went for a walk across the dark, damp fields. He had all the arts of love-making. He was especially good at holding a girl, when he sat with her on a stile in the black, drizzling darkness. He seemed to be holding her in space, against his own warmth and gratification. And his kisses were soft and slow and searching.

So Annie walked out with John Thomas, though she kept her own boy dangling in the distance. Some of the tram-girls chose to be huffy. But there, you must take things as you find them, in this life.

There was no mistake about it, Annie liked John Thomas a good deal. She felt so rich and warm in herself whenever he was near. And John Thomas really liked Annie, more than usual. The soft, melting way in which she could flow into a fellow, as if she melted into his very bones, was something rare and good. He fully appreciated this.

But with a developing acquaintance there began a developing intimacy. Annie wanted to consider him a person, a man; she wanted to take an intelligent interest in him, and to have an intelligent response. She did not want a mere nocturnal presence*, which was what he was so far. And she prided herself that he could not leave her.

Here she made a mistake. John Thomas intended to remain a nocturnal presence; he had no idea of becoming an all-round individual to her. When she started to take an intelligent interest in him and his life and his character, he sheered off. He hated intelligent interest. And he knew that the only way to stop it was to avoid it. The possessive female was aroused in Annie. And so he left her.

It is no use saying she was not surprised. She was at first startled, thrown out of her count. For she had been so *very* sure of holding him. For a while she was staggered, and everything became uncertain to her. Then she wept with fury, indignation, desolation, and misery. Then she had a spasm of despair. And then, when he came, still impudently, on to her car, still

* nocturnal presence: night-time companion

familiar, but letting her see by the movement of his head that he had gone away to somebody else for the time being, and was enjoying pastures new, then she determined to have her own back.

She had a very shrewd idea what girls John Thomas had taken out. She went to Nora Purdy. Nora was a tall, rather pale, but well-built girl, with beautiful yellow hair. She was rather secretive.

'Hey!' said Annie, accosting her; then softly: 'Who's John Thomas on with now?'

'I don't know,' said Nora.

'Why, tha does,' said Annie, ironically lapsing into dialect. 'Tha knows as well as I do.'

'Well, I do, then,' said Nora. 'It isn't me, so don't bother.'

'It's Cissy Meakin, isn't it?'

'It is, for all I know.'

'Hasn't he got a face on him?' said Annie. 'I don't half like his cheek. I could knock him off the foot-board when he comes round at me.'

'He'll get dropped on one of these days,' said Nora.

'Ay, he will, when somebody makes up their mind to drop it on him. I should like to see him taken down a peg or two, shouldn't you?'

'I shouldn't mind,' said Nora.

'You've got quite as much cause to as I have,' said Annie. 'But we'll drop on him one of these days, my girl. What? Don't you want to?'

'I don't mind,' said Nora.

But as a matter of fact, Nora was much more vindictive than Annie.

One by one Annie went the round of the old flames. It so happened that Cissy Meakin left the tramway service in quite a short time. Her mother made her leave. Then John Thomas was on the *qui vive**. He cast his eyes over his old flock. And his eyes lighted on Annie. He thought she would be safe now. Besides, he liked her.

She arranged to walk home with him on Sunday night. It so happened that her car would be in the depot at half past nine: the last car would come in at 10.15. So John Thomas was to wait for her there.

At the depot the girls had a little waiting-room of their own. It was quite rough, but cosy, with a fire and an oven and a mirror, and table and wooden chairs. The half-dozen girls who knew John Thomas only too well had arranged to take service this Sunday afternoon. So, as the cars began to come in, early, the girls dropped into the waiting-room. And instead of hurrying off home, they sat around the fire and had a cup of tea. Outside was the darkness and lawlessness of wartime.

John Thomas came on the car after Annie, at about a quarter to ten. He poked his head easily into the girls' waiting-room.

'Prayer-meeting?' he asked.

'Ay,' said Laura Sharp. 'Ladies only.'

'That's me!' said John Thomas. It was one of his favourite exclamations.

'Shut the door, boy,' said Muriel Baggaley.

'Oh, which side of me?' said John Thomas.

'Which tha likes,' said Polly Birkin.

He had come in and closed the door behind him. The girls moved in their circle, to make a place for him near the fire. He took off his great-coat and pushed back his hat.

'Who handles the teapot?' he said.

* *qui vive*: the alert

Nora Purdy silently poured him out a cup of tea.

'Want a bit o' my bread and drippin'?' said Muriel Baggaley to him.

'Ay, give us a bit.'

And he began to eat his piece of bread.

'There's no place like home, girls,' he said.

They all looked at him as he uttered this piece of impudence. He seemed to be sunning himself in the presence of so many damsels.

'Especially if you're not afraid to go home in the dark,' said Laura Sharp.

'Me! By myself I am.'

They sat till they heard the last tram come in. In a few minutes Emma Houselay entered.

'Come on, my old duck!' cried Polly Birkin.

'It *is* perishing,' said Emma, holding her fingers to the fire.

'But – I'm afraid to, go home in, the dark,' sang Laura Sharp, the tune having got into her mind.

'Who're you going with tonight, John Thomas?' asked Muriel Baggaley coolly.

'Tonight?' said John Thomas. 'Oh, I'm going home by myself tonight – all on my lonely-o.'

'That's me!' said Nora Purdy, using his own ejaculation.

The girls laughed shrilly.

'Me as well, Nora,' said John Thomas.

'Don't know what you mean,' said Laura.

'Yes, I'm toddling,' said he, rising and reaching for his overcoat.

'Nay,' said Polly. 'We're all here waiting for you.'

'We've got to be up in good time in the morning,' he said, in the benevolent official manner.

They all laughed.

'Nay,' said Muriel. 'Don't leave us all lonely, John Thomas. Take one!'

'I'll take the lot, if you like,' he responded gallantly.

'That you won't, either,' said Muriel. 'Two's company; seven's too much of a good thing.'

'Nay – take one,' said Laura. 'Fair and square, all above board and say which.'

'Ay,' cried Annie, speaking for the first time. 'Pick, John Thomas; let's hear thee.'

'Nay,' he said. 'I'm going home quiet tonight. Feeling good, for once.'

'Whereabouts?' said Annie. 'Take a good 'un, then. But tha's got to take one of us!'

'Nay, how can I take one,' he said, laughing uneasily. 'I don't want to make enemies.'

'You'd only make *one*,' said Annie.

'The chosen *one*,' added Laura.

'Oh, my! Who said girls!' exclaimed John Thomas, again turning, as if to escape. 'Well – good night.'

'Nay, you've got to make your pick,' said Muriel. 'Turn your face to the wall, and say which one touches you. Go on – we shall only just touch your back – one of us. Go on – turn your face to the wall, and don't look, and say which one touches you.'

He was uneasy, mistrusting them. Yet he had not the courage to break away. They pushed him to a wall and stood him there with his face to it. Behind his back they all grimaced, tittering. He looked so comical. He looked around uneasily.

'Go on!' he cried.

'You're looking – you're looking!' they shouted.

He turned his head away. And suddenly, with a movement like a swift cat, Annie went forward and fetched him a box on the side of the head that sent his cap flying and himself staggering. He started round.

But at Annie's signal they all flew at him, slapping him, pinching him, pulling his hair, though more in fun than in spite or anger. He, however, saw red. His blue eyes flamed with strange fear as well as fury, and he butted through the girls to the door. It was locked. He wrenched at it. Roused, alert, the girls stood round and looked at him. He faced them, at bay. At that moment they were rather horrifying to him, as they stood in their short uniforms. He was distinctly afraid.

'Come on, John Thomas! Come on! Choose!' said Annie.

'What are you after? Open the door,' he said.

'We shan't – not till you've chosen!' said Muriel.

'Chosen what?' he said.

'Chosen the one you're going to marry,' she replied.

He hesitated a moment.

'Open the blasted door,' he said, 'and get back to your senses.' He spoke with official authority.

'You've got to choose,' cried the girls.

'Come on!' cried Annie, looking him in the eye. 'Come on! Come on!'

He went forward, rather vaguely. She had taken off her belt, and swinging it, she fetched him a sharp blow over the head with the buckle end. He sprang and seized her. But immediately the other girls rushed upon him, pulling and tearing and beating him. Their blood was now thoroughly up. He was their sport now. They were going to have their own back, out of him. Strange, wild creatures, they hung on him and rushed at him to bear him down. His tunic was torn right up the back, Nora had hold at the back of his collar, and was actually strangling him. Luckily the button burst. He struggled in a wild frenzy of fury and terror, almost mad terror. His tunic was simply torn off his back, his shirt-sleeves were torn away, his arms were naked. The girls rushed at him, clenched their hands on him and pulled at him: or they rushed at him and pushed him, butted him with all their might: or they struck him wild blows. He ducked and cringed and struck sideways. They became more intense.

At last he was down. They rushed on him, kneeling on him. He had neither breath nor strength to move. His face was bleeding with a long scratch, his brow was bruised.

Annie knelt on him, the other girls knelt and hung on to him. Their faces were flushed, their hair wild, their eyes were all glittering strangely. He lay at last quite still, with face averted, as an animal lies when it is defeated and at the mercy of the captor. Sometimes his eye glanced back at the wild faces of the girls. His breast rose heavily, his wrists were torn.

'Now, then, my fellow!' gasped Annie at length. 'Now then – now –'

At the sound of her terrifying, cold triumph, he suddenly started to struggle as an animal might, but the girls threw themselves upon him with unnatural strength and power, forcing him down.

'Yes – now, then!' gasped Annie at length.

And there was a dead silence, in which the thud of heart-beating was to be heard. It was a suspense of pure silence in every soul.

'Now you know where you are,' said Annie.

The sight of his white, bare arm maddened the girls. He lay in a kind of trance of fear and antagonism. They felt themselves filled with supernatural strength.

Suddenly Polly started to laugh – to giggle wildly – helplessly – and Emma and Muriel joined in. But Annie and Nora and Laura remained the same, tense, watchful, with gleaming eyes. He winced away from these eyes.

'Yes,' said Annie, in a curious low tone, secret and deadly: 'Yes! You've got it now. You know what you've done, don't you? You know what you've done.'

He made no sound nor sign, but lay with bright, averted eyes and averted, bleeding face.

'You ought to be *killed*, that's what you ought,' said Annie tensely. 'You ought to be *killed*.' And there was a terrifying lust in her voice.

Polly was ceasing to laugh, and giving long-drawn Oh-h-hs and sighs as she came to herself.

'He's got to choose,' she said vaguely.

'Oh, yes, he has,' said Laura, with vindictive decision.

'Do you hear – do you hear?' said Annie. And with a sharp movement, that made him wince, she turned his face to her.

'Do you hear?' she repeated.

But he was quite dumb. She fetched him a sharp slap on the face. He started, and his eyes widened. Then his face darkened with defiance, after all.

'Do you hear?' she repeated.

He only looked at her with hostile eyes.

'Speak!' she said, putting her face devilishly near his.

'What?' he said, almost overcome.

'You've got to *choose*!' she cried, as if it were some terrible menace, and as if it hurt her that she could not exact more.

'What?' he said, in fear.

'Choose your girl, Coddy. You've got to choose her now. And you'll get your neck broken if you play any more of your tricks, my boy. You're settled now.'

There was a pause. Again he averted his face. He was cunning in his overthrow. He did not give in to them really – no, not if they tore him to bits.

'All right, then,' he said, 'I choose Annie.' His voice was strange and full of malice. Annie let go of him as if he had been a hot coal.

'He's chosen Annie!' said the girls in chorus.

'Me!' cried Annie. She was still kneeling, but away from him. He was still lying, prostrate, with averted face. The girls grouped uneasily around.

'Me!' repeated Annie, with a terrible bitter accent.

Then she got up, drawing away from him with strange disgust and bitterness.

'I wouldn't touch him,' she said.

But her face quivered with a kind of agony, she seemed as if she would fall. The other girls turned aside. He remained lying on the floor, with his torn clothes and bleeding, averted face.

'Oh, if he's chosen –' said Polly.

'I don't want him – he can choose again,' said Annie, with the same rather bitter hopelessness.

'Get up,' said Polly, lifting his shoulder. 'Get up.'

He rose slowly, a strange, ragged, dazed creature. The girls eyed him from a distance, curiously, furtively, dangerously.

'Who wants him?' cried Laura, roughly.

'Nobody,' they answered, with contempt. Yet each of them waited for him to look at her, hoped he would look at her. All except Annie, and something was broken in her.

He, however, kept his face closed and averted from them all. There was a silence of the end. He picked up the torn pieces of his tunic, without knowing what to do with them. The girls stood about uneasily, flushed, panting, tidying their hair and their dress unconsciously, and watching him. He looked at none of them. He espied his cap in a corner, and went and picked it up. He put it on his head, and one of the girls burst into a shrill, hysteric laugh at the sight he presented. He, however, took no heed, but went straight to where his overcoat hung on a peg. The girls moved away from contact with him as if he had been an electric wire. He put on his coat and buttoned it down. Then he rolled his tunic-rags into a bundle, and stood before the locked door, dumbly.

'Open the door, somebody,' said Laura.

'Annie's got the key,' said one.

Annie silently offered the key to the girls. Nora unlocked the door.

'Tit for tat, old man,' she said. 'Show yourself a man, and don't bear a grudge.'

But without a word or sign he had opened the door and gone, his face closed, his head dropped.

'That'll learn him,' said Laura.

'Coddy!' said Nora.

'Shut up, for God's sake!' cried Annie fiercely, as if in torture.

'Well, I'm about ready to go, Polly. Look sharp!' said Muriel.

The girls were all anxious to be off. They were tidying themselves hurriedly, with mute, stupefied* faces.

* stupefied: stunned

Murder Mysteries

Lamb to the Slaughter by Roald Dahl
(1954)

The Speckled Band by Sir Arthur Conan Doyle
(1892)

Lamb to the Slaughter

Roald Dahl

The room was warm and clean, the curtains drawn, the two table lamps alight – hers and the one by the empty chair opposite. On the sideboard behind her, two tall glasses, soda water, whisky. Fresh ice cubes in the Thermos bucket.

Mary Maloney was waiting for her husband to come home from work.

Now and again she would glance up at the clock, but without anxiety, merely to please herself with the thought that each minute gone by made it nearer the time when he would come. There was a slow smiling air about her, and about everything she did. The drop of the head as she bent over her sewing was curiously tranquil. Her skin – for this was her sixth month with child – had acquired a wonderful translucent quality, the mouth was soft, and the eyes, with their new placid look, seemed larger, darker than before.

When the clock said ten minutes to five, she began to listen, and a few moments later, punctually as always, she heard the tyres on the gravel outside, and the car door slamming, the footsteps passing the window, the key turning in the lock. She laid aside her sewing, stood up, and went forward to kiss him as he came in.

'Hullo, darling,' she said.

'Hullo,' he answered.

She took his coat and hung it in the closet. Then she walked over and made the drinks, a strongish one for him, a weak one for herself; and soon she was back again in her chair with the sewing, and he in the other, opposite, holding the tall glass with both his hands, rocking it so the ice cubes tinkled against the side.

For her, this was always a blissful time of day. She knew he didn't want to speak much until the first drink was finished, and she, on her side, was content to sit quietly, enjoying his company after the long hours alone in the house. She loved to luxuriate in the presence of this man, and to feel – almost as a sunbather feels the sun – that warm male glow that came out of him to her when they were alone together. She loved him for the way he sat loosely in a chair, for the way he came in a door, or moved slowly across the room with long strides. She loved the intent, far look in his eyes when they rested on her, the funny shape of the mouth, and especially the way he remained silent about his tiredness, sitting still with himself until the whisky had taken some of it away.

'Tired, darling?'

'Yes,' he said. 'I'm tired.' And as he spoke, he did an unusual thing. He lifted his glass and drained it in one swallow although there was still half of it, at least half of it, left. She wasn't really watching him but she knew what he had done because she heard the ice cubes falling back against the bottom of the empty glass when he lowered his arm. He paused a moment, leaning forward in the chair, then he got up and went slowly over to fetch himself another.

'I'll get it!' she cried, jumping up.

'Sit down,' he said.

When he came back, she noticed that the new drink was dark amber with the quantity of whisky in it.

'Darling, shall I get your slippers?'

'No.'

She watched him as he began to sip the dark yellow drink, and she could see little oily swirls in the liquid because it was so strong.

'I think it's a shame,' she said, 'that when a policeman gets to be as senior as you, they keep him walking about on his feet all day long.'

He didn't answer, so she bent her head again and went on with her sewing; but each time he lifted the drink to his lips, she heard the ice cubes clinking against the side of the glass.

'Darling,' she said. 'Would you like me to get you some cheese? I haven't made any supper because it's Thursday.'

'No,' he said.

'If you're too tired to eat out,' she went on, 'it's still not too late. There's plenty of meat and stuff in the freezer, and you can have it right here and not even move out of the chair.'

Her eyes waited on him for an answer, a smile, a little nod, but he made no sign.

'Anyway,' she went on, 'I'll get you some cheese and crackers first.'

'I don't want it,' he said.

She moved uneasily in her chair, the large eyes still watching his face. 'But you *must* have supper. I can easily do it here. I'd like to do it. We can have lamb chops. Or pork. Anything you want. Everything's in the freezer.'

'Forget it,' he said.

'But, darling, you *must* eat! I'll fix it anyway, and then you can have it or not, as you like.'

She stood up and placed her sewing on the table by the lamp.

'Sit down,' he said. 'Just for a minute, sit down.'

It wasn't till then that she began to get frightened.

'Go on,' he said. 'Sit down.'

She lowered herself back slowly into the chair, watching him all the time with those large, bewildered eyes. He had finished the second drink and was staring into the glass, frowning.

'Listen,' he said, 'I've got something to tell you.'

'What is it, darling? What's the matter?'

He had become absolutely motionless, and he kept his head down so that the light from the lamp beside him fell across the upper part of his face, leaving the chin and mouth in shadow. She noticed there was a little muscle moving near the corner of his left eye.

'This is going to be a bit of a shock to you, I'm afraid,' he said. 'But I've thought about it a good deal and I've decided the only thing to do is tell you right away. I hope you won't blame me too much.'

And he told her. It didn't take long, four or five minutes at most, and she sat very still through it all, watching him with a kind of dazed horror as he went further and further away from her with each word.

'So there it is,' he added. 'And I know it's kind of a bad time to be telling you, but there simply wasn't any other way. Of course I'll give you money and see you're looked after. But there needn't really be any fuss. I hope not anyway. It wouldn't be very good for my job.'

Her first instinct was not to believe any of it, to reject it all. It occurred to her that perhaps he hadn't even spoken, that she herself had imagined the whole thing. Maybe, if she went about her business and acted as though she hadn't been listening, then later, when she sort of woke up again, she might find none of it had ever happened.

'I'll get the supper,' she managed to whisper, and this time he didn't stop her.

When she walked across the room she couldn't feel her feet touching the floor. She couldn't feel anything at all – except a slight nausea and a desire to vomit. Everything was automatic now – down the stairs to the cellar, the light switch, the deep freeze, the hand inside the cabinet taking hold of the first object it met. She lifted it out, and looked at it. It was wrapped in paper, so she took off the paper and looked at it again.

A leg of lamb.

All right then, they would have lamb for supper. She carried it upstairs, holding the thin bone-end of it with both her hands, and as she went through the living-room, she saw him standing over by the window with his back to her, and she stopped.

'For God's sake,' he said, hearing her, but not turning round, 'Don't make supper for me. I'm going out.'

At that point, Mary Maloney simply walked up behind him and without any pause she swung the big frozen leg of lamb high in the air and brought it down as hard as she could on the back of his head.

She might just as well have hit him with a steel club.

She stepped back a pace, waiting, and the funny thing was that he remained standing there for at least four or five seconds, gently swaying. Then he crashed to the carpet.

The violence of the crash, the noise, the small table overturning, helped bring her out of the shock. She came out slowly, feeling cold and surprised, and she stood for a while blinking at the body, still holding the ridiculous piece of meat tight with both hands.

All right, she told herself. So I've killed him.

It was extraordinary, now, how clear her mind became all of a sudden. She began thinking very fast. As the wife of a detective, she knew quite well what the penalty would be. That was fine. It made no difference to her. In fact, it would be a relief. On the other hand, what about the child? What were the laws about murderers with unborn children? Did they kill them both – mother and child? Or did they wait until the tenth month? What did they do?

Mary Maloney didn't know. And she certainly wasn't prepared to take a chance.

She carried the meat into the kitchen, placed it in a pan, turned the oven on high, and shoved it inside. Then she washed her hands and ran upstairs to the bedroom. She sat down before the mirror, tidied her face, touched up her lips and face. She tried a smile. It came out rather peculiar. She tried again.

'Hullo Sam,' she said brightly, aloud.

The voice sounded peculiar too.

'I want some potatoes please, Sam. Yes, and I think a can of peas.'

That was better. Both the smile and the voice were coming out better now. She rehearsed it several times more. Then she ran downstairs, took her coat, went out the back door, down the garden, into the street.

It wasn't six o'clock yet and the lights were still on in the grocery shop.

'Hullo Sam,' she said brightly, smiling at the man behind the counter.

'Why, good evening, Mrs Maloney. How're *you*?'

'I want some potatoes please, Sam. Yes, and I think a can of peas.'

The man turned and reached up behind him on the shelf for the peas.

'Patrick's decided he's tired and doesn't want to eat out tonight,' she told him. 'We usually go out Thursdays, you know, and now he's caught me without any vegetables in the house.'

'Then how about meat, Mrs Maloney?'

'No, I've got meat, thanks. I got a nice leg of lamb, from the freezer.'

'Oh.'

'I don't much like cooking it frozen, Sam, but I'm taking a chance on it this time. You think it'll be all right?'

'Personally,' the grocer said, 'I don't believe it makes any difference. You want these Idaho potatoes?'

'Oh yes, that'll be fine. Two of those.'

'Anything else?' The grocer cocked his head on one side, looking at her pleasantly. 'How about afterwards? What you going to give him for afterwards?'

'Well – what would you suggest, Sam?'

The man glanced around his shop. 'How about a nice big slice of cheesecake? I know he likes that.'

'Perfect,' she said. 'He loves it.'

And when it was all wrapped and she had paid, she put on her brightest smile and said, 'Thank you, Sam. Good night.'

'Good night, Mrs Maloney. And thank *you*.'

And now, she told herself as she hurried back, all she was doing now, she was returning home to her husband and he was waiting for his supper; and she must cook it good, and make it as tasty as possible because the poor man was tired; and if, when she entered the house, she happened to find anything unusual, or tragic, or terrible, then naturally it would be a shock and she'd become frantic with grief and horror. Mind you, she wasn't *expecting* to find anything. She was just going home with the vegetables. Mrs Patrick Maloney going home with the vegetables on Thursday evening to cook supper for her husband.

That's the way, she told herself. Do everything right and natural. Keep things absolutely natural and there'll be no need for any acting at all.

Therefore, when she entered the kitchen by the back door, she was humming a little tune to herself and smiling.

'Patrick!' she called. 'How are you, darling?'

She put the parcel down on the table and went through into the living-room; and when she saw him lying there on the floor with his legs doubled up and one arm twisted back underneath his body, it really was rather a shock. All the old love and longing for him welled up inside her, and she ran over to him, knelt down beside him, and began to cry her heart out. It was easy. No acting was necessary.

A few minutes later she got up and went to the phone. She knew the number of the police station, and when the man at the other end answered, she cried to him, 'Quick! Come quick! Patrick's dead!'

'Who's speaking?'

'Mrs Maloney. Mrs Patrick Maloney.'

'You mean Patrick Maloney's dead?'

'I think so,' she sobbed. 'He's lying on the floor and I think he's dead.'

'Be right over,' the man said.

The car came very quickly, and when she opened the front door, two policemen walked in. She knew them both – she knew nearly all the men at the precinct – and she fell right into Jack Noonan's arms, weeping hysterically. He put her gently into a chair, then went over to join the other one, who was called O'Malley, kneeling by the body.

'Is he dead?' she cried

'I'm afraid he is. What happened?'

Briefly, she told her story about going out to the grocer and coming back to find him on the floor. While she was talking, crying and talking, Noonan discovered a small patch of congealed blood on the dead man's head. He showed it to O'Malley who got up at once and hurried to the phone.

Soon, other men began to come into the house. First a doctor, then two detectives, one of whom she knew by name. Later, a police photographer arrived and took pictures, and a man who knew about fingerprints. There was a great deal of whispering and muttering beside the corpse, and the detectives kept asking her a lot of questions. But they always treated her kindly. She told her story again, this time right from the beginning, when Patrick had come in, and she was sewing, and he was tired, so tired he hadn't wanted to go out for supper. She told how she'd put the meat in the oven – 'it's there now, cooking' – and how she'd slipped out to the grocer for vegetables, and come back to find him lying on the floor.

'Which grocer?' one of the detectives asked.

She told him, and he turned and whispered something to the other detective who immediately went outside into the street.

In fifteen minutes he was back with a page of notes, and there was more whispering, and through her sobbing she heard a few of the whispered phrases – '. . . acted quite normal . . . very cheerful . . . wanted to give him a good supper . . . peas . . . cheesecake . . . impossible that she . . . '

After a while, the photographer and the doctor departed and two other men came in and took the corpse away on a stretcher. Then the fingerprint man went away. The two detectives remained, and so did the two policemen. They were exceptionally nice to her, and Jack Noonan asked if she wouldn't rather go somewhere else, to her sister's house perhaps, or to his own wife who would take care of her and put her up for the night.

No, she said. She didn't feel she could move even a yard at the moment. Would they mind awfully if she stayed just where she was until she felt better? She didn't feel too good at the moment, she really didn't.

Then hadn't she better lie down on the bed? Jack Noonan asked.

No, she said, she'd like to stay right where she was, in this chair. A little later perhaps, when she felt better, she would move.

So they left her there while they went about their business, searching the house. Occasionally one of the detectives asked her another question. Sometimes Jack Noonan spoke to her gently as he passed by. Her husband, he told her, had been killed by a blow on the back of the head administered with a heavy blunt instrument, almost certainly a large piece of metal. They were looking for the weapon. The murderer may have taken it with him, but on the other hand he may've thrown it away or hidden it somewhere on the premises.

'It's the old story,' he said. 'Get the weapon, and you've got the man.'

Later, one of the detectives came up and sat beside her. Did she know, he asked, of anything in the house that could've been used as the weapon? Would she mind having a look around to see if anything was missing – a very big spanner, for example, or a heavy metal vase.

They didn't have any heavy metal vases, she said.

'Or a big spanner?'

She didn't think they had a big spanner. But there might be some things like that in the garage.

The search went on. She knew that there were other policemen in the garden all around the house. She could hear their footsteps on the gravel outside, and sometimes she saw the flash of a torch through a chink in the curtains. It began to get late, nearly nine she noticed by the clock on the mantel. The four men searching the rooms seemed to be growing weary, a trifle exasperated.

'Jack,' she said, the next time Sergeant Noonan went by. 'Would you mind giving me a drink?'

'Sure I'll give you a drink. You mean this whisky?'

'Yes, please. But just a small one. It might make me feel better.'

He handed her the glass.

'Why don't you have one yourself,' she said. 'You must be awfully tired. Please do. You've been very good to me.'

'Well,' he answered. 'It's not strictly allowed, but I might take just a drop to keep me going.'

One by one the others came in and were persuaded to take a little nip of whisky. They stood around rather awkwardly with the drinks in their hands, uncomfortable in her presence, trying to say consoling things to her. Sergeant Noonan wandered into the kitchen, came out quickly and said, 'Look, Mrs Maloney. You know that oven of yours is still on, and the meat still inside.'

'Oh *dear* me!' she cried. 'So it is!'

'I better turn it off for you, hadn't I?'

'Will you do that, Jack. Thank you so much.'

When the sergeant returned the second time, she looked at him with her large, dark, tearful eyes. 'Jack Noonan,' she said.

'Yes?'

'Would you do me a small favour – you and these others?'

'We can try, Mrs Maloney.'

'Well,' she said. 'Here you all are, and good friends of dear Patrick's too, and helping to catch the man who killed him. You must be terribly hungry by now because it's long past your supper time, and I know Patrick would never forgive me, God bless his soul, if I allowed you to remain in his house without offering you decent hospitality. Why don't you eat up that lamb that's in the oven? It'll be cooked just right by now.'

'Wouldn't dream of it,' Sergeant Noonan said.

'Please,' she begged. 'Please eat it. Personally I couldn't touch a thing, certainly not what's been in the house when he was here. But it's all right for you. It'd be a favour to me if you'd eat it up. Then you can go on with your work again afterwards.'

There was a good deal of hesitating among the four policemen, but they were clearly hungry, and in the end they were persuaded to go into the kitchen and help themselves. The woman stayed where she was, listening to them through the open door, and she could hear them speaking among themselves, their voices thick and sloppy because their mouths were full of meat.

'Have some more, Charlie?'

'No. Better not finish it.'

'She *wants* us to finish it. She said so. Be doing her a favour.'

'Okay then. Give me some more.'

'That's the hell of a big club the guy must've used to hit poor Patrick,' one of them was saying. 'The doc says his skull was smashed all to pieces just like from a sledge-hammer.'

'That's why it ought to be easy to find.'

'Exactly what I say.'

'Whoever done it, they're not going to be carrying a thing like that around with them longer than they need.'

One of them belched.

'Personally, I think it's right here on the premises.'

'Probably right under our very noses. What do you think, Jack?'

And in the other room, Mary Maloney began to giggle.

The Speckled Band

Sir Arthur Conan Doyle

In glancing over my notes of the seventy-odd cases in which I have during the last eight years studied the methods of my friend Sherlock Holmes, I find many tragic, some comic, a large number merely strange, but none commonplace; for, working as he did rather for the love of his art than for the acquirement of wealth, he refused to associate himself with any investigation which did not tend towards the unusual, and even the fantastic. Of all these varied cases, however, I cannot recall any which presented more singular features than that which was associated with the well-known Surrey family of the Roylotts of Stoke Moran. The events in question occurred in the early days of my association with Holmes, when we were sharing rooms as bachelors, in Baker Street. It is possible that I might have placed them upon record before, but a promise of secrecy was made at the time, from which I have only been freed during the last month by the untimely death of the lady to whom the pledge was given. It is perhaps as well that the facts should now come to light, for I have reasons to know there are widespread rumours as to the death of Dr Grimesby Roylott which tend to make the matter even more terrible than the truth.

It was early in April, in the year '83, that I woke one morning to find Sherlock Holmes standing, fully dressed, by the side of my bed. He was a late riser as a rule, and, as the clock on the mantelpiece showed me that it was only a quarter past seven, I blinked up at him in some surprise, and perhaps just a little resentment, for I was myself regular in my habits.

'Very sorry to knock you up, Watson,' said he, 'but it's the common lot this morning. Mrs Hudson has been knocked up, she retorted upon me, and I on you.'

'What is it, then? A fire?'

'No, a client. It seems that a young lady has arrived in a considerable state of excitement, who insists upon seeing me. She is waiting now in the sitting-room. Now, when young ladies wander about the metropolis at this hour of the morning, and knock sleepy people up out of their beds, I presume that it is something very pressing which they have to communicate. Should it prove to be an interesting case, you would, I am sure, wish to follow it from the outset. I thought at any rate that I should call you, and give you the chance.'

'My dear fellow, I would not miss it for anything.'

I had no keener pleasure than in following Holmes in his professional investigations, and in admiring the rapid deductions, as swift as intuitions, and yet always founded on a logical basis, with which he unravelled the problems which were submitted to him. I rapidly threw on my clothes, and was ready in a few minutes to accompany my friend down to the sitting-room. A lady dressed in black and heavily veiled, who had been sitting in the window, rose as we entered.

'Good morning, madam,' said Holmes cheerily. 'My name is Sherlock Holmes. This is my intimate friend and associate, Dr Watson, before whom you can speak as freely as before myself. Ha, I am glad to see that Mrs Hudson has had the good sense to light the fire. Pray draw up to it, and I shall order you a cup of hot coffee, for I observe that you are shivering.'

'It is not cold which makes me shiver,' said the woman in a low voice, changing her seat as requested.

'What then?'

'It is fear, Mr Holmes. It is terror.' She raised her veil as she spoke, and we could see that she was indeed in a pitiable state of agitation, her face all drawn and grey, with restless, frightened eyes, like those of some hunted animal. Her features and figure were those of a woman of thirty, but her hair was shot with premature grey, and her expression was weary and haggard. Sherlock Holmes ran her over with one of his quick, all-comprehensive glances.

'You must not fear,' said he soothingly, bending forward and patting her forearm. 'We shall soon set matters right, I have no doubt. You have come in by train this morning, I see.'

'You know me, then?'

'No, but I observe the second half of a return ticket in the palm of your left glove. You must have started early, and yet you had a good drive in a dog-cart*, along heavy roads, before you reached the station.'

The lady gave a violent start, and stared in bewilderment at my companion.

'There is no mystery, my dear madam,' said he, smiling. 'The left arm of your jacket is spattered with mud in no less than seven places. The marks are perfectly fresh. There is no vehicle save a dog-cart which throws up mud in that way, and then only when you sit on the left-hand side of the driver.'

'Whatever your reasons may be, you are perfectly correct,' said she. 'I started from home before six, reached Leatherhead at twenty past, and came in by the first train to Waterloo. Sir, I can stand this strain

* dog-cart: light two-wheeled carriage

no longer, I shall go mad if it continues. I have no one to turn to – none, save only one, who cares for me, and he, poor fellow, can be of little aid. I have heard of you, Mr Holmes; I have heard of you from Mrs Farintosh, whom you helped in the hour of her sore need. It was from her that I had your address. Oh, sir, do you not think you could help me too, and at least throw a little light through the dense darkness which surrounds me? At present it is out of my power to reward you for your services, but in a month or two I shall be married, with the control of my own income, and then at least you shall not find me ungrateful.'

Holmes turned to his desk, and unlocking it, drew out a small case-book which he consulted.

'Farintosh,' said he. 'Ah, yes, I recall the case; it was concerned with an opal tiara. I think it was before your time, Watson. I can only say, madam, that I shall be happy to devote the same care to your case as I did to that of your friend. As to reward, my profession is its reward; but you are at liberty to defray* whatever expenses I may be put to, at the time which suits you best. And now I beg that you will lay before us everything that may help us in forming an opinion upon the matter.'

'Alas!' replied our visitor. 'The very horror of my situation lies in the fact that my fears are so vague, and my suspicions depend so entirely upon small points, which might seem trivial to another, that even he to whom of all others I have a right to look for help and advice looks upon all that I tell him about it as the fancies of a nervous woman. He does not say so, but I can read it from his soothing answers and averted eyes. But I have heard, Mr Holmes, that you can see

* defray: make good, repay

deeply into the manifold wickedness of the human heart. You may advise me how to walk amid the dangers which encompass me.'

'I am all attention, madam.'

'My name is Helen Stoner, and I am living with my stepfather, who is the last survivor of one of the oldest Saxon families in England, the Roylotts of Stoke Moran, on the western border of Surrey.'

Holmes nodded his head. 'The name is familiar to me,' said he.

'The family was at one time among the richest in England, and the estate extended over the borders into Berkshire in the north and Hampshire in the west. In the last century, however, four successive heirs were of a dissolute and wasteful disposition, and the family ruin was eventually completed by a gambler, in the days of the Regency. Nothing was left save a few acres of ground and the two-hundred-year-old house, which is itself crushed under a heavy mortgage. The last squire dragged out his existence there, living the horrible life of an aristocratic pauper; but his only son, my stepfather, seeing that he must adapt himself to the new conditions, obtained an advance from a relative, which enabled him to take a medical degree, and went out to Calcutta, where, by his professional skill and his force of character, he established a large practice. In a fit of anger, however, caused by some robberies which had been perpetrated in the house, he beat his native butler to death, and narrowly escaped a capital sentence. As it was, he suffered a long term of imprisonment, and afterwards returned to England a morose and disappointed man.

'When Dr Roylott was in India he married my mother, Mrs Stoner, the young widow of Major-General Stoner, of the Bengal Artillery. My sister Julia and I were twins, and we were only two years old at the time of my mother's re-marriage. She had a considerable sum of money, not less than a thousand a year, and this she bequeathed to Dr Roylott entirely whilst we resided with him, with a provision that a certain annual sum should be allowed to each of us in the event of our marriage. Shortly after our return to England my mother died – she was killed eight years ago in a railway accident near Crewe. Dr Roylott then abandoned his attempts to establish himself in practice in London, and took us to live with him in the ancestral house at Stoke Moran. The money which my mother had left was enough for all our wants, and there seemed no obstacle to our happiness.

'But a terrible change came over our stepfather about this time. Instead of making friends and exchanging visits with our neighbours, who had at first been overjoyed to see a Roylott of Stoke Moran back in the old family seat, he shut himself up in his house, and seldom came out save to indulge in ferocious quarrels with whoever might cross his path. Violence of temper approaching to mania has been hereditary in the men of the family, and in my stepfather's case it had, I believe, been intensified by his long residence in the tropics. A series of disgraceful brawls took place, two of which ended in the police-court, until at last he became the terror of the village, and the folks would fly at his approach, for he is a man of immense strength, and absolutely uncontrollable in his anger.

'Last week he hurled the local blacksmith over a parapet into a stream and it was only by paying over all the money that I could gather together that I was able to avert another public exposure. He had no friends at all save the wandering gipsies, and he would give these vagabonds leave to encamp upon the few acres of bramble-covered land which represent the family estate, and would accept in return the hospitality of their tents, wandering away with them sometimes for weeks on end. He has a passion also for Indian animals, which are sent over to him by a correspondent, and he has at this moment a cheetah and a baboon, which wander freely over his grounds, and are feared by the villagers almost as much as their master.

'You can imagine from what I say that my poor sister Julia and I had no great pleasure in our lives. No servant would stay with us, and for a long time we did all the work of the house. She was but thirty at the time of her death, and yet her hair had already begun to whiten, even as mine has.'

'Your sister is dead, then?'

'She died just two years ago, and it is of her death that I wish to speak to you. You can understand that, living the life which I have described, we were little likely to see anyone of our own age and position. We had, however, an aunt, my mother's maiden sister, Miss Honoria Westphail, who lives near Harrow, and we were occasionally allowed to pay short visits at this lady's house. Julia went there at Christmas two years ago, and met there a half-pay Major of Marines, to whom she became engaged. My stepfather learned of the engagement when my sister returned, and offered no objection to the marriage; but within a fortnight of the day which had been fixed for the wedding, the terrible event occurred which has deprived me of my only companion.'

Sherlock Holmes had been leaning back in his chair with his eyes closed, and his head sunk in a cushion, but he half opened his lids now, and glanced across at his visitor.

'Pray be precise as to details,' said he.

'It is easy for me to be so, for every event of that dreadful time is seared into my memory. The manor house is, as I have already said, very old, and only one wing is now inhabited. The bedrooms in this wing are on the ground floor, the sitting-rooms being in the central block of the buildings. Of these bedrooms, the first is Dr Roylott's, the second my sister's, and the third my own. There is no communication between them, but they all open out into the same corridor. Do I make myself plain?'

'Perfectly so.'

'The windows of the three rooms open out upon the lawn. That fatal night Dr Roylott had gone to his room early, though we knew that he had not retired to rest, for my sister was troubled by the smell of the strong Indian cigars which it was his custom to smoke. She left her room, therefore, and came into mine, where she sat for some time, chatting about her approaching wedding. At eleven o'clock she rose to leave me, but she paused at the door and looked back.

'"Tell me, Helen," said she, 'have you ever heard anyone whistle in the dead of the night?"

'"Never," said I.

'"I suppose that you could not possibly whistle yourself in your sleep?"

'"Certainly not. But why?"

'"Because during the last few nights I have always, about three in the morning, heard a low clear whistle. I am a light sleeper, and it has awakened me. I cannot tell where it came from – perhaps from the next room, perhaps from the lawn. I thought that I would just ask you whether you had heard it."

'"No, I have not. It must be those wretched gipsies in the plantation."

'"Very likely. And yet if it were on the lawn I wonder that you did not hear it also."

'"Ah, but I sleep more heavily than you."

'"Well, it is of no great consequence, at any rate," she smiled back at me, closed my door, and a few moments later I head her key turn in the lock.'

'Indeed,' said Holmes. 'Was it your custom always to lock yourselves in at night?'

'Always.'

'And why?'

'I think that I mentioned to you that the Doctor kept a cheetah and a baboon. We had no feeling of security unless our doors were locked.'

'Quite so. Pray proceed with your statement.'

'I could not sleep that night. A vague feeling of impending misfortune impressed me. My sister and I, you will recollect, were twins, and you know how subtle are the links which bind two souls which are so closely allied. It was a wild night. The wind was howling outside, and the rain was beating and splashing against the windows. Suddenly, amidst all the hubbub of the gale, there burst forth the wild scream of a terrified woman. I knew that it was my sister's voice. I sprang from my bed, wrapped a shawl round me, and rushed into the corridor. As I opened my door I seemed to hear a low whistle, such as my sister described, and a few moments later a clanging sound, as if a mass of metal had fallen. As I ran down the passage my sister's door was unlocked, and revolved slowly upon its hinges. I stared at it horror-stricken, not knowing what was about to issue from it. By the light of the corridor lamp I saw my sister appear at the opening, her face blanched with terror, her hands groping for help, her whole figure swaying to and fro like that of a drunkard. I ran to her and threw my arms round her, but at that moment her knees seemed to give way and she fell to the ground. She writhed as one who is in terrible pain, and her limbs were dreadfully convulsed. At first I thought that she had not recognized me, but as I bent over her she suddenly shrieked out in a voice which I shall never forget, "O, my God! Helen! It was the band! The speckled band!" There was something else which she would fain* have said, and she stabbed with her finger into the air in the direction of the Doctor's room, but a fresh convulsion seized her and choked her words. I rushed out, calling loudly for my stepfather, and I met him hastening from his room in his dressing-gown. When he reached my sister's side she was unconscious, and though he poured brandy down her throat, and sent for medical aid from the village, all efforts were in vain, for she slowly sank and died without having recovered her consciousness. Such was the dreadful end of my beloved sister.'

'One moment,' said Holmes; 'are you sure about this whistle and metallic sound? Could you swear to it?'

'That was what the county coroner asked me at the inquiry. It is my strong impression that I heard it, and yet among the crash of the gale, and the creaking of an old house, I may possibly have been deceived.'

'Was your sister dressed?'

'No, she was in her nightdress. In her right hand was found the charred stump of a match, and in her left a matchbox.'

'Showing that she had struck a light and looked about her when the alarm took place. This is

* would fain: would like to

important. And what conclusions did the coroner come to?'

'He investigated the case with great care, for Dr Roylott's conduct had long been notorious in the county, but he was unable to find any satisfactory cause of death. My evidence showed that the door had been fastened upon the inner side, and the windows were blocked by old-fashioned shutters with broad iron bars, which were secured every night. The walls were carefully sounded, and were shown to be quite solid all round, and the flooring was also thoroughly examined, with the same result. The chimney is wide, but is barred up by four large staples. It is certain, therefore, that my sister was quite alone when she met her end. Besides, there were no marks of any violence upon her.'

'How about poison?'

'The doctors examined her for it, but without success.'

'What do you think that this unfortunate lady died of, then?'

'It is my belief that she died of pure fear and nervous shock, though what it was which frightened her I cannot imagine.'

'Were there gypsies in the plantation at the time?'

'Yes, there are nearly always some there.'

'Ah, and what did you gather from this allusion to a band – a speckled band?'

'Sometimes I have thought that it was merely the wild talk of delirium, sometimes that it may have referred to some band of people, perhaps to these very gipsies in the plantation. I do not know whether the spotted handkerchiefs which so many of them wear over their heads might have suggested the strange adjective which she used.'

Holmes shook his head like a man who is far from being satisfied.

'These are very deep waters,' said he; 'pray go on with your narrative.'

'Two years have passed since then, and my life has been until lately lonelier than ever. A month ago, however, a dear friend, whom I have known for many years, has done me the honour to ask my hand in marriage. His name is Armitage – Percy Armitage – the second son of Mr Armitage, of Crane Water, near Reading. My stepfather has offered no opposition to the match, and we are to be married in the course of the spring. Two days ago some repairs were started in the west wing of the building, and my bedroom wall has been pierced, so that I have had to move into the chamber in which my sister died, and to sleep in the very bed in which she slept. Imagine, then, my thrill of terror when last night, as I lay awake, thinking over her terrible fate, I suddenly heard in the silence of the night the low whistle which had been the herald of her own death. I sprang up and lit the lamp, but nothing was to be seen in the room. I was too shaken to go to bed again, however, so I dressed, and as soon as it was daylight I slipped down, got a dog-cart at the Crown Inn, which is opposite, and drove to Leatherhead, from whence I have come on this morning, with the one object of seeing you and asking your advice.'

'You have done wisely,' said my friend. 'But have you told me all?'

'Yes, all.'

'Miss Stoner, you have not. You are screening your stepfather.'

'Why, what do you mean?'

For answer Holmes pushed back the frill of black lace which fringed the hand that lay upon our visitor's knee. Five little livid spots, the marks of four fingers and a thumb, were printed upon the white wrist.

'You have been cruelly used,' said Holmes.

The lady coloured deeply, and covered over her injured wrist. 'He is a hard man,' she said, 'and perhaps he hardly knows his own strength.'

There was a long silence, during which Holmes leaned his chin upon his hands and stared into the crackling fire.

'This is very deep business,' he said at last. 'There are a thousand details which I should desire to know before I decide upon our course of action. Yet we have not a moment to lose. If we were to come to Stoke Moran today, would it be possible for us to see over these rooms without the knowledge of your stepfather?'

'As it happens, he spoke of coming into town today upon some most important business. It is probable that he will be away all day, and that there would be nothing to disturb you. We have a housekeeper now, but she is old and foolish, and I could easily get her out of the way.'

'Excellent. You are not averse to this trip, Watson?'

'By no means.'

'Then we shall both come. What are you going to do yourself?'

'I have one or two things which I would wish to do now that I am in town. But I shall return by the twelve o'clock train, so as to be there in time for your coming.'

'And you may expect us early in the afternoon. I have myself some small business matters to attend to. Will you not wait and breakfast?'

'No, I must go. My heart is lightened already since I have confided my trouble to you. I shall look forward to seeing you again this afternoon.' She dropped her thick black veil over her face, and glided from the room.

'And what do you think of it all, Watson?' asked Sherlock Holmes, leaning back in his chair.

'It seems to me to be a most dark and sinister business.'

'Dark enough and sinister enough.'

'Yet if the lady is correct in saying that the flooring and walls are sound, and that the door, window, and chimney are impassable, then her sister must have been undoubtedly alone when she met her mysterious end.'

'What becomes, then, of these nocturnal whistles, and what of the very peculiar words of the dying woman?'

'I cannot think.'

'When you combine the ideas of whistles at night, the presence of a band of gipsies who are on intimate terms with this old doctor, the fact that we have every reason to believe that the doctor has an interest in preventing his stepdaughter's marriage, the dying allusion to a band, and finally, the fact that Miss Helen Stoner heard a metallic clang, which might have been caused by one of those metal bars which secured the shutters falling back into their place, I think there is good ground to think that the mystery may be cleared along those lines.'

'But what, then, did the gipsies do?'

'I cannot imagine.'

'I see many objections to any such a theory.'

'And so do I. It is precisely for that reason that we are going to Stoke Moran this day. I want to see whether the objections are fatal, or if they may be explained away. But what, in the name of the devil!'

The ejaculation had been drawn from my companion by the fact that our door had been suddenly dashed open, and that a huge man framed himself in the aperture*. His costume was a peculiar mixture of the professional and of the agricultural, having a black top-hat, a long frock-coat, and a pair of high gaiters*, with a hunting-crop swinging in his hand. So tall was he that his hat actually brushed the cross-bar of the doorway, and his breadth seemed to span it across from side to side. A large face, seared with a thousand wrinkles, burned yellow with the sun, and marked with every evil passion, was turned from one to the other of us, while his deep-set, bile-shot eyes, and the high thin fleshless nose, gave him somewhat the resemblance to a fierce old bird of prey.

'Which of you is Holmes?' asked this apparition.

'My name, sir, but you have the advantage of me,' said my companion quietly.

'I am Dr Grimesby Roylott, of Stoke Moran.'

'Indeed, Doctor,' said Holmes blandly. 'Pray take a seat.'

'I will do nothing of the kind. My stepdaughter has been here. I have traced her. What has she been saying to you?'

'It is a little cold for the time of the year,' said Holmes.

'What has she been saying to you?' screamed the old man furiously.

'But I have heard that the crocuses promise well,' continued my companion imperturbably.

'Ha! You put me off, do you?' said our new visitor, taking a step forward, and shaking his hunting-crop. 'I

* aperture: opening gaiters: protective leggings

know you, you scoundrel! I have heard of you before. You are Holmes the meddler.'

My friend smiled.

'Holmes the busybody.'

His smile broadened.

'Holmes the Scotland Yard jack-in-office.'

Holmes chuckled heartily. 'Your conversation is most entertaining,' said he. 'When you go out close the door, for there is a decided draught.'

'I will go when I have had my say. Don't you dare to meddle with my affairs. I know that Miss Stoner has been here – I traced her! I am a dangerous man to fall foul of! See here.' He stepped swiftly forward, seized the poker, and bent it into a curve with his huge brown hands.

'See that you keep yourself out of my grip,' he snarled, and hurling the twisted poker into the fireplace, he strode out of the room.

'He seems a very amiable person,' said Holmes, laughing. 'I am not quite so bulky, but if he had remained I might have shown him that my grip was not much more feeble than his own.' As he spoke he picked up the steel poker, and with a sudden effort straightened it out again.

'Fancy his having the insolence to confound me with the official detective force! This incident gives zest to our investigation, however, and I only trust that our little friend will not suffer from her imprudence in allowing this brute to trace her. And now, Watson, we shall order breakfast, and afterwards I shall walk down to Doctors' Commons, where I hope to get some data which may help us in this matter.'

It was nearly one o'clock when Sherlock Holmes returned from his excursion. He held in his hand a sheet of blue paper, scrawled over with notes and figures.

'I have seen the will of the deceased wife,' said he. 'To determine its exact meaning I have been obliged to work out the present prices of the investments with which it is concerned. The total income, which at the time of the wife's death was little short of £1,100, is now through the fall in agricultural prices not more than £750. Each daughter can claim an income of £250, in case of marriage. It is evident, therefore, that if both girls had married this beauty would have had a mere pittance*, while even one of them would cripple him to a serious extent. My morning's work has not been wasted, since it has proved that he has the very strongest motives for standing in the way of anything of the sort. And now, Watson, this is too serious for dawdling, especially as the old man is aware that we are interesting ourselves in his affairs, so if you are ready we shall call a cab and drive to Waterloo. I should be very much obliged if you would slip your revolver into your pocket. An Eley's No. 2 is an excellent argument with gentlemen who can twist steel pokers into knots. That and a tooth-brush are, I think, all that we need.'

At Waterloo we were fortunate in catching a train for Leatherhead, where we hired a trap at the station inn, and drove for four or five miles through the lovely Surrey lanes. It was a perfect day, with a bright sun and a few fleecy clouds in the heavens. The trees and wayside hedges were just throwing out their first green shoots, and the air was full of the pleasant smell of the moist earth. To me at least there was a strange contrast between the sweet promise of the spring and

* pittance: small allowance of money

this sinister quest upon which we were engaged. My companion sat in front of the trap, his arms folded, his hat pulled down over his eyes, and his chin sunk upon his breast, buried in the deepest thought. Suddenly, however, he started, tapped me on the shoulder, and pointed over the meadows.

'Look there!' said he.

A heavily timbered park stretched up in a gentle slope, thickening into a grove at the highest point. From amidst the branches there jutted out the grey gables and high roof-tree of a very old mansion.

'Stoke Moran?' said he.

'Yes, sir, that be the house of Dr Grimesby Roylott,' remarked the driver.

'There is some building going on there,' said Holmes; 'that is where we are going.'

'There's the village,' said the driver, pointing to a cluster of roofs some distance to the left; 'but if you want to get to the house, you'll find it shorter to go over this stile, and so by the footpath over the fields. There it is, where the lady is walking.'

'And the lady, I fancy, is Miss Stoner,' observed Holmes, shading his eyes. 'Yes, I think we had better do as you suggest.'

We got off, paid our fare, and the trap rattled back on its way to Leatherhead.

'I thought it as well,' said Holmes, as we climbed the stile, 'that this fellow should think we had come here as architects, or on some definite business. It may stop his gossip. Good afternoon, Miss Stoner. You see that we have been as good as our word.'

Our client of the morning had hurried forward to meet us with a face which spoke her joy. 'I have been waiting so eagerly for you,' she cried, shaking hands with us warmly. 'All has turned out splendidly.

Dr Roylott has gone to town, and it is unlikely that he will be back before evening.'

'We have had the pleasure of making the Doctor's acquaintance,' said Holmes, and in a few words he sketched out what had occurred. Miss Stoner turned white to the lips as she listened.

'Good heavens!' she cried, 'he has followed me, then.'

'So it appears.'

'He is so cunning that I never know when I am safe from him. What will he say when he returns?'

'He must guard himself, for he may find that there is someone more cunning than himself upon his track. You must lock yourself from him to-night. If he is violent, we will take you away to your aunt's at Harrow. Now, we must make the best use of our time, so kindly take us at once to the rooms which we are to examine.'

The building was of grey, lichen-blotched stone, with a high central portion, and two curving wings, like the claws of a crab, thrown out on each side. In one of these wings the windows were broken, and blocked with wooden boards, while the roof was partly caved in, a picture of ruin. The central portion was in little better repair, but the right-hand block was comparatively modern, and the blinds in the windows, with the blue smoke curling up from the chimneys, showed that this was where the family resided. Some scaffolding had been erected against the end wall, and the stonework had been broken into, but there were no signs of any workmen at the moment of our visit. Holmes walked slowly up and down the ill-trimmed lawn, and examined with deep attention the outsides of the windows.

'This, I take it, belongs to the room in which you used to sleep, the centre one to your sister's, and the one next to the main building to Dr Roylott's chamber?'

'Exactly so. But I am now sleeping in the middle one.'

'Pending the alterations, as I understand. By the way, there does not seem to be any very pressing need for repairs at the end wall.'

'There were none. I believe that it was an excuse to move me from my room.'

'Ah! that is suggestive. Now, on the other side of this narrow wing runs the corridor from which these three rooms open. There are windows in it, of course?'

'Yes, but very small ones. Too narrow for anyone to pass through.'

'As you both locked your doors at night, your rooms were unapproachable from that side. Now, would you have the kindness to go into your room, and to bar your shutters.'

Miss Stoner did so, and Holmes, after a careful examination through the open window, endeavoured in every way to force the shutter open, but without success. There was no slit through which a knife could be passed to raise the bar. Then with his lens he tested the hinges, but they were of solid iron, built firmly into the massive masonry. 'Hum!' said he, scratching his chin in some perplexity, 'my theory certainly presents some difficulties. No one could pass these shutters if they were bolted. Well, we shall see if the inside throws any light upon the matter.'

A small side-door led into the whitewashed corridor from which the three bedrooms opened. Holmes refused to examine the third chamber, so we passed at once to the second, that in which Miss Stoner was now sleeping, and in which her sister had met her fate. It was a homely little room, with a low ceiling and a gaping fireplace, after the fashion of old country houses. A brown chest of drawers stood in one corner, a narrow white-counterpaned bed in another, and a dressing-table on the left-hand side of the window. These articles, with two small wickerwork chairs, made up all the furniture in the room, save for a square of Wilton carpet in the centre. The boards round and the panelling of the walls were brown, worm-eaten oak, so old and discoloured that it may have dated from the original building of the house. Holmes drew one of the chairs into a corner and sat silent, while his eyes travelled round and round and up and down, taking in every detail of the apartment.

'Where does that bell communicate with?' he asked at last, pointing to a thick bell-rope which hung down beside the bed, the tassel actually lying upon the pillow.

'It goes to the housekeeper's room.'

'It looks newer than the other things?'

'Yes, it was only put there a couple of years ago.'

'Your sister asked for it, I suppose?'

'No, I never heard of her using it. We used always to get what we wanted for ourselves.'

'Indeed, it seemed unnecessary to put so nice a bell-pull there. You will excuse me for a few minutes while I satisfy myself as to this floor.' He threw himself down upon his face with his lens in his hand, and crawled swiftly backwards and forwards, examining minutely the cracks between the boards. He did the same with the woodwork with which the chamber was panelled. Then he walked over to the bed and spent some time in staring at it, and in running his eye up and down the wall. Finally he took the bell-rope in his hand and gave it a brisk tug.

'Why, it's a dummy,' said he.

'Won't it ring?'

'No, it is not even attached to a wire. This is very interesting. You can see now that it is fastened to a hook just above where the little opening of the ventilator is.'

'How very absurd! I never noticed that before.'

'Very strange!' muttered Holmes, pulling at the rope. 'There are one or two very singular points about this room. For example, what a fool a builder must be to open a ventilator in another room, when, with the same trouble, he might have communicated with the outside air!'

'That is also quite modern,' said the lady.

'Done about the same time as the bell-rope,' remarked Holmes.

'Yes, there were several little changes carried out about that time.'

'They seem to have been of a most interesting character – dummy bell-ropes, and ventilators which do not ventilate. With your permission, Miss Stoner, we shall now carry our researches into the inner apartment.'

Dr Grimesby Roylott's chamber was larger than that of his stepdaughter, but was as plainly furnished. A camp bed, a small wooden shelf full of books, mostly of a technical character, an arm-chair beside the bed, a plain wooden chair against the wall, a round table, and a large iron safe were the principal things which met the eye. Holmes walked slowly round and examined each and all of them with the keenest interest.

'What's in here?' he asked, tapping the safe.

'My stepfather's business papers.'

'Oh! you have seen inside, then?'

'Only once, some years ago. I remember that it was full of papers.'

'There isn't a cat in it, for example?'

'No. What a strange idea!'

'Well, look at this!' He took up a small saucer of milk which stood on the top of it.

'No; we don't keep a cat. But there is a cheetah and a baboon.'

'Ah, yes, of course! Well, a cheetah is just a big cat, and yet a saucer of milk does not go very far in satisfying its wants, I daresay. There is one point which I should wish to determine.' He squatted down in front of the wooden chair, and examined the seat of it with the greatest attention.

'Thank you. That is quite settled,' said he, rising and putting his lens in his pocket. 'Hullo! here is something interesting!'

The object which had caught his eye was a small dog lash hung on one corner of the bed. The lash, however, was curled upon itself, and tied so as to make a loop of whipcord.

'What do you make of that, Watson?'

'It's a common enough lash. But I don't know why it should be tied.'

'That is not quite so common, is it? Ah, me! it's a wicked world, and when a clever man turns his brain to crime it is the worst of all. I think that I have seen enough now, Miss Stoner, and, with your permission, we shall walk out upon the lawn.'

I had never seen my friend's face so grim, or his brow so dark, as it was when we turned from the scene of this investigation. We had walked several times up and down the lawn, neither Miss Stoner nor myself liking to break in upon his thoughts before he roused himself from his reverie*.

'It is very essential, Miss Stoner,' said he, 'that you should absolutely follow my advice in every respect.'

'I shall most certainly do so.'

'The matter is too serious for any hesitation. Your life may depend upon your compliance.'

'I assure you that I am in your hands.'

'In the first place, both my friend and I must spend the night in your room.'

Both Miss Stoner and I gazed at him in astonishment.

'Yes, it must be so. Let me explain. I believe that that is the village inn over there?'

'Yes, that is the "Crown".'

'Very good. Your windows would be visible from there?'

'Certainly.'

'You must confine yourself to your room, on pretence of a headache, when your stepfather comes back. Then when you hear him retire for the night, you must open the shutters of your window, undo the hasp, put your lamp there as a signal to us, and then withdraw with everything which you are likely to want into the room which you used to occupy. I have no doubt that, in spite of the repairs, you could manage there for one night.'

'Oh, yes, easily.'

'The rest you will leave in our hands.'

'But what will you do?'

'We shall spend the night in your room, and we shall investigate the cause of this noise which has disturbed you.'

* reverie: meditation

'I believe, Mr Holmes, that you have already made up your mind,' said Miss Stoner, laying her hand upon my companion's sleeve.

'Perhaps I have.'

'Then for pity's sake tell me what was the cause of my sister's death.'

'I should prefer to have clearer proofs before I speak.'

'You can at least tell me whether my own thought is correct, and if she died from some sudden fright.'

'No, I do not think so. I think that there was probably some more tangible cause. And now, Miss Stoner, we must leave you, for if Dr Roylott returned and saw us, our journey would be in vain. Good-bye, and be brave, for if you will do what I have told you, you may rest assured that we shall soon drive away the dangers that threaten you.'

Sherlock Holmes and I had no difficulty in engaging a bedroom and sitting-room at the Crown Inn. They were on the upper floor, and from our window we could command a view of the avenue gate, and of the inhabited wing of Stoke Moran Manor House. At dusk we saw Dr Grimesby Roylott drive past, his huge form looming up beside the little figure of the lad who drove him. The boy had some slight difficulty in undoing the heavy iron gates, and we heard the hoarse roar of the Doctor's voice, and saw the fury with which he shook his clenched fists at him. The trap drove on, and a few minutes later we saw a sudden light spring up among the trees as the lamp was lit in one of the sitting-rooms.

'Do you know, Watson,' said Holmes, as we sat together in the gathering darkness, 'I have really some scruples as to taking you to-night. There is a distinct element of danger.'

'Can I be of assistance?'

'Your presence might be invaluable.'

'Then I shall certainly come.'

'It is very kind of you.'

'You speak of danger. You have evidently seen more in these rooms than was visible to me.'

'No, but I fancy that I may have deduced a little more. I imagine that you saw all that I did.'

'I saw nothing remarkable save the bell-rope, and what purpose that could answer I confess is more than I can imagine.'

'You saw the ventilator, too?'

'Yes, but I do not think that it is such a very unusual thing to have a small opening between two rooms. It was so small that a rat could hardly pass through.'

'I knew that we should find a ventilator before ever we came to Stoke Moran.'

'My dear Holmes!'

'Oh, yes, I did. You remember in her statement she said that her sister could smell Dr Roylott's cigar. Now, of course that suggests at once that there must be a communication between the two rooms. It could only be a small one, or it would have been remarked upon at the coroner's inquiry. I deduced a ventilator.'

'But what harm can there be in that?'

'Well, there is at least a curious coincidence of dates. A ventilator is made, a cord is hung, and a lady who sleeps in the bed dies. Does not that strike you?'

'I cannot as yet see any connection.'

'Did you observe anything very peculiar about that bed?'

'No.'

'It was clamped to the floor. Did you ever see a bed fastened like that before?'

'I cannot say that I have.'

'The lady could not move her bed. It must always be in the same relative position to the ventilator and to the rope – for so we may call it, since it was clearly never meant for a bell-pull.'

'Holmes,' I cried, 'I seem to see dimly what you are hinting at. We are only just in time to prevent some subtle and horrible crime.'

'Subtle enough and horrible enough. When a doctor does go wrong he is the first of criminals. He has nerve and he has knowledge. Palmer and Pritchard were among the heads of their profession. This man strikes even deeper, but I think, Watson, that we shall be able to strike deeper still. But we shall have horrors enough before the night is over: for goodness' sake let us have a quiet pipe, and turn our minds for a few hours to something more cheerful.'

About nine o'clock the light among the trees was extinguished, and all was dark in the direction of the Manor House. Two hours passed slowly away, and then, suddenly, just at the stroke of eleven, a single bright light shone out right in front of us.

'That is our signal,' said Holmes, springing to his feet; 'it comes from the middle window.'

As we passed out he exchanged a few words with the landlord, explaining that we were going on a late visit to an acquaintance, and that it was possible that we might spend the night there. A moment later we were out on the dark road, a chill wind blowing in our faces, and one yellow light twinkling in front of us through the gloom to guide us on our sombre errand.

There was little difficulty in entering the grounds, for unrepaired breaches* gaped in the old park wall.

* breaches: gaps

Making our way among the trees, we reached the lawn, crossed it, and were about to enter through the window, when out from a clump of laurel bushes there darted what seemed to be a hideous and distorted child, who threw itself on the grass with writhing limbs, and then ran swiftly across the lawn into the darkness.

'My God!' I whispered, 'did you see it?'

Holmes was for the moment as startled as I. His hand closed like a vice upon my wrist in his agitation. Then he broke into a low laugh, and put his lips to my ear.

'It is a nice household,' he murmured, 'that is the baboon.'

I had forgotten the strange pets which the Doctor affected*. There was a cheetah, too; perhaps we might find it upon our shoulders at any moment. I confess that I felt easier in my mind when, after following Holmes's example and slipping off my shoes, I found myself inside the bedroom. My companion noiselessly closed the shutters, moved the lamp on to the table, and cast his eyes round the room. All was as we had seen it in the day-time. Then creeping up to me and making a trumpet of his hand, he whispered into my ear again so gently that it was all that I could do to distinguish the words:

'The least sound would be fatal to our plans.'

I nodded to show that I had heard.

'We must sit without a light. He would see it through the ventilator.'

I nodded again.

'Do not go to sleep; your very life may depend upon it. Have your pistol ready in case we should need it. I will sit on the side of the bed, and you in that chair.'

* affected: preferred

I took out my revolver and laid it on the corner of the table.

Holmes had brought up a long thin cane, and this he placed upon the bed beside him. By it he laid the box of matches and the stump of a candle. Then he turned down the lamp and we were left in darkness.

How shall I ever forget that dreadful vigil? I could not hear a sound, not even the drawing of a breath, and yet I knew that my companion sat open-eyed, within a few feet of me, in the same state of nervous tension in which I was myself. The shutters cut off the least ray of light, and we waited in absolute darkness. From outside came the occasional cry of a night-bird, and once at our very window a long drawn, cat-like whine, which told us that the cheetah was indeed at liberty. Far away we could hear the deep tones of the parish clock, which boomed out every quarter of an hour. How long they seemed, those quarters! Twelve o'clock, and one, and two, and three, and still we sat waiting silently for whatever might befall.

Suddenly there was the momentary gleam of a light up in the direction of the ventilator, which vanished immediately, but was succeeded by a strong smell of burning oil and heated metal. Someone in the next room had lit a dark lantern. I heard a gentle sound of movement, and then all was silent once more, though the smell grew stronger. For half an hour I sat with straining ears. Then suddenly another sound became audible – a very gentle, soothing sound, like that of a small jet of steam escaping continually from a kettle. The instant that we heard it, Holmes sprang from the bed, struck a match, and lashed furiously with his cane at the bell-pull.

'You see it, Watson?' he yelled. 'You see it?'

But I saw nothing. At the moment when Holmes struck the light I heard a low, clear whistle, but the sudden glare flashing into my weary eyes made it impossible for me to tell what it was at which my friend lashed so savagely. I could, however, see that his face was deadly pale, and filled with horror and loathing.

He had ceased to strike, and was gazing up at the ventilator, when suddenly there broke from the silence of the night the most horrible cry to which I have ever listened. It swelled up louder and louder, a hoarse yell of pain and fear and anger all mingled in the one dreadful shriek. They say that away down in the village, and even in the distant parsonage, that cry raised the sleepers from their beds. It struck cold to our hearts, and I stood gazing at Holmes, and he at me, until the last echoes of it had died away into the silence from which it rose.

'What can it mean?' I gasped.

'It means that it is all over,' Holmes answered. 'And perhaps, after all, it is for the best. Take your pistol, and we shall enter Dr Roylott's room.'

With a grave face he lit the lamp, and led the way down the corridor. Twice he struck at the chamber door without any reply from within. Then he turned the handle and entered, I at his heels, with the cocked pistol in my hand.

It was a singular sight which met our eyes. On the table stood a dark lantern with the shutter half open, throwing a brilliant beam of light upon the iron safe, the door of which was ajar. Beside this table, on the wooden chair, sat Dr Grimesby Roylott, clad in a long grey dressing-gown, his bare ankles protruding beneath, and his feet thrust into red heelless Turkish slippers. Across his lap lay the short stock with the long lash which we had noticed during the day. His chin was cocked upwards, and his eyes were fixed in a dreadful rigid stare at the corner of the ceiling. Round his brow he had a peculiar yellow band, with brownish speckles, which seemed to be bound tightly round his head. As we entered he made neither sound nor motion.

'The band! the speckled band!' whispered Holmes.

I took a step forward. In an instant his strange headgear began to move, and there reared itself from among his hair the squat diamond-shaped head and puffed neck of a loathsome serpent.

'It is a swamp adder!' cried Holmes – 'the deadliest snake in India. He has died within ten seconds of being bitten. Violence does, in truth, recoil upon the violent, and the schemer falls into the pit which he digs for another. Let us thrust this creature back into its den, and we can then remove Miss Stoner to some place of shelter, and let the county police know what has happened.'

As he spoke he drew the dog whip swiftly from the dead man's lap, and throwing the noose round the reptile's neck, he drew it from its horrid perch, and, carrying it at arm's length, threw it into the iron safe, which he closed upon it.

Such are the true facts of the death of Dr Grimesby Roylott, of Stoke Moran. It is not necessary that I should prolong a narrative which has already run to too great a length, by telling how we broke the sad news to the terrified girl, how we conveyed her by the morning train to the care of her good aunt at Harrow, of how the slow process of official inquiry came to the conclusion that the Doctor met his fate while indiscreetly playing with a dangerous pet. The little which I had yet to learn of the case was told me by Sherlock Holmes as we travelled back next day.

'I had,' said he, 'come to an entirely erroneous conclusion, which shows, my dear Watson, how dangerous it always is to reason from insufficient data. The presence of the gipsies, and the use of the word "band", which was used by the poor girl, no doubt, to explain the appearance which she had caught a horrid glimpse of by the light of her match, were sufficient to put me upon an entirely wrong scent. I can only claim the merit that I instantly reconsidered my position when, however, it became clear to me that whatever danger threatened an occupant of the room could not come either from the window or the door. My attention was speedily drawn, as I have already remarked to you, to this ventilator, and to the bell-rope which hung down to the bed. The discovery that this was a dummy, and that the bed was clamped to the floor, instantly gave rise to the suspicion that the rope was there as a bridge for something passing through the hole, and coming to the bed. The idea of a snake instantly occurred to me, and when I coupled it with my knowledge that the Doctor was furnished with a supply of creatures from India, I felt that I was probably on the right track. The idea of using a form of poison which could not possibly be discovered by any chemical test was just such a one as would occur to a clever and ruthless man who had had an Eastern training. The rapidity with which such a poison would take effect would also, from his point of view, be an advantage. It would be a sharp-eyed coroner indeed who could distinguish the two little dark punctures which would show where the poison fangs had done their work. Then I thought of the whistle. Of course, he must recall the snake before the morning light revealed it to the victim. He had trained it, probably by the use of the milk which we saw, to return to him when summoned. He would put it through the ventilator at the hour that he thought best, with the certainty that it would crawl down the rope, and land on the bed. It might or might not bite the occupant, perhaps she might escape every night for a week, but sooner or later she must fall a victim.

'I had come to these conclusions before ever I had entered his room. An inspection of his chair showed me that he had been in the habit of standing on it, which, of course, would be necessary in order that he should reach the ventilator. The sight of the safe, the saucer of milk, and the loop of whipcord were enough to finally dispel any doubts which may have remained. The metallic clang heard by Miss Stoner was obviously caused by her stepfather hastily closing the door of his safe upon its terrible occupant. Having once made up my mind, you know the steps which I took in order to put the matter to the proof. I heard the creature hiss, as I have no doubt that you did also, and I instantly lit the light and attacked it.'

'With the result of driving it through the ventilator.'

'And also with the result of causing it to turn upon its master at the other side. Some of the blows of my cane came home, and roused its snakish temper, so that it flew upon the first person it saw. In this way I am no doubt indirectly responsible for Dr Grimesby Roylott's death, and I cannot say that it is likely to weigh very heavily upon my conscience.'

Sacrifice

The Son's Veto by Thomas Hardy (1891)

Survival by John Wyndham (1956)

The Son's Veto

Thomas Hardy

I

To the eyes of a man viewing it from behind, the nut-brown hair was a wonder and a mystery. Under the black beaver hat surmounted* by its tuft of black feathers, the long locks, braided and twisted and coiled like the rushes of a basket, composed a rare, if somewhat barbaric, example of ingenious art. One could understand such weavings and coilings being wrought to last intact for a year, or even a calendar month; but that they should be all demolished regularly at bedtime, after a single day of permanence, seemed a reckless waste of successful fabrication.

And she had done it all herself, poor thing. She had no maid, and it was almost the only accomplishment she could boast of. Hence the unstinted pains.

She was a young invalid lady – not so very much of an invalid – sitting in a wheeled chair, which had been pulled up in the front part of a green enclosure, close to a bandstand where a concert was going on, during a warm June afternoon. It had place in one of the minor parks or private gardens that are to be found in the suburbs of London, and was the effort of a local association to raise money for some charity. There are worlds within worlds in the great city, and though nobody outside the immediate district had ever heard of the charity, or the band, or the garden, the enclosure was filled with an interested audience sufficiently informed on all these.

* surmounted: topped

As the strains proceeded many of the listeners observed the chaired lady, whose black hair, by reason of her prominent position, so challenged inspection. Her face was not easily discernible, but the aforesaid cunning tress-weavings, the white ear and poll*, and the curve of a cheek which was neither flaccid nor sallow, were signals that led to the expectation of good beauty in front. Such expectations are not infrequently disappointed as soon as the disclosure comes; and in the present case, when the lady, by a turn of the head, at length revealed herself, she was not so handsome as the people behind her had supposed, and even hoped – they did not know why.

For one thing (alas! the commonness of this complaint), she was less young than they had fancied her to be. Yet attractive her face unquestionably was, and not at all sickly. The revelation of its details came each time she turned to talk to a boy of twelve or thirteen who stood beside her, and the shape of whose hat and jacket implied that he belonged to a well-known public school. The immediate bystanders could hear that he called her 'Mother'.

When the end of the recital was reached, and the audience withdrew, many chose to find their way out by passing at her elbow. Almost all turned their heads to take a full and near look at the interesting woman, who remained stationary in the chair till the way should be clear enough for her to be wheeled out without obstruction. As if she expected their glances, and did not mind gratifying their curiosity, she met the eyes of several of her observers by lifting her own, showing these to be soft, brown, and affectionate orbs, a little plaintive in their regard.

* poll: head

She was conducted out of the gardens, and passed along the pavement till she disappeared from view, the schoolboy walking beside her. To inquiries made by some persons who watched her away, the answer came that she was the second wife of the incumbent of a neighbouring parish, and that she was lame. She was generally believed to be a woman with a story – an innocent one, but a story of some sort or other.

In conversing with her on their way home the boy who walked at her elbow said that he hoped his father had not missed them.

'He have been so comfortable these last few hours that I am sure he cannot have missed us,' she replied.

'*Has*, dear mother – not *have*!' exclaimed the public-schoolboy, with an impatient fastidiousness* that was almost harsh. 'Surely you know that by this time!'

His mother hastily adopted the correction, and did not resent his making it, or retaliate, as she might well have done, by bidding him to wipe that crumby mouth of his, whose condition had been caused by surreptitious attempts to eat a piece of cake without taking it out of the pocket wherein it lay concealed. After this the pretty woman and the boy went onward in silence.

That question of grammar bore upon her history, and she fell into reverie*, of a somewhat sad kind to all appearance. It might have been assumed that she was wondering if she had done wisely in shaping her life as she had shaped it, to bring out such a result as this.

In a remote nook in North Wessex, forty miles from London, near the thriving county town of Aldbrickham, there stood a pretty village with its

* fastidiousness: pickiness reverie: daydream

church and parsonage, which she knew well enough, but her son had never seen. It was her native village, Gaymead, and the first event bearing upon her present situation had occurred at that place when she was only a girl of nineteen.

How well she remembered it, that first act in her little tragi-comedy, the death of her reverend husband's first wife. It happened on a spring evening, and she who now and for many years had filled that first wife's place was then parlour-maid in the parson's house.

When everything had been done that could be done, and the death was announced, she had gone out in the dusk to visit her parents, who were living in the same village, to tell them the sad news. As she opened the white swing-gate and looked towards the trees which rose westward, shutting out the pale light of the evening sky, she discerned, without much surprise, the figure of a man standing in the hedge, though she roguishly exclaimed as a matter of form, 'O, Sam, how you frightened me!'

He was a young gardener of her acquaintance. She told him the particulars of the late event, and they stood silent, these two young people, in that elevated, calmly philosophic mind which is engendered* when a tragedy has happened close at hand, and has not happened to the philosophers themselves. But it had its bearing upon their relations.

'And will you stay on now at the Vicarage, just the same?' asked he.

She had hardly thought of that. 'O yes – I suppose!' she said. 'Everything will be just as usual, I imagine?'

* engendered: caused

He walked beside her towards her mother's. Presently his arm stole round her waist. She gently removed it; but he placed it there again, and she yielded the point. 'You see, dear Sophy, you don't know that you'll stay on; you may want a home; and I shall be ready to offer one some day, though I may not be ready just yet.'

'Why, Sam, how can you be so fast*! I've never even said I liked 'ee; and it is all your own doing, coming after me!'

'Still, it is nonsense to say I am not to have a try at you like the rest.' He stooped to kiss her a farewell, for they had reached her mother's door.

'No, Sam; you shan't!' she cried, putting her hand over his mouth. 'You ought to be more serious on such a night as this.' And she bade him adieu without allowing him to kiss her or to come indoors.

The vicar just left a widower was at this time a man about forty years of age, of good family, and childless. He had led a secluded existence in this college living, partly because there were no resident landowners; and his loss now intensified his habit of withdrawal from outward observation. He was seen still less than heretofore, kept himself still less in time with the rhythm and racket of the movements called progress in the world without*. For many months after his wife's decease the economy of his household remained as before; the cook, the housemaid, the parlour-maid, and the man out-of-doors performed their duties or left them undone, just as Nature prompted them – the vicar knew not which. It was then represented to him that his servants seemed to have nothing to do in his small family of one. He was struck with the truth of

* fast: forward, cheeky without: outside

this representation, and decided to cut down his establishment. But he was forestalled by Sophy, the parlour-maid, who said one evening that she wished to leave him.

'And why?' said the parson.

'Sam Hobson has asked me to marry him, sir.'

'Well – do you want to marry?'

'Not much. But it would be a home for me. And we have heard that one of us will have to leave.'

A day or two after she said: 'I don't want to leave just yet, sir, if you don't wish it. Sam and I have quarrelled.'

He looked up at her. He had hardly ever observed her before, though he had been frequently conscious of her soft presence in the room. What a kitten-like, flexuous*, tender creature she was! She was the only one of the servants with whom he came into immediate and continuous relation*. What should he do if Sophy were gone?

Sophy did not go, but one of the others did, and things went on quietly again.

When Mr Twycott, the vicar, was ill, Sophy brought up his meals to him, and she had no sooner left the room one day than he heard a noise on the stairs. She had slipped down with the tray, and so twisted her foot that she could not stand. The village surgeon was called in; the vicar got better, but Sophy was incapacitated* for a long time; and she was informed that she must never again walk much or engage in any occupation which required her to stand long on her feet. As soon as she was comparatively well she spoke to him alone. Since she was forbidden to walk and

* flexuous: yielding relation: personal contact
incapacitated: crippled

bustle about, and, indeed, could not do so, it became her duty to leave. She could very well work at something sitting down, and she had an aunt a seamstress.

The parson had been very greatly moved by what she had suffered on his account, and he exclaimed, 'No, Sophy; lame or not lame, I cannot let you go. You must never leave me again!'

He came close to her, and, though she could never exactly tell how it happened, she became conscious of his lips upon her cheek. He then asked her to marry him. Sophy did not exactly love him, but she had a respect for him which almost amounted to veneration*. Even if she had wished to get away from him she hardly dared refuse a personage so reverend* and august* in her eyes, and she assented forthwith to be his wife.

Thus it happened that one fine morning, when the doors of the church were naturally open for ventilation, and the singing birds fluttered in and alighted on the tie-beams of the roof, there was a marriage service at the communion-rails, which hardly a soul knew of. The parson and a neighbouring curate had entered at one door, and Sophy at another, followed by two necessary persons, whereupon in a short time there emerged a newly-made husband and wife.

Mr Twycott knew perfectly well that he had committed social suicide by this step, despite Sophy's spotless character, and he had taken his measures accordingly. An exchange of livings had been arranged with an acquaintance who was incumbent* of a church

* veneration: worship
reverend . . . august: worthy of respect and splendid
incumbent: parson

in the south of London, and as soon as possible the couple removed thither, abandoning their pretty home, with trees and shrubs and glebe*, for a narrow, dusty house in a long, straight street, and their fine peal of bells for the wretchedest one-tongued clangour that ever tortured mortal ears. It was all on her account. They were, however, away from every one who had known her former position; and also under less observation from without than they would have had to put up with in any country parish.

Sophy the woman was as charming a partner as a man could possess, though Sophy the lady had her deficiencies. She showed a natural aptitude for little domestic refinements, so far as related to things and manners; but in what is called culture she was less intuitive. She had now been married more than fourteen years, and her husband had taken much trouble with her education; but she still held confused ideas on the use of 'was' and 'were', which did not beget* a respect for her among the few acquaintances she made. Her great grief in this relation was that her only child, on whose education no expense had been and would be spared, was now old enough to perceive these deficiencies in his mother, and not only to see them but to feel irritated at their existence.

Thus she lived on in the city, and wasted hours in braiding her beautiful hair, till her once apple cheeks waned to pink of the very faintest. Her foot had never regained its natural strength after the accident, and she was mostly obliged to avoid walking altogether. Her husband had grown to like London for its freedom and its domestic privacy; but he was twenty years his Sophy's senior, and had latterly been seized with a

* glebe: vicar's plot of land beget: make for

serious illness. On this day, however, he had seemed to be well enough to justify her accompanying her son Randolph to the concert.

II

The next time we get a glimpse of her is when she appears in the mournful attire of a widow.

Mr Twycott had never rallied, and now lay in a well-packed cemetery to the south of the great city, where, if all the dead it contained had stood erect and alive, not one would have known him or recognized his name. The boy had dutifully followed him to the grave*, and was now again at school.

Throughout these changes Sophy had been treated like the child she was in nature though not in years. She was left with no control over anything that had been her husband's beyond her modest personal income. In his anxiety lest her inexperience should be over-reached he had safeguarded with trustees all he possibly could. The completion of the boy's course at the public school, to be followed in due time by Oxford and ordination, had been all previsioned* and arranged, and she really had nothing to occupy her in the world but to eat and drink, and make a business of indolence, and go on weaving and coiling the nut-brown hair, merely keeping a home open for the son whenever he came to her during vacations.

Foreseeing his probable decease long years before her, her husband in his lifetime had purchased for her use a semi-detached villa in the same long, straight road whereon the church and parsonage faced, which

* dutifully followed him to the grave: attended the funeral (women did not then go to funerals)
previsioned: foreseen

was to be hers as long as she chose to live in it. Here she now resided, looking out upon the fragment of lawn in front, and through the railings at the ever-flowing traffic; or, bending forward over the window-sill on the first floor, stretching her eyes far up and down the vista of sooty trees, hazy air, and drab house-façades, along which echoed the noises common to a suburban main thoroughfare.

Somehow, her boy, with his aristocratic school-knowledge, his grammars, and his aversions*; was losing those wide infantine* sympathies, extending as far as to the sun and moon themselves, with which he, like other children, had been born, and which his mother, a child of nature herself, had loved in him; he was reducing their compass to a population of a few thousand wealthy and titled people, the mere veneer* of a thousand million or so of others who did not interest him at all. He drifted further and further away from her. Sophy's *milieu** being a suburb of minor tradesmen and under-clerks, and her almost only companions the two servants of her own house, it was not surprising that after her husband's death she soon lost the little artificial tastes she had acquired from him, and became – in her son's eyes – a mother whose mistakes and origin it was his painful lot as a gentleman to blush for. As yet he was far from being man enough – if he ever would be – to rate these sins of hers at their true infinitesimal* value beside the yearning fondness that welled up and remained penned in her heart till it should be more fully accepted by him, or by some other person or thing. If

* aversions: dislikes — infantine: childish
veneer: surface layer — *milieu*: natural setting
infinitesimal: tiny

he had lived at home with her he would have had all of it; but he seemed to require so very little in present circumstances, and it remained stored.

Her life became insupportably dreary; she could not take walks, and had no interest in going for drives, or, indeed, in travelling anywhere. Nearly two years passed without an event, and still she looked on that suburban road, thinking of the village in which she had been born, and whither she would have gone back – O how gladly! – even to work in the fields.

Taking no exercise she often could not sleep, and would rise in the night or early morning to look out upon the then vacant thoroughfare, where the lamps stood like sentinels* waiting for some procession to go by. An approximation to such a procession was indeed made eagerly every morning about one o'clock, when the country vehicles passed up with loads of vegetables for Covent Garden market. She often saw them creeping along at this silent and dusky hour – waggon after waggon, bearing green bastions* of cabbages nodding to their fall, yet never falling, walls of baskets enclosing masses of beans and peas, pyramids of snow-white turnips, swaying howdahs* of mixed produce – creeping along behind aged night-horses, who seemed ever patiently wondering between their hollow coughs why they had always to work at that still hour when all other sentient creatures were privileged to rest. Wrapped in a cloak, it was soothing to watch and sympathize with them when depression and nervousness hindered sleep, and to see how the fresh green-stuff brightened to life as it came opposite

* sentinels: lookouts bastions: fortifications
howdahs: seats carried on the backs of elephants

the lamp, and how the sweating animals steamed and shone with their miles of travel.

They had an interest, almost a charm, for Sophy, these semi-rural people and vehicles moving in an urban atmosphere, leading a life quite distinct from that of the daytime toilers on the same road. One morning a man who accompanied a waggon-load of potatoes gazed rather hard at the house-fronts as he passed, and with a curious emotion she thought his form was familiar to her. She looked out for him again. His being an old-fashioned conveyance, with a yellow front, it was easily recognizable, and on the third night after she saw it a second time. The man alongside was, as she had fancied, Sam Hobson, formerly gardener at Gaymead, who would at one time have married her.

She had occasionally thought of him, and wondered if life in a cottage with him would not have been a happier lot than the life she had accepted. She had not thought of him passionately, but her now dismal situation lent an interest to his resurrection – a tender interest which it is impossible to exaggerate. She went back to bed, and began thinking. When did these market gardeners, who travelled up to town so regularly at one or two in the morning, come back? She dimly recollected seeing their empty waggons, hardly noticeable amid the ordinary day-traffic, passing down at some hour before noon.

It was only April, but that morning, after breakfast, she had the window opened, and sat looking out, the feeble sun shining full upon her. She affected* to sew, but her eyes never left the street. Between ten and eleven the desired waggon, now unladen, reappeared

* affected: pretended

on its return journey. But Sam was not looking round him then, and drove on in a reverie.

'Sam!' cried she.

Turning with a start, his face lighted up. He called to him a little boy to hold the horse, alighted, and came and stood under the window.

'I can't come down easily, Sam, or I would!' she said. 'Did you know I lived here?'

'Well, Mrs Twycott, I knew you lived along here somewhere. I have often looked out for 'ee.'

He briefly explained his own presence on the scene. He had long since given up his gardening in the village near Aldbrickham, and was now manager at a market gardener's on the south side of London, it being part of his duty to go up to Covent Garden with waggon-loads of produce two or three times a week. In answer to her curious inquiry, he admitted that he had come to this particular district because he had seen in the Aldbrickham paper, a year or two before, the announcement of the death in South London of the aforetime vicar of Gaymead, which had revived an interest in her dwelling-place that he could not extinguish, leading him to hover about the locality till his present post had been secured.

They spoke of their native village in dear old North Wessex, the spots in which they had played together as children. She tried to feel that she was a dignified personage now, that she must not be too confidential with Sam. But she could not keep it up, and the tears hanging in her eyes were indicated in her voice.

'You are not happy, Mrs Twycott, I'm afraid?' he said.

'O, of course not! I lost my husband only the year before last.'

'Ah! I meant in another way. You'd like to be home again?'

'This is my home – for life. The house belongs to me. But I understand' – She let it out then. 'Yes, Sam, I long for home – *our* home! I *should* like to be there, and never leave it, and die there.' But she remembered herself. 'That's only a momentary feeling. I have a son, you know, a dear boy. He's at school now.'

'Somewhere handy, I suppose? I see there's lots on 'em along this road.'

'O no! Not in one of these wretched holes! At a public school – one of the most distinguished in England.'

'Chok' it all! of course! I forget, ma'am, that you've been a lady for so many years.'

'No, I am not a lady,' she said sadly. 'I never shall be. But he's a gentleman, and that – makes it – O how difficult for me!'

III

The acquaintance thus oddly reopened proceeded apace*. She often looked out to get a few words with him, by night or by day. Her sorrow was that she could not accompany her one old friend on foot a little way, and talk more freely than she could do while he paused before the house. One night, at the beginning of June, when she was again on the watch after an absence of some days from the window, he entered the gate and said softly, 'Now, wouldn't some air do you good? I've only half a load this morning. Why not ride up to Covent Garden with me? There's a nice seat on the cabbages, where I've spread a sack. You can be home again in a cab before anybody is up.'

She refused at first, and then, trembling with excitement, hastily finished her dressing, and wrapped

* apace: rapidly

herself up in cloak and veil, afterwards sidling downstairs by the aid of the handrail, in a way she could adopt on an emergency. When she had opened the door she found Sam on the step, and he lifted her bodily on his strong arm across the little forecourt into his vehicle. Not a soul was visible or audible in the infinite length of the straight, flat highway, with its ever-waiting lamps converging to points in each direction. The air was fresh as country air at this hour, and the stars shone, except to the north-eastward, where there was a whitish light – the dawn. Sam carefully placed her in the seat and drove on.

They talked as they had talked in old days, Sam pulling himself up now and then, when he thought himself too familiar. More than once she said with misgiving that she wondered if she ought to have indulged in the freak. 'But I am so lonely in my house,' she added, 'and this makes me so happy!'

'You must come again, dear Mrs Twycott. There is no time o' day for taking the air like this.'

It grew lighter and lighter. The sparrows became busy in the streets, and the city waxed denser around them. When they approached the river it was day, and on the bridge they beheld the full blaze of morning sunlight in the direction of St Paul's, the river glistening towards it, and not a craft stirring.

Near Covent Garden he put her into a cab, and they parted, looking into each other's faces like the very old friends they were. She reached home without adventure, limped to the door, and let herself in with her latch-key unseen.

The air and Sam's presence had revived her: her cheeks were quite pink – almost beautiful. She had something to live for in addition to her son. A woman of pure instincts, she knew there had been nothing really wrong in the journey, but supposed it conventionally to be very wrong indeed.

Soon, however, she gave way to the temptation of going with him again, and on this occasion their conversation was distinctly tender, and Sam said he never should forget her, notwithstanding that she had served him rather badly at one time. After much hesitation he told her of a plan it was in his power to carry out, and one he should like to take in hand, since he did not care for London work: it was to set up as a master greengrocer down at Aldbrickham, the county town of their native place. He knew of an opening – a shop kept by aged people who wished to retire.

'And why don't you do it, then, Sam?' she asked with a slight heartsinking.

'Because I'm not sure if – you'd join me. I know you wouldn't – couldn't! Such a lady as ye've been so long, you couldn't be a wife to a man like me.'

'I hardly suppose I could!' she assented, also frightened at the idea.

'If you could,' he said eagerly, 'you'd on'y have to sit in the back parlour and look through the glass partition when I was away sometimes – just to keep an eye on things. The lameness wouldn't hinder that . . . I'd keep you as genteel as ever I could, dear Sophy – if I might think of it!' he pleaded.

'Sam, I'll be frank,' she said, putting her hand on his. 'If it were only myself I would do it, and gladly, though everything I possess would be lost to me by marrying again.'

'I don't mind that! It's more independent.'

'That's good of you, dear, dear Sam. But there's something else. I have a son . . . I almost fancy when I am miserable sometimes that he is not really mine, but one I hold in trust for my late husband. He seems to belong so little to me personally, so entirely to his dead father. He is so much educated and I so little that I do not feel dignified enough to be his mother . . . Well, he would have to be told.'

'Yes. Unquestionably.' Sam saw her thought and her fear. 'Still, you can do as you like, Sophy – Mrs Twycott,' he added. 'It is not you who are the child, but he.'

'Ah, you don't know! Sam, if I could, I would marry you, some day. But you must wait a while, and let me think.'

It was enough for him, and he was blithe* at their parting. Not so she. To tell Randolph seemed impossible. She could wait till he had gone up to Oxford, when what she did would affect his life but little. But would he ever tolerate the idea? And if not, could she defy him?

She had not told him a word when the yearly cricket match came on at Lord's between the public schools, though Sam had already gone back to Aldbrickham. Mrs Twycott felt stronger than usual: she went to the match with Randolph, and was able to leave her chair and walk about occasionally. The bright idea occurred to her that she could casually broach the subject while moving round among the spectators, when the boy's spirits were high with interest in the game, and he would weigh domestic matters as feathers in the scale beside the day's victory. They promenaded under the lurid July sun, this pair, so wide apart, yet so near, and Sophy saw the large proportion of boys like her own, in their broad white collars and dwarf hats, and all around the rows of great coaches under which was jumbled the *débris* of luxurious luncheons; bones,

* blithe: cheerful

pie-crusts, champagne bottles, glasses, plates, napkins, and the family silver; while on the coaches sat the proud fathers and mothers; but never a poor mother like her. If Randolph had not appertained to* these, had not centred all his interests in them, had not cared exclusively for the class they belonged to, how happy would things have been! A great huzza* at some small performance with the bat burst from the multitude of relatives, and Randolph jumped wildly into the air to see what had happened. Sophy fetched up the sentence that had been already shaped; but she could not get it out. The occasion was, perhaps, an inopportune* one. The contrast between her story and the display of fashion to which Randolph had grown to regard himself as akin* would be fatal. She awaited a better time.

It was on an evening when they were alone in their plain suburban residence, where life was not blue but brown, that she ultimately broke silence, qualifying her announcement of a probable second marriage by assuring him that it would not take place for a long time to come, when he would be living quite independently of her.

The boy thought the idea a very reasonable one, and asked if she had chosen anybody? She hesitated; and he seemed to have a misgiving. He hoped his stepfather would be a gentleman? he said.

'Not what you call a gentleman,' she answered timidly. 'He'll be much as I was before I knew your father;' and by degrees she acquainted* him with the whole. The youth's face remained fixed for a moment;

* appertained to: identified with
huzza: cheer
inopportune: badly timed
akin: related, part of
acquainted: familiarized

then he flushed, leant on the table, and burst into passionate tears.

His mother went up to him, kissed all of his face that she could get at, and patted his back as if he were still the baby he once had been, crying herself the while. When he had somewhat recovered from his paroxysm* he went hastily to his own room and fastened the door.

Parleyings* were attempted through the keyhole, outside which she waited and listened. It was long before he would reply, and when he did it was to say sternly at her from within: 'I am ashamed of you! It will ruin me! A miserable boor! a churl! a clown! It will degrade me in the eyes of all the gentlemen of England!'

'Say no more – perhaps I am wrong! I will struggle against it!' she cried miserably.

Before Randolph left her that summer a letter arrived from Sam to inform her that he had been unexpectedly fortunate in obtaining the shop. He was in possession; it was the largest in the town, combining fruit with vegetables, and he thought it would form a home worthy even of her some day. Might he not run up to town to see her?

She met him by stealth, and said he must still wait for her final answer. The autumn dragged on, and when Randolph was home at Christmas for the holidays she broached the matter again. But the young gentleman was inexorable*.

It was dropped for months; renewed again; abandoned under his repugnance; again attempted; and thus the gentle creature reasoned and pleaded till four or five long years had passed. Then the faithful

* paroxysm: outburst parleyings: negotiations
inexorable: unyielding

Sam revived his suit with some peremptoriness*. Sophy's son, now an undergraduate, was down from Oxford one Easter, when she again opened the subject. As soon as he was ordained*, she argued, he would have a home of his own, wherein she, with her bad grammar and her ignorance, would be an encumbrance* to him. Better obliterate* her as much as possible.

He showed a more manly anger now, but would not agree. She on her side was more persistent, and he had doubts whether she could be trusted in his absence. But by indignation and contempt for her taste he completely maintained his ascendancy*; and finally taking her before a little cross and altar that he had erected in his bedroom for his private devotions, there bade her kneel, and swear that she would not wed Samuel Hobson without his consent. 'I owe this to my father!' he said.

The poor woman swore, thinking he would soften as soon as he was ordained and in full swing of clerical work. But he did not. His education had by this time sufficiently ousted* his humanity to keep him quite firm; though his mother might have led an idyllic life with her faithful fruiterer and greengrocer, and nobody have been anything the worse in the world.

Her lameness became more confirmed as time went on, and she seldom or never left the house in the long southern thoroughfare, where she seemed to be pining her heart away. 'Why mayn't I say to Sam that I'll marry him? Why mayn't I?' she would murmur plaintively to herself when nobody was near.

* peremptoriness: impatience
ordained: made a vicar
encumbrance: burden
obliterate: erase
ascendancy: dominance
ousted: got the better of

Some four years after this date a middle-aged man was standing at the door of the largest fruiterer's shop in Aldbrickham. He was the proprietor, but today, instead of his usual business attire, he wore a neat suit of black; and his window was partly shuttered. From the railway station a funeral procession was seen approaching: it passed his door and went out of the town towards the village of Gaymead. The man, whose eyes were wet, held his hat in his hand as the vehicle moved by; while from the mourning coach a young smooth-shaven priest in a high waistcoat looked black as a cloud at the shopkeeper standing there.

Survival

John Wyndham

As the spaceport bus trundled unhurriedly over the mile or more of open field that separated the terminal buildings from the embarkation hoist, Mrs Feltham stared intently forward across the receding row of shoulders in front of her. The ship stood up on the plain like an isolated silver spire. Near its bow she could see the intense blue light which proclaimed it all but ready to take off. Among and around the great tailfins, dwarf vehicles and little dots of men moved in a fuss of final preparations. Mrs Feltham glared at the scene, at this moment loathing it and all the inventions of men, with a hard, hopeless hatred.

Presently she withdrew her gaze from the distance and focused it on the back of her son-in-law's head, a yard in front of her. She hated him, too.

She turned, darting a swift glance at the face of her daughter in the seat beside her. Alice looked pale; her lips were firmly set, her eyes fixed straight ahead.

Mrs Feltham hesitated. Her glance returned to the spaceship. She decided on one last effort. Under cover of the bus noise she said:

'Alice, darling, it's not too late, even now, you know.'

The girl did not look at her. There was no sign that she had heard, save that her lips compressed a little more firmly. Then they parted.

'Mother, please!' she said.

But Mrs Feltham, once started, had to go on.

'It's for your own sake, darling. All you have to do is to say you've changed your mind.'

The girl held a protesting silence.

'Nobody would blame you,' Mrs Feltham persisted. 'They'd not think a bit worse of you. After all, everybody knows that Mars is no place for –'

'Mother, please stop it,' interrupted the girl. The sharpness of her tone took Mrs Feltham aback for a moment. She hesitated. But time was growing too short to allow herself the luxury of offended dignity. She went on:

'You're not used to the sort of life you'll have to live there, darling. Absolutely primitive. No kind of life for any woman. After all, dear, it is only a five-year appointment for David. I'm sure if he really loves you he'd rather know that you *are* safe here and waiting –'

The girl said, harshly:

'We've been over all this before, Mother. I tell you it's no good. I'm not a child. I've thought it out, and I've made up my mind.'

Mrs Feltham sat silent for some moments. The bus swayed on across the field, and the rocket ship seemed to tower further into the sky.

'If you had a child of your own –' she said, half to herself. '– Well, I expect some day you will. Then you will begin to understand . . .'

'I think it's you who don't understand,' Alice said. 'This is hard enough, anyway. You're only making it harder for me.'

'My darling, I love you. I gave birth to you. I've watched over you always and I *know* you. I *know* this can't be the kind of life for you. If you were a hard, hoydenish* kind of girl, well, perhaps – but you aren't, darling. You know quite well you aren't.'

'Perhaps you don't know me quite as well as you imagine you do, Mother.'

* hoydenish: tomboyish

Mrs Feltham shook her head. She kept her eyes averted, boring jealously into the back of her son-in-law's head.

'He's taken you right away from me,' she said dully.

'That's not true, Mother. It's – well, I'm no longer a child. I'm a woman with a life of my own to live.'

'"Whither thou goest, I will go . . ."' said Mrs Feltham reflectively. 'But that doesn't really hold now, you know. It was all right for a tribe of nomads, but nowadays the wives of soldiers, sailors, pilots, spacemen –'

'It's more than that, Mother. You don't understand. I must become adult and real to myself . . .'

The bus rolled to a stop, puny and toylike beside the ship that seemed too large ever to lift. The passengers got out and stood staring upwards along the shining side. Mr Feltham put his arms round his daughter. Alice clung to him, tears in her eyes. In an unsteady voice he murmured:

'Good-bye, my dear. And all the luck there is.'

He released her, and shook hands with his son-in-law.

'Keep her safe, David. She's everything –'

'I know. I will. Don't you worry.'

Mrs Feltham kissed her daughter farewell, and forced herself to shake hands with her son-in-law.

A voice from the hoist called: 'All passengers aboard, please!'

The doors of the hoist closed. Mr Feltham avoided his wife's eyes. He put his arm round her waist, and led her back to the bus in silence.

As they made their way, in company with a dozen other vehicles, back to the shelter of the terminal, Mrs Feltham alternately dabbed her eyes with a wisp of white handkerchief and cast glances back at the spaceship standing all inert, and apparently deserted now. Her hand slid into her husband's.

'I can't believe it even now,' she said. 'It's so utterly unlike her. Would you ever have thought that our little Alice . . .? Oh, why did she have to marry him . . .?' Her voice trailed to a whimper.

Her husband pressed her fingers, without speaking.

'It wouldn't be so surprising with some girls,' she went on. 'But Alice was always so quiet. I used to worry because she was so quiet – I mean in case she might become one of those timid bores. Do you remember how the other children used to call her Mouse?

'And now this! Five years in that dreadful place! Oh, she'll never stand it, Henry. I know she won't, she's not the type. Why didn't you put your foot down, Henry? They'd have listened to you. You could have stopped it.'

Her husband sighed. 'There are times when one can give advice, Miriam, though it's scarcely ever popular, but what one must not do is to try to live other people's lives for them. Alice is a woman now, with her own rights. Who am I to say what's best for her?'

'But you could have stopped her going.'

'Perhaps – but I didn't care for the price.'

She was silent for some seconds, then her fingers tightened on his hand.

'Henry – Henry, I don't think we shall ever see them again. I feel it.'

'Come, come, dear. They'll be back safe and sound, you'll see.'

'You don't really believe that, Henry. You're just trying to cheer me up. Oh, why, why must she go to that horrible place? She's so young. She could have waited five years. Why is she so stubborn, so hard – not like my little Mouse at all?'

Her husband patted her hand reassuringly.

'You must try to stop thinking of her as a child, Miriam. She's not; she's a woman now and if all our women were mice, it would be a poor outlook for our survival . . .'

The Navigating Officer of the s/r *Falcon* approached his captain.

'The deviation, sir.'

Captain Winters took the piece of paper held out to him.

'One point three six five degrees,' he read out. 'H'm. Not bad. Not at all bad, considering. South-east sector again. Why are nearly all deviations in the S.E. sector, I wonder, Mr Carter?'

'Maybe they'll find out when we've been at the game a bit longer, sir. Right now it's just one of those things.'

'Odd, all the same. Well, we'd better correct it before it gets any bigger.'

The Captain loosened the expanding book-rack in front of him and pulled out a set of tables. He consulted them and scribbled down the result.

'Check, Mr Carter.'

The navigator compared the figures with the table, and approved.

'Good. How's she lying?' asked the Captain.

'Almost broadside, with a very slow roll, sir.'

'You can handle it. I'll observe visually. Align her and stabilize. Ten seconds on starboard laterals at force two. She should take about thirty minutes, twenty seconds to swing over, but we'll watch that. Then neutralize with the port laterals at force two. Okay?'

'Very good, sir.' The Navigating Officer sat down in the control chair, and fastened the belt. He looked over the keys and switches carefully.

'I'd better warn 'em. May be a bit of a jolt,' said the Captain. He switched on the address system, and pulled the microphone bracket to him.

'Attention all! Attention all! We are about to correct course. There will be several impulses. None of them will be violent, but all fragile objects should be secured, and you are advised to seat yourselves and use the safety belts. The operation will take approximately half an hour and will start in five minutes from now. I shall inform you when it has been completed. That is all.' He switched off.

'Some fool always thinks the ship's been holed by a meteor if you don't spoon it out,' he added. 'Have that woman in hysterics, most likely. Doesn't do any good.' He pondered idly. 'I wonder what the devil she thinks she's doing out here, anyway. A quiet little thing like that; what she ought to be doing is sitting in some village back home, knitting.'

'She knits here,' observed the Navigating Officer.

'I know – and think what it implies! What's the idea of that kind going to Mars? She'll be as homesick as hell, and hate every foot of the place on sight. That husband of hers ought to have had more sense. Comes damn near cruelty to children.'

'It mightn't be his fault, sir. I mean, some of those quiet ones can be amazingly stubborn.'

The Captain eyed his officer speculatively.

'Well, I'm not a man of wide experience, but I know what I'd say to my wife if she thought of coming along.'

'But you can't have a proper ding-dong with those quiet ones, sir. They kind of featherbed the whole thing, and then get their own way in the end.'

'I'll overlook the implication of the first part of that remark, Mr Carter, but out of this extensive knowledge of women can you suggest to me why the devil she is here if he didn't drag her along? It isn't as if Mars were domestically hazardous, like a convention.'

'Well, sir – she strikes me as the devoted type. Scared of her own shadow ordinarily, but with an awful amount of determination when the right string's pulled. It's sort of – well, you've heard of ewes facing lions in defence of their cubs, haven't you?'

'Assuming that you mean lambs,' said the Captain, 'the answers would be, A: I've always doubted it; and B: she doesn't have any.'

'I was just trying to indicate the type, sir.'

The Captain scratched his cheek with his forefinger.

'You might be right, but I know if I were going to take a wife to Mars, which heaven forbid, I'd feel a tough, gun-toting Momma was less of a liability. What's his job there?'

'Taking charge of a mining company office, I think.'

'Office hours, huh? Well, maybe it'll work out some way, but I still say the poor little thing ought to be in her own kitchen. She'll spend half the time scared to death, and the rest of it pining for home comforts.' He glanced at the clock. 'They've had enough time to batten down the chamber-pots now. Let's get busy.'

He fastened his own safety-belt, swung the screen in front of him on its pivot, switching it on as he did so, and leaned back watching the panorama of stars move slowly across it.

'All set, Mr Carter?'

The Navigating Officer switched on a fuel line, and poised his right hand above a key.

'All set, sir.'

'Okay. Straighten her up.'

The Navigating Officer glued his attention to the pointers before him. He tapped the key beneath his fingers experimentally. Nothing happened. A slight double furrow appeared between his brows. He tapped again. Still there was no response.

'Get on with it, man,' said the Captain irritably.

The Navigating Officer decided to try twisting her the other way. He tapped one of the keys under his left hand. This time there was response without delay. The whole ship jumped violently sideways and trembled. A crash jangled back and forth through the metal members* around them like a diminishing echo.

Only the safety belt kept the Navigating Officer in his seat. He stared stupidly at the gyrating* pointers before him. On the screen the stars were streaking across like a shower of fireworks. The Captain watched the display in ominous silence for a moment, then he said coldly:

'Perhaps when you have had your fun, Mr Carter, you will kindly straighten her up.'

The navigator pulled himself together. He chose a key, and pressed it. Nothing happened. He tried another. Still the needles on the dials revolved smoothly. A slight sweat broke out on his forehead. He switched to another fuel line, and tried again.

The Captain lay back in his chair, watching the heavens stream across his screen.

'Well?' he demanded curtly.

'There's – no response, sir.'

Captain Winters unfastened his safety-belt and clacked across the floor on his magnetic soles. He jerked his head for the other to get out of his seat, and

* members: structural supports gyrating: revolving

took his place. He checked the fuel line switches. He pressed a key. There was no impulse: the pointers continued to turn without a check. He tried other keys, fruitlessly. He looked up and met the navigator's eyes. After a long moment he moved back to his own desk, and flipped a switch. A voice broke into the room:

'– would I know? All I know is that the old can's just bowling along head over elbow, and that ain't no kind of way to run a bloody spaceship. If you ask me –'

'Jevons,' snapped the Captain.

The voice broke off abruptly.

'Yes, sir?' it said, in a different tone.

'The laterals aren't firing.'

'No, sir,' the voice agreed.

'Wake up, man. I mean they *won't* fire. They've packed up.'

'What – all of 'em, sir?'

'The only ones that have responded are the port laterals – and they shouldn't have kicked the way they did. Better send someone outside to look at 'em. I didn't like that kick.'

'Very good, sir.'

The Captain flipped the communicator switch back, and pulled over the announcement mike.

'Attention, please. You may release all safety-belts and proceed as normal. Correction of course has been postponed. You will be warned before it is resumed. That is all.'

Captain and navigator looked at one another again. Their faces were grave, and their eyes troubled . . .

Captain Winters studied his audience. It comprised everyone aboard the *Falcon*. Fourteen men and one woman. Six of the men were his crew; the rest passengers. He watched them as they found themselves places in the ship's small living-room. He would have been happier if his cargo had consisted of more freight and fewer passengers. Passengers, having nothing to occupy them, were always making mischief one way and another. Moreover, it was not a quiet, subservient type of man who recommended himself for a job as a miner, prospector, or general adventurer on Mars.

The woman could have caused a great deal of trouble aboard had she been so minded. Luckily she was diffident, self-effacing. But even though at times she was irritatingly without spirit, he thanked his luck that she had not turned out to be some incendiary* blonde who would only add to his troubles.

All the same, he reminded himself, regarding her as she sat beside her husband, she could not be quite as meek as she looked. Carter must have been right when he spoke of a stiffening motive somewhere – without that she could never have started on the journey at all, and she would certainly not be coming through steadfast and uncomplaining so far. He glanced at the woman's husband. Queer creatures, women. Morgan was all right, but there was nothing about him, one would have said, to lead a woman on a trip like this . . .

He waited until they had finished shuffling around and fitting themselves in. Silence fell. He let his gaze dwell on each face in turn. His own expression was serious.

'Mrs Morgan and gentlemen,' he began. 'I have called you here together because it seemed best to me that each of you should have a clear understanding of our present position.

* incendiary: provocative

'It is this. Our lateral tubes have failed. They are, for reasons which we have not yet been able to ascertain, useless. In the case of the port laterals they are burnt out, and irreplaceable.

'In case some of you do not know what that implies, I should tell you that it is upon the laterals that the navigation of the ship depends. The main drive tubes give us the initial impetus for take-off. After that they are shut off, leaving us in free fall. Any deviations from the course plotted are corrected by suitable bursts from the laterals.

'But it is not only for steering that we use them. In landing, which is an infinitely more complex job than take-off, they are essential. We brake by reversing the ship and using the main drive to check our speed. But I think you can scarcely fail to realize that it is an operation of the greatest delicacy to keep the huge mass of such a ship as this perfectly balanced upon the thrust of her drive as she descends. It is the laterals which make such balance possible. Without them it cannot be done.'

A dead silence held the room for some seconds. Then a voice asked, drawling:

'What you're saying, Captain, is, the way things are, we can neither steer nor land – is that it?'

Captain Winters looked at the speaker. He was a big man. Without exerting himself, and, apparently, without intention, he seemed to possess a natural domination over the rest.

'That is exactly what I mean,' he replied.

A tenseness came over the room. There was the sound of a quickly drawn breath here and there.

The man with the slow voice nodded, fatalistically. Someone else asked:

'Does that mean that we might crash on Mars?'

'No,' said the Captain. 'If we go on travelling as we are now, slightly off course, we shall miss Mars altogether.'

'And so go on out to play tag with the asteroids,' another voice suggested.

'That is what would happen if we did nothing about it. But there is a way we can stop that, if we can manage it.' The Captain paused, aware that he had their absorbed attention. He continued:

'You must all we well aware from the peculiar behaviour of space as seen from our ports that we are now tumbling along all ars – er – head over heels. This is due to the explosion of the port laterals. It is a highly unorthodox method of travelling, but it does mean that by an impulse from our main tubes given at exactly the critical moment we should be able to alter our course approximately as we require.'

'And how much good is that going to do us if we can't land?' somebody wanted to know. The Captain ignored the interruption. He continued:

'I have been in touch by radio with both home and Mars, and have reported our state. I have also informed them that I intend to attempt the one possible course open to me. That is of using the main drive in an attempt to throw the ship into an orbit about Mars.

'If that is successful we shall avoid two dangers – that of shooting on towards the outer parts of the system, and of crashing on Mars. I think we have a good chance of bringing it off.'

When we stopped speaking he saw alarm in several faces, thoughtful concentration in others. He noticed Mrs Morgan holding tightly to her husband's hand, her face a little paler than usual. It was the man with the drawl who broke the silence.

'You *think* there is a good chance?' he repeated questioningly.

'I do. I also think it is the only chance. But I'm not going to try to fool you by pretending complete confidence. It's too serious for that.'

'And if we do get into this orbit?'

'They will try to keep a radar fix on us, and send help as soon as possible.'

'H'm,' said the questioner. 'And what do you personally think about that, Captain?'

'I – well, it isn't going to be easy. But we're all in this together, so I'll tell you just what they told me. At the very best we can't expect them to reach us for some months. The ship will have to come from Earth. The two planets are well past conjunction now. I'm afraid it's going to mean quite a wait.'

'Can we – hold out long enough, Captain?'

'According to my calculations we should be able to hold out for about seventeen or eighteen weeks.'

'And that will be long enough?'

'It'll have to be.'

He broke the thoughtful pause that followed by continuing in a brisker manner.

'This is not going to be comfortable, or pleasant. But, if we all play our parts, and keep strictly to the necessary measures, it can be done. Now, there are three essentials: air to breathe – well, luckily we shan't have to worry about that. The regeneration plant and stock of spare cylinders, and cylinders in cargo will look after that for a long time. Water will be rationed. Two pints each every twenty-four hours, for *everything*. Luckily we shall be able to draw water from the fuel tanks, or it would be a great deal less than that. The thing that is going to be our most serious worry is food.'

He explained his proposals further, with patient clarity. At the end he added: 'And now I expect you have some questions?'

A small, wiry man with a weather-beaten face asked:

'Is there no hope at all of getting the lateral tubes to work again?'

Captain Winters shook his head.

'Negligible. The impellent* section of a ship is not constructed to be accessible in space. We shall keep on trying, of course, but even if the others could be made to fire, we should still be unable to repair the port laterals.'

He did his best to answer the few more questions that followed in ways that held a balance between easy confidence and despondency. The prospect was by no means good. Before help could possibly reach them they were all going to need all the nerve and resolution they had – and out of sixteen persons some must be weaker than others.

His gaze rested again on Alice Morgan and her husband beside her. Her presence was certainly a possible source of trouble. When it came to the pinch the man would have more strain on account of her – and, most likely, fewer scruples.

Since the woman was here, she must share the consequences equally with the rest. There could be no privilege. In a sharp emergency one could afford a heroic gesture, but preferential treatment of any one person in the long ordeal which they must face would create an impossible situation. Make any allowances for her, and you would be called on to make allowances

* impellent: forward drive

for others on health or other grounds – with heaven knew what complications to follow.

A fair chance with the rest was the best he could do for her – not, he felt, looking at her as she clutched her husband's hand and looked at him from wide eyes in a pale face, not a very good best.

He hoped she would not be the first to go under. It would be better for morale if she were not the very first . . .

She was not the first to go. For nearly three months nobody went.

The *Falcon*, by means of skilfully timed bursts on the main tubes, had succeeded in nudging herself into an orbital relationship with Mars. After that, there was little that the crew could do for her. At the distance of equilibrium she had become a very minor satellite, rolling and tumbling on her circular course, destined, so far as anyone could see, to continue this untidy progress until help reached them, or perhaps for ever . . .

Inboard, the complexity of her twisting somersaults was not perceptible unless one deliberately uncovered a port. If one did, the crazy cavortings of the universe outside produced such a sense of bewilderment that one gladly shut the cover again to preserve the illusion of stability within. Even Captain Winters and the Navigating Officer took their observations as swiftly as possible and were relieved when they had shut the whizzing constellations off the screen, and could take refuge in relativity.

For all her occupants the *Falcon* had become a small, independent world, very sharply finite in space, and scarcely less so in time.

It was, moreover, a world with a very low standard of living; a community with short tempers, weakening distempers*, aching bellies, and ragged nerves. It was a group in which each man watched on a trigger of suspicion for a hairsbreadth difference in the next man's ration, and where the little he ate so avidly was not enough to quiet the rumblings of his stomach. He was ravenous when he went to sleep; more ravenous when he woke from dreams of food.

Men who had started from Earth full-bodied were now gaunt and lean, their faces had hardened from curved contours into angled planes and changed their healthy colours for a grey pallor in which their eyes glittered unnaturally. They had all grown weaker. The weakest lay on their couches torpidly*. The more fortunate looked at them from time to time with a question in their eyes. It was not difficult to read the question: 'Why do we go on wasting good food on this guy? Looks like he's booked, anyway.' But as yet no one had taken up that booking.

The situation was worse than Captain Winters had foreseen. There had been bad stowage. The cans in several cases of meat had collapsed under the terrific pressure of other cans above them during take-off. The resulting mess was now describing an orbit of its own around the ship. He had had to throw it out secretly. If the men had known of it, they would have eaten it gladly, maggots and all. Another case shown on his inventory had disappeared. He still did not know how. The ship had been searched for it without trace. Much of the emergency stores consisted of dehydrated foods for which he dared not spare sufficient water, so that though edible they were painfully unattractive. They

* distempers: illnesses torpidly: sluggishly

had been intended simply as a supplement in case the estimated time was overrun, and were not extensive. Little in the cargo was edible, and that mostly small cans of luxuries. As a result, he had had to reduce the rations expected to stretch meagrely over seventeen weeks. And even so, they would not last that long.

The first who did go owed it neither to sickness nor malnutrition, but to accident.

Jevons, the chief engineer, maintained that the only way to locate and correct the trouble with the laterals was to effect an entry into the propellent section of the ship. Owing to the tanks which backed up against the bulkhead separating the sections this could not be achieved from within the ship herself.

It had proved impossible with the tools available to cut a slice out of the hull; the temperature of space and the conductivity of the hull caused all their heat to run away and dissipate itself without making the least impression on the tough skin. The one way he could see of getting in was to cut away round the burnt-out tubes of the port laterals. It was debatable whether this was worth while since the other laterals would still be unbalanced on the port side, but where he found opposition solidly against him was in the matter of using precious oxygen to operate his cutters. He had to accept that ban, but he refused to relinquish his plan altogether.

'Very well,' he said, grimly. 'We're like rats in a trap, but Bowman and I aim to do more than just keep the trap going, and we're going to try, even if we have to cut our way into the damned ship by hand.'

Captain Winters had okayed that; not that he believed that anything useful would come of it, but it would keep Jevons quiet, and do no one else any harm.

So for weeks Jevons and Bowman had got into their spacesuits and worked their shifts. Oblivious after a time of the wheeling heavens about them, they kept doggedly on with their sawing and filing. Their progress, pitifully slow at best, had grown even slower as they became weaker.

Just what Bowman was attempting when he met his end still remained a mystery. He had not confided in Jevons. All that anyone knew about it was the sudden lurch of the ship and the clang of reverberations running up and down the hull. Possibly it was an accident. More likely he had become impatient and laid a small charge to blast an opening.

For the first time for weeks ports were uncovered and faces looked out giddily at the wheeling stars. Bowman came into sight. He was drifting inertly, a dozen yards or more outboard. His suit was deflated, and a large gash showed in the material of the left sleeve.

The consciousness of a corpse floating round and round you like a minor moon is no improver of already lowered morale. Push it away, and it still circles, though at a greater distance. Some day a proper ceremony for the situation would be invented – perhaps a small rocket would launch the poor remains upon their last, infinite voyage. Meanwhile, lacking a precedent, Captain Winters decided to pay the body the decent respect of having it brought inboard. The refrigeration plant had to be kept going to preserve the small remaining stocks of food, but several sections of it were empty . . .

A day and a night by the clock had passed since the provisional interment of Bowman when a modest knock came on the control-room door. The Captain laid blotting paper carefully over his latest entry in the log, and closed the book.

'Come in,' he said.

The door opened just widely enough to admit Alice Morgan. She slipped in, and shut it behind her. He was somewhat surprised to see her. She had kept sedulously* in the background, putting the few requests she had made through the intermediation of her husband. He noticed the changes in her. She was haggard now as they all were, and her eyes anxious. She was also nervous. The fingers of her thin hands sought one another and interlocked themselves for confidence. Clearly she was having to push herself to raise whatever was in her mind. He smiled in order to encourage her.

'Come and sit down, Mrs Morgan,' he invited, amiably.

She crossed the room with a slight clicking from her magnetic soles, and took the chair he indicated. She seated herself uneasily, and on the forward edge.

It had been sheer cruelty to bring her on this voyage, he reflected again. She had been at least a pretty little thing, now she was no longer that. Why couldn't that fool husband of hers have left her in her proper setting – a nice quiet suburb, a gentle routine, a life where she would be protected from exaction* and alarm alike. It surprised him again that she had had the resolution and the stamina to survive conditions on the *Falcon* as long as this. Fate would probably have been kinder to her if it had disallowed that. He spoke to her quietly, for she perched rather than sat, making him think of a bird ready to take off at any sudden movement.

'And what can I do for you, Mrs Morgan?'

* sedulously: carefully exaction: hardship

Alice's fingers twined and intertwined. She watched them doing it. She looked up, opened her mouth to speak, closed it again.

'It isn't very easy,' she murmured apologetically.

Trying to help her, he said:

'No need to be nervous, Mrs Morgan. Just tell me what's on your mind. Has one of them been – bothering you?'

She shook her head.

'Oh, no, Captain Winters. It's nothing like that at all.'

'What is it, then?'

'It's – it's the rations, Captain. I'm not getting enough food.'

The kindly concern froze out of his face.

'None of us is,' he told her, shortly.

'I know,' she said, hurriedly. 'I know, but –'

'But what?' he inquired in a chill tone.

She drew a breath.

'There's the man who died yesterday. Bowman. I thought if I could have his rations –'

The sentence trailed away as she saw the expression on the Captain's face.

He was not acting. He was feeling just as shocked as he looked. Of all the impudent suggestions that ever had come his way, none had astounded him more. He gazed dumbfounded at the source of the outrageous proposition. Her eyes met his, but, oddly, with less timidity than before. There was no sign of shame in them.

'I've *got* to have more food,' she said, intensely.

Captain Winters' anger mounted.

'So you thought you'd just snatch a dead man's share as well as your own! I'd better not tell you in words just where I class that suggestion, young woman. But you can understand this: we share, and we share equally. What Bowman's death means to us is that we can keep on having the same ration for a little longer – that, and only that. And now I think you had better go.'

But Alice Morgan made no move to go. She sat there with her lips pressed together, her eyes a little narrowed, quite still save that her hands trembled. Even through his indignation the Captain felt surprise, as though he had watched a hearth cat suddenly become a hunter. She said stubbornly:

'I haven't asked for any privilege until now, Captain. I wouldn't ask you now if it weren't absolutely necessary. But that man's death gives us a margin now. And I *must* have more food.'

The Captain controlled himself with an effort.

'Bowman's death has not given us a margin, or a windfall – all it has done is to extend by a day or two the chance of our survival. Do you think that every one of us doesn't ache just as much as you do for more food? In all my considerable experience of effrontery* – '

She raised her thin hand to stop him. The hardness of her eyes made him wonder why he had ever thought her timid.

'Captain. Look at me!' she said, in a harsh tone.

He looked. Presently his expression of anger faded into shocked astonishment. A faint tinge of pink stole into her pale cheeks.

'Yes,' she said. 'You see, you've *got* to give me more food. My baby *must* have the chance to live.'

The Captain continued to stare at her as if mesmerized. Presently he shut his eyes, and passed his hand over his brow.

* effrontery: barefaced cheek

'God in heaven. This is terrible,' he murmured.

Alice Morgan said seriously, as if she had already considered that very point:

'No. It isn't terrible – not if my baby lives.' He looked at her helplessly, without speaking. She went on:

'It wouldn't be robbing anyone, you see. Bowman doesn't need his rations any more – but my baby does. It's quite simple, really.' She looked questioningly at the Captain. He had no comment ready. She continued: 'So you couldn't call it unfair. After all, I'm two people now, really, aren't I? I *need* more food. If you don't let me have it you will be murdering my baby. So you *must* . . . *must* . . . My baby has *got* to live – he's got to . . .'

When she had gone Captain Winters mopped his forehead, unlocked his private drawer, and took out one of his carefully hoarded bottles of whisky. He had the self-restraint to take only a small pull on the drinking-tube and then put it back. It revived him a little, but his eyes were still shocked and worried.

Would it not have been kinder in the end to tell the woman that her baby had no chance at all of being born? That would have been honest; but he doubted whether the coiner of the phrase about honesty being the best policy had known a great deal about group morale. Had he told her that, it would have been impossible to avoid telling her why, and once she knew why it would have been impossible for her not to confide it, if only to her husband. And then it would be too late.

The Captain opened the top drawer, and regarded the pistol within. There was always that. He was tempted to take hold of it now and use it. There wasn't much use in playing the silly game out. Sooner or later it would have to come to that, anyway.

He frowned at it, hesitating. Then he put out his right hand and gave the thing a flip with his finger, sending it floating to the back of the drawer, out of sight. He closed the drawer. Not yet . . .

But perhaps he had better begin to carry it soon. So far, his authority had held. There had been nothing worse than safety-valve grumbling. But a time would come when he was going to need the pistol either for them or for himself.

If they should begin to suspect that the encouraging bulletins that he pinned up on the board from time to time were fakes: if they should somehow find out that the rescue ship which they believed to be hurtling through space towards them had not, in fact, even yet been able to take off from Earth – that was when hell would start breaking loose.

It might be safer if there were to be an accident with the radio equipment before long . . .

'Taken your time, haven't you?' Captain Winters asked. He spoke shortly because he was irritable, not because it mattered in the least how long anyone took over anything now.

The Navigating Officer made no reply. His boots clicked across the floor. A key and an identity bracelet drifted towards the Captain, an inch or so above the surface of his desk. He put out a hand to check them.

'I –' he began. Then he caught sight of the other's face. 'Good God, man, what's the matter with you?'

He felt some compunction*. He wanted Bowman's identity bracelet for the record, but there had been no

* compunction: pity

real need to send Carter for it. A man who had died Bowman's death would be a piteous sight. That was why they had left him still in his spacesuit instead of undressing him. All the same, he had thought that Carter was tougher stuff. He brought out a bottle. The last bottle.

'Better have a shot of this,' he said.

The navigator did, and put his head in his hands. The Captain carefully rescued the bottle from its mid-air drift, and put it away. Presently the Navigating Officer said, without looking up:

'I'm sorry, sir.'

'That's okay, Carter. Nasty job. Should have done it myself.'

The other shuddered slightly. A minute passed in silence while he got a grip on himself. Then he looked up and met the Captain's eyes.

'It – it wasn't just that, sir.'

The Captain looked puzzled.

'How do you mean?' he asked.

The officer's lips trembled. He did not form his words properly, and he stammered.

'Pull yourself together. What are you trying to say?' The Captain spoke sharply to stiffen him.

Carter jerked his head slightly. His lips stopped trembling.

'He – he –' he floundered; then he tried again, in a rush. 'He – hasn't any legs, sir.'

'Who? What *is* this? You mean Bowman hasn't any legs?'

'Y – yes, sir.'

'Nonsense, man. I was there when he was brought in. So were you. He had legs, all right.'

'Yes, sir. He did have legs then – but he hasn't now!'

The Captain sat very still. For some seconds there was no sound in the control-room but the clicking of the chronometer. Then he spoke with difficulty, getting no further than two words:

'You mean –?'

'What else could it be, sir?'

'*God in heaven!*' gasped the Captain.

He sat staring with eyes that had taken on the horror that lay in the other man's . . .

Two men moved silently, with socks over their magnetic soles. They stopped opposite the door of one of the refrigeration compartments. One of them produced a slender key. He slipped it into the lock, felt delicately with it among the wards for a moment, and then turned it with a click. As the door swung open a pistol fired twice from within the refrigerator. The man who was pulling the door sagged at the knees, and hung in mid-air.

The other man was still behind the half-opened door. He snatched a pistol from his pocket and slid it swiftly round the corner of the door, pointing into the refrigerator. He pulled the trigger twice.

A figure in a spacesuit launched itself out of the refrigerator, sailing uncannily across the room. The other man shot at it as it swept past him. The spacesuited figure collided with the opposite wall, recoiled slightly, and hung there. Before it could turn and use the pistol in its hand, the other man fired again. The figure jerked, and floated back against the wall. The man kept his pistol trained, but the spacesuit swayed there, flaccid* and inert.

* flaccid: limp

The door by which the men had entered opened with a sudden clang. The Navigating Officer on the threshold did not hesitate. He fired slightly after the other, but he kept on firing . . .

When his pistol was empty the man in front of him swayed queerly, anchored by his boots; there was no other movement in him. The Navigating Officer put out a hand and steadied himself by the doorframe. Then, slowly and painfully, he made his way across to the figure in the spacesuit. There were gashes in the suit. He managed to unlock the helmet and pull it away.

The Captain's face looked somewhat greyer than undernourishment had made it. His eyes opened slowly. He said in a whisper:

'Your job now, Carter. Good luck!'

The Navigating Officer tried to answer, but there were no words, only a bubbling of blood in his throat. His hands relaxed. There was a dark stain still spreading on his uniform. Presently his body hung listlessly swaying beside his Captain's.

'I figured they were going to last a lot longer than this,' said the small man with the sandy moustache.

The man with the drawl looked at him steadily.

'Oh, you did, did you? And do you reckon your figuring's reliable?'

The smaller man shifted awkwardly. He ran the tip of his tongue along his lips.

'Well, there was Bowman. Then those four. Then the two that died. That's seven.'

'Sure. That's seven. Well?' inquired the big man softly. He was not as big as he had been, but he still had a large frame. Under his intent regard the emaciated small man seemed to shrivel a little more.

'Er – nothing. Maybe my figuring was kind of hopeful,' he said.

'Maybe. My advice to you is to quit figuring and keep on hoping. Huh?'

The small man wilted. 'Er – yes. I guess so.'

The big man looked round the living-room, counting heads.

'Okay. Let's start,' he said.

A silence fell on the rest. They gazed at him with uneasy fascination. They fidgeted. One or two nibbled at their fingernails. The big man leaned forward. He put a space-helmet, inverted, on the table. In his customary leisurely fashion he said:

'We shall draw for it. Each of us will take a paper and hold it up unopened until I give the word. *Un*opened. Got that?'

They nodded. Every eye was fixed intently upon his face.

'Good. Now one of those pieces of paper in the helmet is marked with a cross. Ray, I want you to count the pieces there and make sure that there are nine –'

'Eight!' said Alice Morgan's voice sharply.

All the heads turned towards her as if pulled by strings. The faces looked startled, as though the owners might have heard a turtle-dove roar. Alice sat embarrassed under the combined gaze, but she held herself steady and her mouth was set in a straight line. The man in charge of the proceedings studied her.

'Well, well,' he drawled. 'So you don't want to take a hand in our little game!'

'No,' said Alice.

'You've shared equally with us so far – but now we have reached this regrettable stage you don't want to?'

'No,' agreed Alice again.

He raised his eyebrows.

'You are appealing to our chivalry, perhaps?'

'No,' said Alice once more. 'I'm denying the equity of what you call your game. The one who draws the cross dies – isn't that the plan?'

'*Pro bono publico**,' said the big man. 'Deplorable, of course, but unfortunately necessary.'

'But if *I* draw it, two must die. Do you call that equitable?' Alice asked.

The group looked taken aback. Alice waited.

The big man fumbled it. For once he was at a loss.

'Well,' said Alice, 'isn't that so?'

One of the others broke the silence to observe: 'The question of the exact stage when the personality, the soul of the individual, takes form is still highly debatable. Some have held that until there is separate existence –'

The drawling voice of the big man cut him short. 'I think we can leave that point to the theologians, Sam. This is more in the Wisdom of Solomon class. The point would seem to be that Mrs Morgan claims exemption on account of her condition.'

'My baby has a right to live.' Alice said doggedly.

'We all have a right to live. We all want to live,' someone put in.

'Why should you –?' another began; but the drawling voice dominated again:

'Very well, gentlemen. Let us be formal. Let us be democratic. We will vote on it. The question is put: do you consider Mrs Morgan's claim to be valid – or should she take her chance with the rest of us? Those in –'

'Just a minute,' said Alice, in a firmer voice than any of them had heard her use. 'Before you start voting on

* *Pro bono publico*: for the good of everyone (Latin)

that you'd better listen to me a bit.' She looked round, making sure she had the attention of all of them. She had; and their astonishment as well.

'Now the first thing is that I am a lot more important than any of you,' she told them simply. 'No, you needn't smile. I am – and I'll tell you why.

'Before the radio broke down –'

'Before the Captain wrecked it, you mean,' someone corrected her.

'Well, before it became useless,' she compromised. 'Captain Winters was in regular touch with home. He gave them news of us. The news that the Press wanted most was about me. Women, particularly women in unusual situations, are always news. He told me I was in the headlines: GIRL-WIFE IN DOOM ROCKET, WOMAN'S SPACEWRECK ORDEAL, that sort of thing. And if you haven't forgotten how newspapers look, you can imagine the leads, too: "Trapped in their living space tomb, a girl and fifteen men now wheel helplessly around the planet Mars . . ."

'All of you are just men – hulks, like the ship, I am a woman, therefore my position is romantic, so I am young, glamorous, beautiful . . .' Her thin face showed for a moment the trace of a wry smile. 'I am a heroine . . .'

She paused, letting the idea sink in. Then she went on:

'I was a heroine even before Captain Winters told them that I was pregnant. But after that I became a phenomenon. There were demands for interviews, I wrote one, and Captain Winters transmitted it for me. There have been interviews with my parents and my friends, anyone who knew me. And now an enormous number of people know a great deal about me. They are intensely interested in me. They are even more interested in my baby – which is likely to be the first baby ever born in a spaceship . . .

'Now do you begin to see? You have a fine tale ready. Bowman, my husband, Captain Winters, and the rest were heroically struggling to repair the port laterals. There was an explosion. It blew them all away out into space.

'You may get away with that. But if there is no trace of me and my baby – or of our bodies – *then* what are you going to say? How will you explain that?'

She looked round the faces again.

'Well, what *are* you going to say? That I, too, was outside repairing the port laterals? That I committed suicide by shooting myself out into space with a rocket?

'Just think it over. The whole world's press is wanting to know about me – with all the details. It'll have to be a mighty good story to stand up to that. And if it doesn't stand up – well, the rescue won't have done you much good.

'You'll not have a chance in hell. You'll hang, or you'll fry, every one of you – unless it happens they lynch you first . . .'

There was silence in the room as she finished speaking. Most of the faces showed the astonishment of men ferociously attacked by a Pekinese, and at a loss for suitable comment.

The big man sat sunk in reflection for a minute or more. Then he looked up, rubbing the stubble on his sharp-boned chin thoughtfully. He glanced round the others and then let his eyes rest on Alice. For a moment there was a twitch at the corner of his mouth.

'Madam,' he drawled, 'you are probably a great loss to the legal profession.' He turned away. 'We shall have to reconsider this matter before our next meeting. But, for the present, Ray, *eight* pieces of paper as the lady said . . .'

'It's her!' said the Second, over the Skipper's shoulder.

The Skipper moved irritably. 'Of course it's her. What else'd you expect to find whirling through space like a sozzled owl?' He studied the screen for a moment. 'Not a sign. Every port covered.'

'Do you think there's a chance, Skipper?'

'What, after all this time! No, Tommy, not a ghost of it. We're – just the morticians*, I guess.'

'How'll we get aboard her, Skip?'

The Skipper watched the gyrations of the *Falcon* with a calculating eye.

'Well, there aren't any rules, but I reckon if we can get a cable on her we *might* be able to play her gently, like a big fish. It'll be tricky, though.'

Tricky, it was. Five times the magnet projected from the rescue ship failed to make contact. The sixth attempt was better judged. When the magnet drifted close to the *Falcon* the current was switched on for a moment. It changed course, and floated nearer to the ship. When it was almost in contact the switch went over again. It darted forward, and glued itself limpet-like to the hull.

Then followed the long game of playing the *Falcon*; of keeping tension on the cable between the two ships, but not too much tension, and of holding the rescue ship from being herself thrown into a roll by the pull. Three times the cable parted, but at last, after weary hours of adroit manoeuvre by the rescue ship the derelict's motion had been reduced to a slow twist.

* morticians: undertakers

There was still no trace of life aboard. The rescue ship closed a little.

The Captain, the Third Officer, and the doctor fastened on their spacesuits and went outboard. They made their way forward to the winch. The Captain looped a short length of line over the cable, and fastened both ends of it to his belt. He laid hold of the cable with both hands, and with a heave sent himself skimming into space. The others followed him along the guiding cable.

They gathered beside the *Falcon*'s entrance port. The Third Officer took a crank from his satchel. He inserted it in an opening, and began to turn until he was satisfied that the inner door of the airlock was closed. When it would turn no more, he withdrew it, and fitted it into the next opening; that should set the motors pumping air out of the lock – if there were air, and if there were still current to work the motors. The Captain held a microphone against the hull, and listened. He caught a humming.

'Okay. They're running,' he said.

He waited until the humming stopped.

'Right. Open her up,' he directed.

The Third Officer inserted his crank again, and wound it. The main port opened inwards, leaving a dark gap in the shining hull. The three looked at the opening sombrely for some seconds. With a grim quietness the Captain's voice said: 'Well. Here we go!'

They moved carefully and slowly into the blackness, listening.

The Third Officer's voice murmured:

'The silence that is in the starry sky,
The sleep that is among the lonely hills . . .'

Presently the Captain's voice asked:

'How's the air, Doc?'

The doctor looked at his gauges.

'It's okay,' he said, in some surprise. 'Pressure's about six ounces down, that's all.' He began to unfasten his helmet. The others copied him. The Captain made a face as he took his off.

'The place stinks,' he said, uneasily. 'Let's – get on with it.'

He led the way towards the lounge. They entered it apprehensively.

The scene was uncanny and bewildering. Though the gyrations of the *Falcon* had been reduced, every loose object in her continued to circle until it met a solid obstruction and bounced off it upon a new course. The result was a medley of wayward items churning slowly hither and thither.

'Nobody here, anyway,' said the Captain, practically. 'Doc, do you think – ?'

He broke off at the sight of the doctor's strange expression. He followed the line of the other's gaze. The doctor was looking at the drifting flotsam of the place. Among the flow of books, cans, playing-cards, boots, and miscellaneous rubbish, his attention was riveted upon a bone. It was large and clean and had been cracked open.

The Captain nudged him. 'What's the matter, Doc?'

The doctor turned unseeing eyes upon him for a moment, and then looked back at the drifting bone.

'That' – he said in an unsteady voice – 'that, Skipper is a human femur.'

In the long moment that followed while they stared at the grisly relic the silence which had lain over the *Falcon* was broken. The sound of a voice rose, thin, uncertain, but perfectly clear. The three looked incredulously at one another as they listened:

> *'Rock-a-bye baby*
> *On the tree top*
> *When the wind blows*
> *The cradle will rock . . .'*

Alice sat on the side of her bunk, swaying a little, and holding her baby to her. It smiled, and reached up one miniature hand to pat her cheek as she sang:

> *'. . .When the bough breaks*
> *The cradle will fall*
> *Down will – '*

Her song cut off suddenly at the click of the opening door. For a moment she stared as blankly at the three figures in the opening as they at her. Her face was a mask with harsh lines drawn from the points where the skin was stretched tightly over the bones. Then a trace of expression came over it. Her eyes brightened. Her lips curved in a travesty of a smile.

She loosed her arms from about the baby, and it hung there in mid-air, chuckling a little to itself. She slid her right hand under the pillow of the bunk, and drew it out again, holding a pistol.

The black shape of the pistol looked enormous in her transparently thin hand as she pointed it at the men who stood transfixed in the doorway.

'Look, baby,' she said. 'Look there! Food! Lovely food . . .'

ACTIVITIES AND ASSIGNMENTS

Ghost Stories

The Red Room by H G Wells
Farthing House by Susan Hill

1 Spend a little time brainstorming what you think are the ingredients of a good ghost story. Do you expect the story to frighten you? How? Does the story need to surprise or shock you? Why? How important is the setting? Do you prefer ghost stories with traditional settings, such as gloomy old houses, and scenes which make your spine tingle? Or is the setting not important as long as the story has a good plot?

2 At the beginning of *The Red Room* the young man is rather sure of himself and quite boastful. What is his attitude to the old people? Make a table like the one below. Re-read the first three pages of the story and write examples of the young man's descriptions of the old people in the column marked **Evidence.** Then write what each description tells you about his attitude to the old people in the column marked **Attitude.** What does this tell you about the young man's character?

Evidence	Attitude

3 The story is told from the young man's point of view. Yet every story has two sides. What might the old people think of the young man? Imagine you are one of the people left in the housekeeper's room after the young man goes to find the Red Room. Write your diary entry for that evening. You should write about your impressions of the young man and about what you think of his determination to sleep in the Red Room.

4 The young man's boastful character begins to break down as the story progresses. At the same time, the language of the story changes and the level of tension increases. Find the following phrases in the text and, on a scale of 1 to 10, say how frightened you think the young man is at each point (1 is not very frightened at all, 10 is absolutely petrified):

a) '". . . it will take a very tangible ghost to frighten me." And I stood up before the fire with my glass in my hand.'
b) '("This night of all nights!" said the old woman.)'
c) 'Their very existence was spectral.'
d) 'its shadow fell with marvellous distinctness upon the white panelling and gave me the impression of someone crouching to waylay me.'
e) '. . . the memory of that story gave me a sudden twinge of apprehension.'
f) 'My candle was a little tongue of light in its vastness, that failed to pierce the opposite end of the room.'
g) 'I still found the remoter darkness of the place . . . too stimulating for the imagination.'
h) 'By this time I was in a state of considerable nervous tension.'
i) 'The sombre reds and blacks of the room troubled me.'
j) 'With a cry of terror, I dashed at the alcove.'
k) 'There is Fear in that room of hers . . . black Fear.'

5 Do you think the ghost is real or is it a figment of the young man's imagination? Discuss this question in groups and try to arrive at an answer you all agree with.

6 At the end of the story why do we see the old people taking charge, bandaging the young man's wounds and giving him medicine? What is this telling us about the effect the ghost has upon the young man?

7 Read *Farthing House* and then re-read the first few paragraphs. Who is the storyteller? Who is she writing to?

8 The mood of the young male storyteller at the beginning of *The Red Room* could be described as 'very confident'. How would you describe the mood of the storyteller at the beginning of *Farthing House*?

9 What conflicting emotions does the storyteller feel just before entering and just after entering Farthing House (pages 19–20)?

10 Look back at question 4, in which you traced the development of the young man's fear. Now trace the development of the young woman's emotions throughout *Farthing House*. What other emotions does she feel as well as fear? You could use a chart like the one below to help you. Write evidence from the text in Column 1 and describe the emotion she feels in Column 2. (You may like to work in groups for this activity. You should divide the pages of the story between you to find evidence in the text, then come together to complete your chart.)

Evidence	**Emotion**

11 What do you think of the ending of *Farthing House*? Do you think the extra twist in the tale makes the story more interesting?

12 Write the newspaper report which the storyteller sees at the end of *Farthing House*. Remember to think about layout and headings.

13 In *Farthing House* the female storyteller is quite different from the young man in *The Red Room*. Discuss how each storyteller copes with the ghosts in their room. Think about:

- how the young man in *The Red Room* deliberately sets out to confront the ghost
- how the storyteller in *Farthing House* meets the ghost accidentally
- the different types of ghost they meet
- the emotions each storyteller feels about the ghost
- how each storyteller feels after their experience
- the ways in which the storytellers relate their stories. What does this tell us about the type of people they are?

14 Compare the settings for each story. Both are set in old houses but the details are rather different. How does each author make use of the setting to create a sense of tension or mystery?

15 *The Red Room* has a gradual but continuous growth of tension leading to the young man's final terror. In *Farthing House*, the pattern of the story is quite different: tension builds and then falls away, then tension builds again. Try to identify these patterns in each story.

Which story do you think is the most successful ghost story? Which story do you prefer and why?

Assignments

1 Write about how each of the storytellers describes their experiences, and say what their stories tell us about themselves. Think about:

- each storyteller's feelings about the other people they meet in the story
- the emotions each storyteller feels as the stories develop (fear, sympathy, sadness etc.)

- the different types of ghost each storyteller meets and how they react to the ghosts
- the language each storyteller uses to describe their experiences
- the endings, and what they tell us about how each storyteller has reacted to the experience.

2 Discuss how the authors create tension in each of the stories. Which do you think is the more successful ghost story? Think about:
- the setting of each story
- how each author keeps you guessing about what may happen next
- the structure of each story, e.g. the use of twists and turns and the placing of tense moments
- the language each storyteller uses to describe encounters with ghosts
- the feelings you are left with at the end of each story.

Fear

The Whole Town's Sleeping by Ray Bradbury
A Terribly Strange Bed by Wilkie Collins
The Landlady by Roald Dahl

The Whole Town's Sleeping

1 In *The Whole Town's Sleeping*, Lavinia remembers a story from her childhood:

> 'The story about the man coming in your house and you upstairs in bed. And now he's at the *first* step, coming up to your room. Now he's at the second step. Now he's at the third and the fourth, and the *fifth* step! Oh, how you laughed and screamed at that story! And now the horrid man is at the twelfth step, opening your door, and now he's standing by your bed. I got *you*!'

Stories which make us frightened have been popular with both children and adults for hundreds of years. Why do you think this is so?

2 Look at the words and phrases given below and discuss which words best apply to each of the female characters. You may think that some words apply to more than one character. Look for evidence in the text to support your decisions.

- tough
- determined
- nervous
- foolhardy
- calm
- timid
- protective
- sensation-seeking
- anxious
- reasonable

Draw up a chart like the one on the next page to record your evidence:

Lavinia	Francine	Helen
Tough – Lavinia is 'cool as mint ice-cream' and not afraid to walk through the ravine		

3 In this story there is a sharp contrast between descriptions of the town with its ordinary life and descriptions of the ravine. On one side of your piece of paper write down words and phrases from the text which describe the town and on the other write down words and phrases which describe the ravine. How does the author make you feel about the ravine?

4 Tension builds throughout the whole story until the very last paragraph. Yet there are also tense moments in the story followed by relief from tension. In which parts of the story does the tension increase? Which parts offer a moment of light relief?

5 Read the last part of the story again from the point at which Lavinia enters the ravine on her own. How does the author create a real sense of fear in this section? How does he build up suspense? Look at the vocabulary he chooses, the length of the sentences and the thoughts which pass through Lavinia's mind.

6 Debate whether you think it was sensible for Lavinia to enter the ravine on her own. Is she just asking for trouble? Do you think she really wants to tempt fate? Or is she right not to give in to the threat posed by 'the Lonely One'?

7 What is your reaction to the ending? Were you expecting it? Is it too obvious?

A Terribly Strange Bed and *The Whole Town's Sleeping*

1 What impression do you get of the narrator during the first three pages of *A Terribly Strange Bed*? Pick out three or four phrases which help to sum up his character.

2 At the beginning of *A Terribly Strange Bed* the narrator says 'let us go somewhere where we can see a little genuine, blackguard, poverty-stricken gaming, with no false gingerbread glitter thrown over it at all' (page 57). Compare this with Lavinia's words in *The Whole Town's Sleeping*: ' . . . A lady has all too little excitement in her life, especially an old maid, a lady thirty-seven like me, so you don't mind if I enjoy it . . .' (page 45). Discuss the ways in which the desires of these two characters are similar.

3 The narrator begins to win large amounts of Napoleons, and, as he says, he became 'gambling-drunk' (page 60). How does the author create a sense of the rising excitement in this section?

4 What is your first impression of the old soldier? Would you trust him?

5 Look again at the scene in which the canopy of the bed descends (from 'Good God! the man had pulled his hat down on his brows', page 70). How does the author create suspense in this scene? Think about the way the narrator gradually realizes what is happening, the language the author uses and the length of the sentences.

6 It is the day after the police raid on the house. Write the newspaper article which reveals what has been going on in the house. Think of a sensational heading and a spine-tingling opening paragraph. You may wish to include an interview with the narrator, the only victim to survive!

7 You have been asked to produce a version of *A Terribly Strange Bed* for television. However, the television company wants you to set the story in the present time. Discuss how you might do this. In what sort of place might you set the story? A Las Vegas-type casino? Or among a group of gamblers in some other location? How would you suggest the main characters should dress and act? What sort of character would you turn the old soldier into? What sort of trap might you use in place of the bed canopy?
Do you think the story would gain or lose from these changes? How far do you think the story's sense of mystery and suspense depends on its nineteenth-century setting?

8 Discuss the similarities between the two stories. Compare the main characters. How far are they both looking for danger and excitement? How far are they both asking for trouble? Compare the ways in which both authors create a sense of fear and excitement. Which story holds your attention more successfully and why? Which story did you prefer and why?

Assignments

1 Compare Lavinia in *The Whole Town's Sleeping* with the narrator in *A Terribly Strange Bed*. In what ways are they similar characters? Think about:

- what you learn about each character at the beginning of each story
- how far each character deliberately seeks danger and excitement
- the language used to describe each character
- how each character thinks and feels during the attacks
- whether you believe they are to blame for the attacks.

2 Compare *The Whole Town's Sleeping* with *A Terribly Strange Bed*, focusing on the techniques used by each writer to build up tension and create an atmosphere of suspense. Think about:
   - the setting of each story
   - how each author uses the plot to create suspense
   - how the characters' thoughts and feelings create a sense of excitement
   - examples of language which increase the sense of tension in each story
   - your feelings at the climax of each story.

The Landlady and *A Terribly Strange Bed*

1 What do you learn about Billy Weaver at the beginning of this story? Choose three adjectives to describe his character.

2 What do you notice about the boarding house? What strange features make you think all is not as it should be?

3 What strikes you as odd about the landlady? What clues do you gather as the story develops that all is not what it seems? When do you first begin to suspect the landlady of some sort of foul play?

4 Re-read through the story and note every occasion when the landlady comments on Billy's age and physical appearance. Why is this significant?

5 *A Terribly Strange Bed* is written in the first person, that is, the story is told from the narrator's point of view and we know exactly what the narrator is thinking throughout. In *The Landlady* the story is told in the third person and we are not shown exactly what Billy is thinking.
   a) Read the story again from the point at which Billy thinks the name of Christopher Mulholland rings a

bell. What might be going through his mind? At what point do you think he might have begun to get really frightened?

b) Write Billy's 'internal monologue' (that is, the thoughts that are going on inside his head) from the point at which he begins to question the landlady about Christopher Mulholland.

Assignments

1 Compare the 'old soldier' in *A Terribly Strange Bed* with the landlady in Dahl's story. What are the similarities and differences between them? Think about:
- how both characters seem to be at first
- how both characters deceive their unsuspecting victims
- the clues in each text which lead you to suspect each character of foul deeds
- what each author seems to feel about the characters.

2 Compare the settings of *A Terribly Strange Bed* and *The Landlady*. How do these add to the suspense of the stories? Think about:
- the language used to describe the landlady's sitting room and the bedroom
- how the bedroom is described in *A Terribly Strange Bed*
- anything you notice in the setting of each story which makes you think all is not as it might appear.

Men and Women

***Tony Kytes, the Arch-Deceiver* by Thomas Hardy**
***Seeing a Beauty Queen Home* by Bill Naughton**
***Tickets, Please* by D H Lawrence**

Tony Kytes, the Arch-Deceiver

1 Tony Kytes meets three women in this story: Unity, Milly and Hannah. Look again at Tony's meetings with each of the three women. Discuss which of the words or phrases below apply to each woman and why:

- sweet-natured
- friendly
- proud
- bossy
- bad-tempered
- easy to please
- hard to please
- fun to be with
- manipulative

Now think of two extra phrases of your own to describe each woman. Make sure you can find evidence from the text to support your views. Complete a table like the one below to record your evidence:

Unity	**Milly**	**Hannah**
		proud: in a tantrum because a scar might be left on her face

2 In groups, discuss which of the following statements you think is most true of Tony Kytes. Look for evidence in the text to support your opinions. If you think none of the statements is quite right, write your own sentence to sum up Tony's character.

a) Tony Kytes is a likeable character who is a bit confused! The situation he finds himself in is not his fault.

b) Tony Kytes is a selfish character who deliberately sets out to cheat the women.
c) Tony Kytes is a weak character who ends up in a mess because he cannot control the women or events around him.
d) Tony Kytes is an attractive, good-humoured character – but you'd never trust him an inch.

During your discussion, think about what Tony says to each of the women, how he changes his mind, how he asks for and then rejects his father's advice and how he reacts to the situation at the end.

3 Finally, only Milly is willing to accept Tony as a husband, though Hannah was near to accepting his offer. Consider the responses of the three women to Tony's proposals. What do these responses tell us about the women? What might this tell you about the position of women in society during this period?

Seeing a Beauty Queen Home and *Tony Kytes, the Arch-Deceiver*

1 a) Like Tony Kytes, Rudy is presented as a young man who thinks he is very attractive to women. Re-read the first pages of both stories and, using a chart like the one below, write down phrases which tell you about each character and his relationship with women. Then summarize the similarities between them.

Tony	**Rudy**	**Similarities**
O the petticoats went off, and the breeches they went on!	Lend us your body, baby	Both men try to attract women through being flippant.

b) In *Tony Kytes* we learn about Tony through what the narrator tells us. In *Seeing a Beauty Queen Home* we learn about Rudy through his own words. How does this affect our view of each character? Do you believe that Rudy is a success with women?

2 a) *Seeing a Beauty Queen Home* is set in the 1930s and it is interesting to see the men's attitude towards women. What do you think a 'Ladies' Excuse Me' is? How would women react to such a situation today?

b) Many of Rudy's sexist comments are more than a reflection of society's attitude towards women at the time. They actually tell us something about Rudy himself. Look through the story and identify Rudy's patronizing comments (e.g. 'Naturally the dames were all after me', 'I knew I was making their weekend'). What do these comments tell us about Rudy?

3 Tony Kytes weaves a web of half-truths as he meets each woman on his journey. Rudy also shows himself to be quite capable of deceit. Compare the lies each character tells. Who do you think is the more convincing? Why?

4 Rudy manages to fool Maggie's grandmother, although she remains a little suspicious. Rudy is proud of this deception, but Maggie begins to see another side to his character. What does she see?
Work in groups. Choose one person to be Maggie. Hotseat the character. Ask Maggie what was going through her mind as Rudy was lying to her grandmother. Try to find out exactly what made her so angry with Rudy.

5 Compare the ending of *Tony Kytes, the Arch-Deceiver* with the ending of *Seeing a Beauty Queen Home*. What are the similarities and differences between the ways the women react to each male character?

Assignments

1 Describe the characters of Tony Kytes and Rudy. In what ways are the two characters similar? Think about:
- how each character treats the women in the stories
- how each character tries to deceive people
- whether each character is in control of relationships and situations
- how you feel about each character at the end of the stories.

2 Imagine that the women who know Tony Kytes and those who know Rudy all meet together. Write the conversation in which they tell each other about the incidents which occur at the end of each of the stories. (You may introduce some of the other women who would have been in the dance hall in *Seeing a Beauty Queen Home*.) Think about:
- what you know about each woman's character from the stories and what they would want to say about each of the male characters
- adding a few details which are not in the stories, but trying to refer closely to specific details in the texts as well.

Tickets, Please and *Tony Kytes, the Arch-Deceiver*

1 In *Tickets, Please*, Lawrence gives us a vivid impression of the setting of his story before we meet the characters. There is an exciting, daring atmosphere surrounding the trams and the people who work on them. Re-read the first part of the story to the point where we meet Annie (page 120), and identify the words and phrases which create this atmosphere.

2 a) When we meet John Thomas he seems to be a rather daring young man. Read the description of him when he is first introduced (pages 121–122) and the description of him at the fair (pages 123–124). Choose three adjectives from the following list that you think best describe his character. Then find a quotation from the text as evidence to support each word you have chosen:

- wild
- attractive
- irresistible
- irresponsible
- dangerous
- amusing
- warm
- humorous

Now add three adjectives of your own and find evidence to support them.

b) Why does John Thomas back off from his relationship with Annie? What does this tell you about him?

3 Write Annie's diary entry for the day on which she realizes John Thomas has left her. Remember, she had felt very certain that he would stay with her and we are told 'everything became uncertain to her'. What does she think about John Thomas now? What does she think about herself?

Now write her diary entry for a few days later. She has just seen John Thomas on the tram and is 'determined to have her own back'. Write about Annie's plans for her revenge and about how she thinks this will make John Thomas feel.

4 a) Re-read the description of the girls' treatment of Thomas when Lawrence uses phrases such as 'immediately the other girls rushed upon him, pulling and tearing and beating him' (page 130). In what ways has the mood of the story changed and why?

b) Why is 'something broken inside Annie' at the end of the story? How do you think she feels about John Thomas now?

5 Compare the characters of John Thomas and Tony Kytes. How similar are their attitudes to women? Do you think John Thomas is a more manipulative character than Tony Kytes?

6 Re-read the description of Annie's and John Thomas's relationship from 'Of course, during these performances . . .' (page 124) to 'And so he left her' (page 125).
Re-read the description of Tony Kytes' meeting with Hannah from 'Hannah had seen him coming, and waited at the window . . .' (page 98) to '"Something's there . . ."' (page 100).
What are the similarities between these two relationships? How does each author convey the development of each relationship? Think about the words and phrases each author chooses to express the characters' thoughts and feelings.

7 Look back at the work you did on the female characters in *Tony Kytes, the Arch-Deceiver* (question 1 on page 251). Look again at the section in *Tickets, Please* where the women challenge John Thomas in the waiting room. Compare the attitudes of the women in the two stories. Which character in *Tony Kytes* might have behaved most like the women in *Tickets, Please*?

8 What do you learn about the social and cultural background to each story? What can you say about women's position in society and attitudes towards women? (Hardy wrote his story in the 1890s and Lawrence wrote his story in the 1920s).

Assignments

1 Both John Thomas and Tony Kytes are daring characters who try to manipulate the women around them. Yet in the end both are weaker than the women in each story. Compare the two male characters and discuss whether or not you agree with this statement. Think about:
- the similarities between the two men and their attitudes to women

- the differences between the two men, the ways in which they control their relationships with women, and who is in command
- how each man reacts to the incidents at the end of each story
- whether or not the women in the stories really do prove to be stronger than the men
- how far the actions of the men and women in each story are affected by the time in which they live.

2 Compare the female characters in each story. What are the differences and similarities between the ways they react to the male characters? Think about:
- whether the women in *Tony Kytes, the Arch-Deceiver* try to manipulate Tony, and who is really in control of the relationship between Annie and John Thomas in *Tickets, Please*
- how the women react when they feel they have been cheated or deceived
- the language each writer uses to describe the women's emotions and what this tells you about their feelings
- how far the actions of the women in each story are governed by the time in which they live.

3 Compare the relationships between men and women in all three stories in this section. Think about:
- the similarities and differences between the male characters and their attitudes to women
- the similarities and differences between the female characters and how they react to the men
- the similarities and differences between the seriousness of the relationships in each story
- the use of language in each story and how this affects your response to them.

Murder Mysteries

Lamb to the Slaughter by Roald Dahl
The Speckled Band by Sir Arthur Conan Doyle

1 Spend a little time brainstorming what you think are the ingredients of a good murder mystery. You may have seen all sorts of different murder mysteries on television (e.g. *Poirot*, *Murder She Wrote*, *Inspector Morse* and so on).
- What do all of these stories have in common? (Think about the people who solve the mysteries, the kinds of stories you find in each one, how the tension is built up throughout each story, how the stories are usually resolved.)
- Think about the detectives or people who solve the mysteries in each of these programmes. Do they have any particular habits or mannerisms which repeat from week to week?

Lamb to the Slaughter

2 Roald Dahl begins his story by creating a rather cosy picture of Mrs Maloney and her role as a loving wife. Re-read the opening pages and make a list of all the details which show Mrs Maloney in this role, e.g. 'she took his coat and hung it in the closet' and 'Darling, shall I get your slippers'. Why do you think Dahl gives us so many details about her role as a loving wife and home-maker?

3 Re-read the story up until Mr Maloney begins his revelation ('This is going to be a bit of a shock to you . . .'). How can you tell Mr Maloney is on edge? What impression do you get of the relationship between Mr and Mrs Maloney?

4 Does the picture we have built up of Mrs Maloney increase the shock we feel when she kills her husband? If so, why?

5 Write Mr Maloney's diary entries for the few days prior to the evening on which the story is set. In it he should describe his feelings towards Mrs Maloney. How might she irritate him? Might he feel guilty about leaving her – or just relieved?

6 Mrs Maloney takes careful steps to cover her tracks. Do you think she is terribly cold and calculating or slightly (or very) mad? Do you think she feels any guilt at all?

7 How does Roald Dahl create an atmosphere of mystery and suspense in this story? Read the story again and pick out the details which make you want to know what is going to happen next. Did you guess that the policemen were going to eat the lamb?

8 a) Imagine you are one of the detectives who interview Mrs Maloney. Write the police report you produce when you return to the station that evening. In it you must include:

- Mrs Maloney's statement (her account of events)
- an account of the procedure you followed when you arrived at the house, how you and your team looked for evidence, etc.
- your impression of Mrs Maloney's state of mind
- a summary of what you think happened and the next steps you plan to take to solve the murder.

or

b) Work in groups. Imagine you are the detectives who have interviewed Mrs Maloney and you are to be interviewed on local radio or television. Role play and tape-record your interview. Decide who will play the part of the interviewer. Then decide which of you will be asked about the details of the crime, who will be asked about Mrs Maloney's state of mind, and who will be asked about suspects.

The Speckled Band

1 When Holmes first meets Helen Stoner he makes some deductions about her very quickly (page 152). What else do you learn about Helen? Complete a table like the following one:

What we learn about Helen	**Evidence**
She has been very frightened or sad for a long time	*Her features and face were those of a young woman of thirty but her hair was shot with premature grey*

2 During Helen Stoner's account she tells Holmes of a whistle and a metallic sound. All of these details help to build up the mystery and encourage the reader to read on. What other details build up the mystery?

3 a) What are your impressions of Roylott? Look at Helen Stoner's description of him (pages 154–156) and the description of him when he bursts into Holmes' room (pages 164–165). Would you say he is a typical villain?
b) Write a brief character sketch of Roylott. Consider his appearance, personality and way of speaking and acting.

4 How does Conan Doyle build suspense throughout this story?
a) Look at the scene in which Holmes examines the bedroom. Which details intrigue you and make you want to read on?
b) Now re-read the conversation between Holmes and Watson in their room before they return to the house. Which details intrigue you here?

c) Now consider the atmosphere created around Holmes and Watson's secret entrance into the Manor House. How does Sherlock Holmes use detail to build up the tension here?

d) Look at the final scream of Roylott and the revelation about the speckled band. Is this a successful climax to the story?

5 Imagine you are going to produce a short television adaptation of *The Speckled Band.*

a) Choose one of these episodes to focus on: Helen Stoner's visit to Holmes followed by Roylott's visit; Holmes', and Watson's first visit to the Manor House and exploration of the room; Holmes and Watson arriving in the dark until the end of the story.

b) Plan a storyboard for your chosen episode. You will need to decide which parts of your episode are most important to include. Then you will need to decide which shots should be 'long distance' shots, which 'close-ups' and which 'medium range' shots. Finally, you will need to decide which speeches to keep.

6) If you can, watch a television version of *The Speckled Band*. Discuss how the story has been transferred to the screen. Think about:

- whether the characters are as you had imagined them
- whether the settings are appropriate
- whether any of the original story has been changed and why
- which version you prefer and why.

Assignments

1 Both *Lamb to the Slaughter* and *The Speckled Band* share some characteristics of murder mysteries. What are the similarities and differences between the two stories? Did either of the stories make you want to read on more than the other? Think about:

- how far the characters in each story are like 'typical victims' or 'typical detectives'
- how important the settings are to each story (the homely background in *Lamb to the Slaughter* and the old, mysterious house in *The Speckled Band*)
- how each author makes us want to read on
- whether the endings were what you expected or not
- which story seems more successful to you, and why.

2 Both Mrs Maloney and Roylott are clever about the way they hide the evidence of their crimes. Why does Mrs Maloney get away with it while Roylott doesn't? Think about:

- the differences between the two characters (e.g. which one would you be more likely to suspect of murder and why?)
- how the characters hide their evidence
- how the detectives go about their jobs: would Mrs Maloney have stood a chance if Sherlock Holmes was investigating her case?

Sacrifice

The Son's Veto by Thomas Hardy
Survival by John Wyndham

The Son's Veto

1 *The Son's Veto*, like *Survival*, centres on the fate of a woman. What does 'veto' mean, what is being vetoed and by whom?

2 What do we learn about Sophy and her son in the first two pages of the story? What does the conversation about Sophy's use of language ('*Has*, dear mother, not *have*') tell us about Sophy's relationship with her son?

3 Look at the extract 'she roguishly exclaimed as a matter of form, "O, Sam, how you frightened me!"' (page 188). When we see Sophy with Sam before her marriage to Mr Twycott, does she seem different from the way she appears throughout the rest of the story? If so, do we see her at all like this again?

4 The story goes back in time and we see Mr Twycott's proposal to Sophy.

   a) What does the following extract tell us about their marriage?

   'Even if she had wished to get away from him she hardly dared refuse a personage so reverend and august in her eyes, and she assented forthwith to be his wife' (page 191).

   If Sophy had not injured her leg, do you think she and Mr Twycott would have been married?

   b) Hardy writes 'Mr Twycott knew perfectly well that he had committed social suicide by this step' (page 191).

He is writing about the marriage. What does this tell us about their relationship?

5 a) Re-read the scene when we see Sophy and her son at the cricket match. Why is it impossible for Sophy to tell her son of her plans to re-marry?

b) Now re-read the scene in which Sophy does tell her son of her plans. What do you think of the son when we read, 'The youth's face remained fixed for a moment; then he flushed, leant on the table, and burst into passionate tears' (pages 202–203). Is he against his mother re-marrying or just against her marriage to Sam? What are the reasons for his feelings?

6 Write Sophy's diary entry for one of the days when she is waiting and hoping that her son will change his mind. What makes her hope that her son might soften? Does she consider marrying Sam in spite of her son's wishes? Does she consider how Sam might feel?

7 *The Son's Veto* and *Survival* are very different stories but they have something in common. They both tell us about women who do a great deal for their children. Discuss what the women do for their children. Do you think their decisions are justified?

Survival

1 John Wyndham's story is set in the 'future' but John Wyndham was actually writing in 1956 when social attitudes were often quite different from attitudes today. Travelling through space and going to work on another planet are made to seem like normal, everyday events but the presence of a woman on the spaceship seems to be unusual! For example, the captain says 'I wonder what the devil she thinks she's doing out here, anyway?' (page 211). Find other examples which indicate that women do not normally join these expeditions. What does this make you think about the men on board the spaceship?

2 Alice's mother says of her, 'she was so quiet . . . the other children used to call her Mouse'. Alice says 'Perhaps you don't know me quite as well as you imagine you do, Mother'.
The crew learn a lot about Alice as the story develops. Trace opinions of Alice throughout the story and record who says them. Complete a table like the following one:

Comment about Alice	Who said it
what she ought to be doing is sitting in some village back home, knitting	*Captain*
the captain felt surprise, as though he had watched a hearth cat suddenly become a hunter	*Narrator*

3 Write Alice's diary entries for:
a) the day the spaceship takes off. How does she feel about leaving Earth and her parents? How does she feel about the future?
b) the evening after the Captain tells the passengers about the ship's problems. How does she feel about being stuck in space?
c) the day she first realizes she is pregnant. How does she feel about the future?
d) how she feels after she has convinced the men she shouldn't be part of the draw
e) how she feels when she and her baby are the only people left alive on the ship.

4 Re-read the scene in which Alice refuses to take part in the draw. In groups, discuss whether you think she is being fair. Should she have special treatment because she is pregnant? Try to reach a conclusion you all agree with.

Assignments

1 Compare the characters of the two women and write about how far you sympathize with the decision each woman makes. Think about:
- how the characters of both women change throughout the stories (remember that Hardy's story moves backwards and forwards in time)
- the ways in which the men treat the two women and how they react
- how you feel about the sacrifice Sophy makes and how far Alice is prepared to sacrifice other people
- what the authors' attitudes to the women seem to be (look at the language they use to describe them and their actions).

2 *The Son's Veto* and *Survival* are set in very different times. How far are each woman's actions governed by social expectations of women in each period? Think about:
- why Sophy marries the vicar and how she then becomes trapped in a particular social class
- the men's attitude to Alice in *Survival* and how Alice is able to triumph over this attitude
- whether Alice is more assertive because twentieth-century society allows her to be so, or because of the need to protect her unborn child.

NEW WINDMILL SHORT STORY COLLECTIONS

by authors featured in Stories Then and Now

Ray Bradbury	The Golden Apples of the Sun The Illustrated Man
Roald Dahl	The Wonderful World of Henry Sugar
Sir Arthur Conan Doyle	The New Windmill Book of Sherlock Holmes Short Stories
Thomas Hardy	The Withered Arm and Other Wessex Tales
D H Lawrence	Selected Tales
Bill Naughton	The Goalkeeper's Revenge

ALSO IN

Founding Editors: Anne and Ian Serraillier

Chinua Achebe Things Fall Apart
David Almond Skellig
Maya Angelou I Know Why the Caged Bird Sings
Margaret Atwood The Handmaid's Tale
Jane Austen Pride and Prejudice
J G Ballard Empire of the Sun
Stan Barstow Joby; A Kind of Loving
Nina Bawden Carrie's War; Devil by the Sea; Kept in the Dark; The Finding; Humbug
Lesley Beake A Cageful of Butterflies
Malorie Blackman Tell Me No Lies; Words Last Forever
Martin Booth Music on the Bamboo Radio
Ray Bradbury The Golden Apples of the Sun; The Illustrated Man
Betsy Byars The Midnight Fox; The Pinballs; The Not-Just-Anybody Family; The Eighteenth Emergency
Victor Canning The Runaways
Jane Leslie Conly Racso and the Rats of NIMH
Robert Cormier We All Fall Down
Roald Dahl Danny, The Champion of the World; The Wonderful Story of Henry Sugar; George's Marvellous Medicine; The BFG; The Witches; Boy; Going Solo; Matilda; My Year
Anita Desai The Village by the Sea
Charles Dickens A Christmas Carol; Great Expectations; Hard Times; Oliver Twist; A Charles Dickens Selection
Peter Dickinson Merlin Dreams
Berlie Doherty Granny was a Buffer Girl; Street Child
Roddy Doyle Paddy Clarke Ha Ha Ha
Anne Fine The Granny Project
Jamila Gavin The Wheel of Surya
Graham Greene The Third Man and The Fallen Idol; Brighton Rock
Thomas Hardy The Withered Arm and Other Wessex Tales
L P Hartley The Go-Between
Ernest Hemmingway The Old Man and the Sea; A Farewell to Arms
Frances Mary Hendry Chandra
Barry Hines A Kestrel For A Knave
Nigel Hinton Getting Free; Buddy; Buddy's Song; Out of the Darkness
Anne Holm I Am David

Janni Howker Badger on the Barge; The Nature of the Beast; Martin Farrell
Pete Johnson The Protectors
Jennifer Johnston Shadows on Our Skin
Geraldine Kaye Comfort Herself
Daniel Keyes Flowers for Algernon
Clive King Me and My Million
Dick King-Smith The Sheep-Pig
Elizabeth Laird Red Sky in the Morning; Kiss the Dust
D H Lawrence The Fox and The Virgin and the Gypsy; Selected Tales
George Layton The Swap
Harper Lee To Kill a Mockingbird
Julius Lester Basketball Game
C Day Lewis The Otterbury Incident
Joan Lingard Across the Barricades; The File on Fraulein Berg
Penelope Lively The Ghost of Thomas Kempe
Jack London The Call of the Wild; White Fang
Bernard MacLaverty Cal; The Best of Bernard Mac Laverty
Margaret Mahy The Haunting
Anthony Masters Wicked
James Vance Marshall Walkabout
Ian McEwan The Daydreamer; A Child in Time
Pat Moon The Spying Game
Michael Morpurgo My Friend Walter; The Wreck of the Zanzibar; The War of Jenkins' Ear; Why the Whales Came; Arthur, High King of Britain
Beverley Naidoo No Turning Back
Bill Naughton The Goalkeeper's Revenge
New Windmill A Charles Dickens Selection
New Windmill Book of Classic Short Stories
New Windmill Book of Fiction and Non-fiction: Taking Off!
New Windmill Book of Haunting Tales
New Windmill Book of Humorous Stories: Don't Make Me Laugh
New Windmill Book of Nineteenth Century Short Stories
New Windmill Book of Non-fiction: Get Real!
New Windmill Book of Non-fiction: Real Lives, Real Times
New Windmill Book of Scottish Short Stories
New Windmill Book of Short Stories: Fast and Curious
New Windmill Book of Short Stories: Tales with a Twist

How many have you read?